THE LONG FALL

The Long Fall

PENELOPE WILCOCK

MINSTREL

Eastbourne

Front cover illustration by Margery May

ISBN 0 85476 296 5

Minstrel is an imprint of Kingsway Publications Ltd,
Lottbridge Drove, Eastbourne, E Sussex BN23 6NT.
Typeset by Nuprint Ltd, Harpenden, Herts.
Printed in Great Britain by Richard Clay Ltd,
Bungay, Suffolk.

For
Mark and Gill Barrett

CONTENTS

I	The Last of the Summer	11
II	The Wake of the Storm	29
III	Picking up the Pieces	57
IV	Out of Silence	87
V	A Promise	121
VI	Sore	147
VII	The Course Run	179
VIII	Winter	203

'The worst of partialities is to withhold oneself, the worst ignorance is not to act, the worst lie is to steal away.'

Charles Péguy

I

The Last of the Summer

July 22nd. The blackberries are in flower. Pink. They are pink, and I thought they were white; but these new, tender, thrusting shoots are burdened with clusters of tight, grey-green buds, and here and there a flower of sharp pink.

The raspberries grow thick and luscious this year, all that rain. It's raining now: fat drops of rain spattering into the languid warmth of the evening, hissing in the flames of the bonfire. The honeysuckle sprawls over the fence, its sweet, heavy scent mingling with the woodsmoke. The fragrance of it in the warm, damp stillness of the evening is decadent, feminine, overpowering.

The sage is in flower, its purple-blue petals shining brighter as afternoon drifts into dusk and the sun fades. The borage flowers too are bright stars of blue, and the dropping clusters of pink and blue comfrey flowers hang motionless from the thick, hairy stems. The elderflower is nearly finished now, the umbels of dense blossom give way to a plentiful load of berries. The roses are still a mad profusion of beauty, a good promise there too of fruit. Rose-hip syrup, elderberry cordial—there'll be plenty for the winter.

In the physic garden, the feverfew is a mass of yellow and white, and the calendula growing up radiant among it. Flowers, everywhere flowers. What a summer it's been.

The hay was half-ruined in the rain, just a bit left standing to come in. The grain harvests look good now, though, and the beans are looking healthy, which is just as well. There was nothing to them last year, and what we dried was scarce enough to eke through the winter months. Ah, but the honey will be good this year! The flowers ardent with life on their stems, nothing faded or limp. There should be enough nectar in there to put a smile on any bee's face.

Evening coming down now: a rumble of thunder threatening in the distance. The sound of the cows lowing as they come down from the pasture to the byre. Brother Stephen was late with milking again, then. He needed more help, really, this time of year. Further away, the voices of the sheep on the hills. What must it be like to live where there are no sheep; not to hear the sound of the ewes calling their lambs, and the lonely cry of the curlew overhead, and the sweet, rising song of the lark?

Brother Tom forked the last wayward straggles of leaves over the smoking fire. The Office bell was ringing for Compline. The wind changed, and the smoke from Tom's bonfire engulfed him suddenly. He turned away choking, his eyes stinging with it.

'Serves you right, standing here dreaming when you should be on your way to chapel,' he told himself. He left the pitchfork leaning against the fence, and walked down through the garden to the abbey buildings. The bell had stopped ringing, but he was not hurrying even now. It just wasn't that kind of evening.

At thirty-three years old, Brother Tom had been a fully professed brother of St Alcuin's Abbey on the edge of the Yorkshire moors for eleven years now, serving God under the Rule of St Benedict, learning the rhythm of spirituality which sees prayer as work and work as prayer. He had had his early struggles, like most men, but he was contented in the life now. His time was for the most part occupied with his duties in the abbot's house, but he was a big, brawny man, raised on a farm, and there were not many days he let pass without doing some work out of doors in the garden, or on the farm, or up on the hill pastures at lambing time.

He looked with satisfaction at the patch he had weeded, as he strolled down towards the cloister. He paused to tie up a white rose that was straggling across the path, the slender stem bowing under the weight of its blossom. He rummaged in his pocket for the end of twine that was in there somewhere, cut it in half with the knife that every brother kept in his belt for a hundred and one uses, and tied the rose back neatly. He bent to breathe in its perfume before he left it and disappeared into the passageway that led through to the cloister. There was a little door in the wall of the passage, through which he entered the vestry and sacristy of the abbey church.

Tom stood for a moment, accustoming his eyes to the change as he left behind the dim fragrance of the summer dusk, and stepped into the chapel with its smells of stone and beeswax and incense, the echo of its silences widening out about him, an immense, deep cave of breathing dark.

In the choir, the tranquil chant of the psalm was ringing. Tom listened carefully: '...*frumenti, vini, et olei sui multiplicati sunt. In pace in idipsum dormiam...*'

'Faith, they're on the last verse already,' he muttered to himself. 'I'd better move.'

The reading from the Rule at the morning's Chapter had been concerned with punctuality at the Office, and the abbot's homily on the chapter they had heard had dwelt at some length on punctuality as a golden rule of courtesy, and courtesy as a jewel in the crown of Christian charity.

Brother Tom had not listened to the homily with the closest attention, being familiar through long experience with this particular bee in his abbot's bonnet. Anything that Father Peregrine took to be a necessity for courtesy was insisted upon punctiliously. Brother Tom, having held the obedience of abbot's esquire for eleven years now, had heard a great deal in the course of time on the subject of courtesy and punctuality.

He moved briskly across the Lady Chapel into the choir, and slid into his place with an appropriately submissive air just as they were singing the final phrase of the Gloria from the first psalm. He could not, then, technically be said to be late, but it was only by the skin of his teeth. He could feel his abbot's eyes on him, and risked a glance at him. Father Peregrine was shaking his head at him in disapproval, but the amusement and affection in his face were plain enough. Brother Tom knew better than to presume on it though, and bent his head meekly, joining in the chant of the psalm: '*Non accedet ad te malum: et flagelum non appropinquabit tabernaculo tuo. Quoniam angelis suis mandavit de te: ut custodiant te in omnibus viis tuis...*' ('Upon you no evil shall fall: no plague approach where you dwell. For you has he commanded his angels: to keep you in all your ways...')

Brother Tom had often wondered what his abbot made of the promises of that psalm, and all the other promises like it that were scattered throughout the Scriptures. How did Father Peregrine feel when he sang those words, Brother Tom wondered; Father Peregrine whose left leg had been lamed and his hands crippled by an attack of thugs. He had borne the disablement thirteen years now, limping about the place on a crutch, struggling with the handicap of his awkward, deformed hands; yet he sang those promises in the psalm with equanimity.

Brother Tom wondered if the abbot's soul ever raged against God, '*Where was your protection when I needed you? Where were your angels for me?*' Probably; but he kept such things, like most things, to himself. Brother Tom sighed. He loved his abbot, but being his personal attendant was no easy job. He was not an easy man, with the storm and fire of his moods, the quick flare of his temper, and his high standards of spirituality. Still, Tom knew no one like him for compassion and tenderness when a man was broken by grief, or weariness, or defeated by weakness and despair. It was that particular quality of his gentleness with men in trouble that betrayed the nightmare of his own suffering. But—did his soul ever rage against God? Tom wondered. Maybe not. Father Peregrine's favourite text from the whole of Scripture was Pilate's brief sentence *'Ecce homo'*, 'Behold the man'; spoken as Pilate brought out the flogged and battered figure of Jesus, decorated with Roman spittle, crowned with thorns. Behold the man, Emmanuel, God with us. Tom had heard Father Peregrine recall the minds of the brethren again and again to this living icon of the love of God. Maybe he regarded his sufferings as some kind of offering to this wounded deity.

'He is the God of the broken heart,' the abbot would tell his monks, 'the God of the bruised spirit, and the shattered body. Those are his shrines where the power of his presence dwells, not the relics of the dead or the altars built by human hands.'

Tom looked across the chapel at him now. He looked weary. He always looked weary. Last night when Brother Tom had got out of bed at the ringing of the bell for the Night Office, he had looked for his abbot, whose chamber he shared, and found his bed not slept in. As he passed to the cloister through the great room which was Father Peregrine's centre of operations, he found him rising stiffly from his table spread with plans and accounts relating to the abbey farm. It was the same in the morning when the bell was ringing for Prime and the morrow Mass.

Brother Tom had scolded his superior as he washed him and shaved him before they went into Chapter.

'You're fussy enough about everyone else keeping the rules, you should keep them yourself. Any other brother in this house that drove himself as you do, and wasn't in his bed where he ought to be at night, and you'd be on his back like a ton of bricks. What's so special about you?'

'I'm the abbot of this community; that's what's so

special about me. If I don't get all this business about the
farm buildings right, we shall be into debt again, and have
I not worked these fifteen years to get this community
back into solvency and keep us that way?'

Brother Tom washed the last traces of soap from his
abbot's face.

'You look a wreck. Your eyes are that shadowed you
look as though you've been in a fight. You're losing
weight. You look horrible. You're sixty years old this
September, you can't go burning the candle at both ends
at your time of life. You'll make yourself ill—you *will*,
don't look at me like that. You're a monk. You're supposed to be humble and put your trust in God and go to
bed at night and eat up your dinner like a good lad. If I
were your superior instead of you mine, I'd bawl you out
for your flouting of the Rule.'

'My superior? Since when have you waited to be my
superior to bawl me out? Hark at you! Brother Thomas, I
swear living with you is like being married without any of
the fun. Peace, man, for pity's sake. Come now, will you
carry some of these documents to Chapter for me? I'll be
here with them today with Brother Ambrose and everyone
who knows the details of it, but I must give some indica-
tion to the community of what we're about.'

After the Chapter meeting, where the bare bones of the
situation had been laid before the brethren, the abbot met
with Brother Ambrose his cellarer, Father Chad his prior,
Brother Stephen and old Brother Prudentius from the
farm, and Father Bernard who was learning the difficult
and complex job of the cellarer with a view to taking it
over from Brother Ambrose who, though as shrewd and
competent as ever, was none the less getting very old. One
of the abbey's tenant farmers, who helped with the farm
management in lieu of part of his rent, was also with them;
and Brother Tom had the job of fetching and carrying
plans, deeds and letters as required.

The plans under discussion concerned some of the farm

buildings, which had for some while been in need of repair. The need was becoming urgent, but the coffers of the abbey had been heavily bled by Papal taxes and the King's war taxes in the past year. In addition to this, the hay harvest had all but failed throughout the region in the rains of the early summer, which meant buying and transporting in hay from elsewhere for the winter months.

Brother Thomas had listened to all this with some interest. The business talk of his superiors usually failed to engage his attention at all, but the subject of farming was one near to his heart, and he understood it well.

'...in addition to this, we lost fifty-eight ewes from the blowfly after we moved them down from the hill pasture to the orchard. That wasn't our fault. We had to move them because of Sir Geoffrey d'Ebassier's wretched hunting dogs harassing the sheep. The Cistercians at Mount Hope will sell us some ewes in lamb this autumn, when we have the money from the wool we sell of this summer's shearing. Theirs is all good stock, but we can expect no favours. We shall have to pay through the nose for them.

'Brother Stephen is adamant that we must replace the beasts' field shelters here...and here. The repairs to the byre will have to wait. We must pray for a good winter, that's all.

'Another call on our finances is the urgent repair to the masonry of the main drain from the reredorter. That can't wait. The morale of any community is only as good as its latrines.

'There is also the matter of the repair of the tower at the church of St Mary the Virgin. The tower, Brother. It was damaged in the gales during the spring, if you recall. So was the roof at the east end of the church. Father Chad said Easter Mass for them with drips of rain dancing on his pate, which entertained the people vastly no doubt, but we have responsibility for repairs there, and also we are liable for the priest's house.

'Further to that, Bishop Eric and his retinue will be

here for six weeks in February; that means fires, and winter feed for his horses, and a mountain of provisions at the leanest time of the year.

'Also, we are bound to send at least two of the junior monks to university this year. We won't get away with pleading poverty another year. Brother James, probably, and maybe Brother Damien. I'm not sure. I have friends at Ely who will put them up in the abbey's hostel at Cambridge, which will cut down the expense a little.

'We could look at increasing the rents again, but that'll go down like a dish of toenails as usual. Other than that, I don't know. I'm hoping you have some suggestions for me. But if they include building a barn with three threshing floors like the one at Barlbridge Manor and a new dovecote, which is what I've heard rumoured, you can forget it. Brother Stephen?'

Brother Stephen cleared his throat. 'Well…with all due respect, Father, I do feel the dovecote is a matter of some urgency. We left it last year, and the year before that. The pigeons do us very well for meat all through. As you just pointed out, the bishop will be here, and we shall have to feed him. If half the birds have died of cold, it'll only mean slaughtering more sheep or cockerels. If we rebuild it, and build larger, we can accommodate more birds, which we really ought to do.'

Father Peregrine sighed. You're too tired, thought Tom. You can't think straight, can you? He watched the tension around his abbot's eyes, the persistent twitching of the left eye. Your head's aching, and you feel sick with it.

'Oh, very well. Does it truly have to be rebuilt? Can we not repair it?'

Brother Prudentius shook his head. 'The roof has been in holes through several winters. Some of the timbers have rot, and the nesting boxes the same.'

'Yes, but if we repair it, the rot will stop, won't it?'

Brother Prudentius said nothing, meekly lowering his eyes.

'Won't it?' snapped the abbot.

'Yes, Father,' Brother Stephen responded resignedly.

'Thank you. The roof, I grant you, must be repaired. We can do that.

'The field shelters, then. Brother Stephen?'

'The one out on the hills...here...is tumbling down. It needs rebuilding, but it is all stone. Brother Thomas and I can do that after the harvest, if you will spare him for me. This one also is in a bad state. The great ash tree fell on it in the spring gale. Again, those timbers and the stonework are not beyond us, but I shall need Brother Thomas. We can make new piers for it I should think, wouldn't you, Brother?'

Brother Tom nodded. 'I've done it before.'

Brother Stephen smiled encouragingly at his abbot, who did not respond, but sat scowling in thought at the plans of the abbey estate in front of him. Brother Stephen exchanged a quick glance with the farm manager, and then embarked cautiously on the proposal about which he had the least optimism: 'If you'll look at the outlying buildings to the west there, Father—there near the boundary. I doubt if you have been out there yourself for some years.' It was said respectfully, but it was a barbed shaft designed to get Brother Stephen his own way, and it made its mark. The tension in Peregrine's face increased, and the tightness about his mouth and jaw was a warning with which Brother Tom was all too familiar.

'Yes?' There was not much that the abbot could not accomplish, disabled though he was, but it was true he had not ventured out to this steep and rough terrain since he had been lame. Brother Stephen, Tom thought, was unlikely to win himself much sympathy by rubbing his abbot's nose in his disabilities.

'The shelter shed there is large, and in need of extensive repair. Not to put too fine a point on it, it is falling down. The barn has worm in some of the aisle joists. The lift is

rotted through, and the pigs and poultry from the neigh-
bouring land can come and go as they please. Also, if we
took it down now, while some of the timbers will still serve
us, and built a larger barn with two, maybe three, threshing floors and a porch with a granary over, we could cut
down on transport of feedstuffs and straw—'

'Brother Stephen.' The abbot spoke quietly. 'Over my
dead body will you tear down a perfectly good barn to
pursue some grandiose scheme of your own. May I remind
you we are sworn to holy poverty. It is not the most
convenient building, and I am prepared to consider
enlarging it if that is within our means when all the repairs
are done; but that is all. The joists and the lift to keep out
the animals, we will replace.'

Brother Stephen said nothing. The farm manager
opened his mouth to speak. Peregrine looked at him,
silently. The man closed his mouth, and nodded.

The atmosphere in the room as the men rose to attend
midday Office, was not entirely happy.

Things did not improve after the midday meal as they
got down to close inspection of financial possibilities.

'My Lord, we could always' (Peregrine raised one eyebrow in sardonic response to Brother Ambrose's obse-
quious approach) 'sell corrodies, as we used to—'

Save your breath, thought Tom, in the split second
before the abbot thundered, '*No!* The years I laboured to
reclaim this abbey from its debts! I am not now going to
encumber it with unwanted inhabitants mingling with the
brothers to their spiritual detriment and weighing round
our necks for ever, just to raise ready money now!'

Brother Ambrose raised his hands. 'So be it, so be it.
We are back to pulling our belts in and raising the rents,
then.'

'Yes. Yes we are, until we have achieved the stability
we need to afford the improvements we would like—
always providing those are sufficiently modest to be in
keeping with our vows of poverty.'

They had finished before Vespers, Father Peregrine insisting on restricting all expenditure to the most frugal necessary repairs. The men were disappointed, but they trusted and respected him, and accepted his judgement with the best grace they could muster.

Brother Tom was left alone with the abbot as the others went their way. Peregrine sat staring at the accounts and plans spread before him.

Tom seated himself opposite him, in the chair Brother Prudentius had vacated.

'Have you ever noticed, Father,' he said, 'what an ill view of life a man has when he is dog-tired, and his head is throbbing, and his headache has made him feel sick so that he's hardly eaten for two days? Have you ever noticed how short with his brothers a man like that can be, speaking sharply to them and not having the kindness, as he normally might, to hear out their points of view?'

'Brother Thomas, are you lecturing me?'

'Would I dare to? I simply wanted to remind you that a man without sleep, food and leisure is indistinguishable from a man without charity, patience or a sense of humour.'

'Well, thank you very much. Now, I have some work to do with these accounts. No doubt you also have some work to be getting on with.'

'Perhaps I should have said, "...without charity, patience, a sense of humour, or any other kind of sense, including common sense".'

'Brother Thomas, that is impertinent. You are presuming too much upon my goodwill, and you are testing my patience sorely. That is enough. Go and weed your garden, or whatever it is you want to do.'

Brother Tom gave up, and left him to it.

Now, as Peregrine sat in chapel at Compline, his face was drawn in hard lines of weariness, his eyes and mouth tight in tension and pain.

After Compline, the brethren retired to bed in silence.

Tom gave his abbot ten minutes to return to his house, then rose from his knees in the chapel and followed him in. He found him seated once again at his table, the accounts spread out. Tom sat down opposite him. Peregrine raised his head. He lifted his eyebrows in enquiry. He did not speak. They were in silence now.

'Go to bed,' said Brother Tom.

Peregrine frowned. 'Brother Thomas, we are in silence.'

'Please; go to bed.'

The abbot hesitated. 'Brother, to tell you the truth, I don't feel very well. I must get this straight in my head before I go to bed, in case I have a fever or something in the morning. I promise you, after I have done these last few things, I will spend a day or two searching out my lost common sense, not to mention my sense of humour and all the rest. I can hardly keep my mind to it as it is. You go to your bed. I shall be finished before Matins. I will get some sleep before morning.'

The brothers had to be abed early if they were to be up for the Night Office at midnight, and it was still no later than ten o'clock when Brother Tom unfastened his sandals and his belt, took off his habit and climbed into bed in his drawers and undershirt. The Rule laid down that the brethren must sleep clothed saving the knives in their belts which might wound them as they slept, but Tom had no intention of going to bed in a habit on a hot summer night. Outside, dusk was only just deepening into night, though it was dark enough in the chamber of the abbot's house, with its tiny slits of windows.

Tom kicked off his blanket. It was sultry weather, and oppressive even in the cool of the monastery buildings with their thick walls of stone. In the distance, he could hear a low rumbling of thunder. He could not get comfortable in his bed, and lay shifting about restlessly for a while. 'Wish it would rain,' he said to himself; 'I can hardly breathe.' The few, fat, heavy drops that had fallen earlier had come to nothing, and the night waited in sullen stillness for the storm. Tom lay on his back, his knees drawn up and his hands clasped behind his head, staring into the dark. 'I'll never get to sleep on a night like this,' he thought.

He was woken by a tremendous rending crash of thunder. Lightning flashed blue through the narrow window, and the air was full of the sweet freshness of rain. Tom lay listening to the torrential wetness of it on the sloping roof of the abbot's chamber, built on as a single-storey after-thought projecting from the rest of the building. He rolled onto his side, raising himself on one elbow, listening. The deluge of rain and the rolling of thunder were loud enough to obscure the sound of anyone's breathing, but he was sure he was alone. Another flash of lightning illuminated the room; a split second, but long enough for him to see his abbot's bed, empty and unruffled. Tom frowned. 'Whatever's he doing?' he muttered.

He slid out of bed and pulled on his habit, fastened his belt, then went through into the main room of the abbot's house. The great oak table was a litter of plans and accounts still, but Father Peregrine had gone.

The door into the cloister was closed, but someone had opened wide the little door at the back of the room, beside where the scribe's desk stood under the window.

Brother Tom crossed the room and looked out through the low, narrow doorway into the streaming dark. Peregrine was standing on the flagged path, leaning on his wooden crutch, his face held up to the pouring rain. The thunder growled and crashed around him, the flashes of lightning intermittently illuminating the path awash with rain and the wet leaves of the birch tree tossing in the storm.

'Come inside, you crazy fool!' Tom called. 'What the devil are you doing?'

Peregrine turned round at the sound of Tom's voice. In the momentary illumination of the lightning, Tom saw his face radiant with exultation, laughing in the wildness of the storm.

'Man, truly I wonder if you're quite sound in the head,' Brother Tom grumbled at him as he came and stood in the doorway, the fringe of hair around the tonsure plastered to his skin, the whole of him drenched, from head to foot. Tom stared at him incredulously. 'Father, I...oh, you witless...witless... Here, let me go fetch a towel: don't you dare cross that threshold till I'm back.'

He went out through the main door of the room, that led into the cloister, and down to the lavatorium beside the kitchen entrance, where the stack of towels lay neatly folded for the morning. He grabbed two from the top and hurried back to the abbot's house.

Peregrine stood in the doorway still, his back turned to the house, looking out at the deluging night.

'Come and dry yourself now; you'll be catching your death of cold. Look at you, just look at you! No, wait; let me come to you—you're wringing wet, and it's me, not you, will have to mop this floor in the morning.

'Oh, Father, the state of you! You're wet to the skin! I'll have to find you something dry to wear. Have you a habit in your chest in the chamber?'

Peregrine was rubbing his head with one towel while Tom scrubbed him down with the other, having peeled his dripping clothes from him and flung them in a soggy bundle onto the doorstep. Peregrine looked at Tom, his eyes dancing, his face still full of the wildness and jubilation of the storm. 'I don't know,' he said. 'You're my esquire. You're supposed to know about that sort of thing.' He grinned at Tom happily. 'It was the joy of the rain,' he said apologetically, 'the passion and grandeur of the storm. I didn't mean to put you to any trouble.'

'It'll be no trouble to me at all, Father. You'll have to go to Chapel naked if I can't find anything, that's all.'

Tom lit a candle and went back into the chamber. He opened the chest against the wall, setting the candle down beside him so he could see well enough to rummage for some clothes.

'Your old habit is there,' he said to Peregrine as he returned. 'It'll do till morning. Patched and stained it is, this one, but never mind, it's dark, no one will see. There's an undershirt here too, about fit for a scarecrow, but it'll serve for now. Drawers you'll have to live without until the morning. Come and sit in this chair then, so you can put that crutch down.'

He helped his abbot into the dry clothes, and dried his belt and sandals with the towel.

'I've no idea what the time is. Should we go to Chapel or back to bed? Oh, there's the bell now. There, you look reasonable, which is more than you are. Let me fasten that door before we go. Did you get your work done?'

'I did. It's sorted in my mind now. I can see how to do what's needful within a year without incurring debts. I'll go through it with Brother Ambrose and Father Chad in the morning. But hush now, we're breaking silence shamelessly. No more talk.'

'Except—Brother Thomas, thank you. For everything, I mean.'

During the Office, in the long chanting of the Gospel, Brother Tom watched the abbot's eyelids drooping irresistibly; the little shake of his head as he fought valiantly to stay awake. He lasted through to the end of Matins, but by the time the bell was ringing again for Lauds he leaned sideways in his stall, his head lolling, fast asleep.

Tom left his place in the choir and crossed over to Father Peregrine. He shook his shoulder gently. Peregrine sighed and stirred, opened his eyes and looked up sleepily at Tom. 'Mm?' His eyes were drowsing again.

'Father—' Tom bent over him, his hand on his shoulder. Peregrine would be deeply embarrassed to be caught dozing once Lauds had begun. 'Father—'

The abbot's head rolled and he murmured something, then his body sagged completely, sliding down in his stall.

Tom squatted down beside him, taking hold of his arms: 'Father...Mother of God, he's convulsing...'

He looked back over his shoulder, and saw with relief Brother John coming into Chapel. The infirmary brothers were not always there for the Night Office. Whether they were free to come depended on whom they had in their care.

'Brother John!' Tom spoke urgently, but not loud. Even so, his voice overrode the whisper of robes and the shuffling of sandals as the brethren made their way back into the choir for the second Office of the night. All round the choir, cowled heads lifted, and Brother John strode to his side in the stillness of a watching, listening silence.

'He's in some kind of a fit—I don't know—he's convulsing...'

'Let me squeeze past you. Yes, hold on to him. I want to try and get a look at his face. Look, if I lift under his arms, will you take his legs? Lay him on his side, not on his back. Can you manage?'

The calmness of Brother John's voice eased Tom's fear. They lifted him down from his stall, and laid him on the ground.

'No vomit in his mouth. His eyes are all over the place, look. Face very grey. Hmm. He doesn't look too good, Tom. Can I come where you are? Let me have a look at his body. Oh...yes. Can you see how all this right side is awry? And his face, look—twisted the same. I've seen seizures like this before. He might well come through...but...there, the convulsion has stopped now. Breathing very, very slow. Faith, he's a horrible colour, isn't he—even by candlelight.

'We'll carry him to the infirmary. Bring the bier round from the parish side. We'll take him on that. Send someone ahead of us to the infirmary to give Brother Michael word to expect us—someone sensible; Brother Francis or someone. And Tom! Tell Father Chad to start the Office, will you? This silent audience is giving me the creeps.'

The chapel was full of heaviness as the tense, despondent silence of the gathered community roused itself into the ancient duty of worship. They had already seen death that year: Father Matthew, in the spring, and old Father Lucanus six weeks after him, in Whitsuntide. The brothers' voices rose and fell with the chant, but their thoughts were with the unconscious form of their abbot as the bier trundled out of the south door of the choir to the infirmary, under the sombre speculation of their gaze.

In the infirmary, night-lights were burning in the still, warm dark. Brother Michael had made ready for them, prepared a bed already in a room where no other patients slept. Like Brother John, he moved in unruffled efficiency; he was used to men, fearful and ill, needing his reassuring calm as much as they needed bones splinting or fever physicking, or muscles rubbing. It was part of the nursing care the infirmary offered, and Brother Michael, aware of Tom's agitation, made available to him the soothing peace of his own competence.

Tom hovered anxiously, watching Brother John's face while he and Brother Michael put the abbot into a clean bed and stripped him of his habit. Peregrine's body was as limp and unwieldy as a corpse now, offering neither co-operation nor resistance. His eyes were open, but rolling independently, and his breathing rasped slow and stertorous. Brother John's face, observant and purposeful, gave nothing away as he went about his work.

'That's his old tunic,' Tom explained. He was aware of his voice gabbling nervously, but not able to slow it down. 'He went out in the rain tonight and got himself wet through. That's an old undershirt too. I couldn't find him any drawers, it was the middle of the night. I was expecting to find him some presentable clothes in the morning. He—'

Brother John looked up at Tom. 'It's all right. He won't be needing to wear drawers here for a while. He won't need his habit either, and we've a whole cupboard full of undershirts. Don't worry yourself, Brother. I suggest you go and get a bit of rest. If there's any change, I'll send you word. He may be quite a time like this, and then it could go either way. Be prepared for that.'

'I told him. I told him he was working too hard and he'd be ill if he didn't slow down.'

Brother John shook his head. 'It probably would have happened anyway, Tom. He's not getting any younger. These things can sometimes be hastened or delayed—but not by very much. We'll do our best for him, don't fret.'

Brother Tom nodded, and stood there a moment longer. 'I'll go then,' he said. 'There's nothing else I can do. Let me know.'

As he went back out into the night rain, he was gripped by a sense of deep loss. There had grown between himself and Father Peregrine over the years a bond of trust and love. Prepare yourself, Brother John had warned. It would not be all that easy to prepare himself to lose the dry wit and warm compassion, the honesty and courage and faith, of the man he had come to know so well.

Brother Tom did not return to his bed. He went back to the chapel. There was nothing he could do, but he could pray, and sleep would be an impossibility. It was the sight of Peregrine's eyes that haunted him: rolling in the grey, sagging face. Sleep would be exiled by that memory. He pushed open the door, and walked slowly back into the choir.

There he found the rest of the community, who in silent unanimity had remained in prayer. They stayed there, united in anxious intercession, until the morning.

II

The Wake of the Storm

'It would make more sense for you to be on the farm than working in a job like this, wouldn't it?' asked Father Chad.

'Yes. It would. I'd like to be on the farm just now.' Brother Tom stood before the great oak table in the abbot's house. Father Chad had it considerably tidier than Father Peregrine ever had. He had been Father Peregrine's prior for so many years now, and the community was now so stable both economically and pastorally, that he had been able to step smoothly into the role of abbot, filling his superior's place in time of sickness. Brother Tom looked down at the tidy table, and at Father Chad supplanting Peregrine in the abbot's chair. The resentment he felt was, he knew, the danger of particular friendships. As part of his vow of chastity, keeping his heart guarded against human affection, he ought now to contemplate the prospect of another man filling Father Peregrine's place with equanimity. He did not. There was no point trying to deceive himself.

'Thank you,' he said. 'I think I'd rather be on the farm. There are two strips of hay still standing because of the rain in June. They need to get it down and stacked as quickly as possible, and they need someone to thatch the ricks besides Brother Stephen. We want to begin work on the field shelters in the least sheltered places before harvest, too. Once the harvest is over and the fall is on us, the weather will be more uncertain, and we shall need to get started with the ploughing, and—'

'All right, Brother Thomas! I can see you're itching to get underway. I'll ask Brother Josephus and Brother Thaddeus to take your place here. It's not really advisable to have just the one attendant these days anyway; people expect at least two. I know Father liked to keep to just the one—humility and poverty, and so forth—but there are lots of good reasons why having two is more practical. You have done good service here, Brother. I have often thought it was hard to keep you to the obedience of abbot's esquire when your heart is for the land, but Father would have it so. He relied on you as he relied on no one else. The change will be good for you. You can go up to the farm this morning if you like. I've no visitors. I shall be eating in refectory with the brethren at midday.'

'Thank you, Father.'

Father Chad smiled at Tom, and Tom obliged with a smile in return, but his heart was sore. It was true, all summer he had fretted to be out on the farm, as he always did, but now he had what he wanted, there was no joy in it.

Earlier in the summer, in June, when they had been struggling to harvest what hay they could before the rain defeated them, his obedience had weighed like chains. Most of the able-bodied men had been out in the fields all day, and he had been able to snatch only a couple of hours in the afternoons. The rest of his time had been taken up in the abbot's house, where a seemingly endless procession of wealthy pilgrims availed themselves of the abbey's hospitality, day after day. He had chafed under the tedious restriction of waiting at table, standing unobtrusively to one side to pour wine. Father Peregrine had seen it.

'Would you rather be on the farm, Brother Thomas?' he had asked.

'Yes,' Tom had responded shortly. And he had watched the familiar tightening of tension about his superior's jaw as he replied evenly, avoiding Tom's eyes, 'Brother, it would be the work of a moment to release you to the farm. I can have Brother Francis or someone to help me here.'

Eventually Tom's silence had forced the abbot to look him in the eye, revealing the anxious vulnerability of his incapacity. Tom knew that anyway. He knew how Peregrine needed someone who was very familiar with the limitations his disability imposed on him, to smooth the path with guests, and to a certain extent with the brethren. He knew, too, that Peregrine needed someone who could read his moods, see through his defences, to help him live with his own stormy spirit, its occasional moods of anguish and blackness.

Tom had shaken his head. 'Don't distress yourself. My work is here. I'll help with the ploughing in the fall. That'll do me.'

And Peregrine, who with anyone else would have dismissed it, sent them to the work they were best fitted for, sat with the anxiety twitching his mouth, looking at Tom, helpless, his eyes begging understanding. 'Thank you,' he had said stiffly, at last. He needed Tom. Both of them knew that.

Tom plodded away from the cloister buildings, and up to the farm. Only a week. It did not seem possible. Only a week, and the gap was closing behind him...another man in his chair...another man's rule making little changes...another man's style in the abbot's chapter at the morning meeting. It was as though he'd died. Worse, maybe.

It was four days since Tom himself had been to see Father Peregrine in the infirmary. There was nothing to go for. He lay mute and paralysed, beyond communication.

The first day of Peregrine's illness, Brother Tom had been at the infirmary at six o'clock in the morning, as soon as he had eaten his breakfast; and that had stuck in his craw like sawdust, as he ate in anxious haste.

Martin Jonson, the village man who came every day to help in the infirmary, greeted him at the door.

'Good day to you, Brother Thomas. Have you come to see how Father Columba is?'

'What? Oh—yes.' Columba was Peregrine's name in religion; the name he had been given when he took his monastic vows. His brothers all called him Father Peregrine, which was his baptismal name, agreeing that Peregrine the hawk was more in keeping with the man than Columba, the dove; he could be gentle and merciful, but he was no dove. Even his compassion burned with the fierce ardour of his spirit. No dove. But as a matter of propriety, outsiders to the community knew him as Father Columba.

'Yes. Can I see him?'

'Well...' Martin pulled a long face. 'I wouldn't, not if I were you, Brother. I don't want to upset you, but he's not right, like. He's as limp and floppy as a stick of wilted rhubarb; his eyes turned up in his head, and as helpless as a baby, too, if you know what I mean. There's no point in speaking to him, not really. He'd not know you.'

'I see. Thank you.' Brother Tom turned away. He could not now remember the rest of that day. The events of it all gave way to the dull pain of sadness. It must have been like any day, shaped by the round of prayer and work, but all he could remember of it was lying in his bed in the abbot's chamber that night, listening to the regular breathing of Father Chad's peaceful sleep; wanting to cry, and telling himself not to be so silly, wanting the familiar comfort of Peregrine's grey eyes watching him shrewdly as he poured out his troubles.

'This is a big one, Father,' he whispered into the sleeping dark. 'I need your counsel to help me through this.' And he remembered the senseless anger and indignation he had felt that Peregrine was not there, now when he needed him.

At Mass in the morning he had sat in his stall gazing up at the great wooden crucifix, as he had seen Peregrine do, times beyond counting. But it was nothing, only lifeless wood. God seemed as far away as the sun in the sky, shimmering in remote, impassive glory on the half of the world that was not engulfed in the night of sickness and confusion and distress.

After Chapter, where he had listened with aching resentment to Father Chad, sitting in the abbot's chair, giving the abbot's address, he had gone again to the infirmary, and found Martin Jonson sitting out in the morning sunshine, sorting through a great bag of absorbent sphagnum moss.

'Good morning to you, Brother Thomas! Not much change I'm afraid, if it's Father Columba you're asking after. He's a little better, maybe. Not so limp today, but his right side is all stiff: apoplexy, Brother John says it is. They've only just started on washes and physic dosing and what have you. Truth to tell, you'd be wasting your time waiting. We'll let you know.'

'Thank you,' Tom had said miserably, and trailed slowly back down the path to the cloister buildings. That day he could remember. He remembered sweeping the floor in the abbot's house, moving out his bed into the dorter upstairs, because Father Chad did not need him in the night to help him dress and fasten his shoes, as Peregrine had.

'You don't think he'll be back, then?' he had asked Father Chad, trying to keep his voice casual, trying to make it sound like a friendly enquiry. The sick pain of sorrow that wept inside him was too private to share with anyone. He did not want Father Chad to see it. He thought of all the times he had come into the abbot's house, in perplexity, in heartache, in temptation— 'Father, can I talk to you?'—and Peregrine putting aside

his work, looking at him affectionately, perceptively—
'Tell me about it.'

Father Chad shook his head doubtfully. 'Brother John thinks not. He's paralysed all down one side, you see, and he can't speak. They think he can see and hear, but...no, Brother. I'm sure he won't be back.'

'No,' said Tom. 'No, of course not. I'll move the bed.'

He remembered waiting on Father Chad at table, the concerned enquiries of guests, and Father Chad's discreet, reassuring answers: 'Not too well—overwork—complete rest for a while. No, we're not at all sure...yes, he will be delighted to know you were here and greeted him. Yes, I will pass on your good wishes with all my heart...no; no visitors, I'm afraid.'

When he was free to go, Tom went early into chapel for Compline. He sat in his stall, thinking nothing, holding the sadness inside him like a great weight; sitting very still lest the rolling weight of sorrow topple his equilibrium completely.

Suddenly aware of someone beside him, he looked up, into Brother Michael's face. Brother Michael, Brother John's assistant in the infirmary, had been with Brother Tom in the novitiate for a short while, and they had the ease between them of men who had trained together, even though years had passed since those days.

'Are you not coming to see him, then?' Brother Michael asked. His gentle friendliness undermined most men's defences. Tom felt the tears welling in his eyes.

'I came. Martin said...' he couldn't finish the sentence.

'Martin Jonson sent you away?'

Tom nodded.

'I'm sorry. He had no business to. Come in the morning, after High Mass.' Brother Michael paused. 'And what about you, Tom? This must be distressing you. Have you talked to anyone about it?'

'No.' Brother Tom replied dully. 'There's no one I want to talk to.'

Brother Michael looked at him, quietly taking in the harshness of pain in his face.

'You know where to find Brother John and me, if you need us. I'll see you in the morning then, yes?'

Brother Tom nodded. He did not trust himself to speak. The Compline bell was ringing, and the chapel beginning to fill up. He did not want to make a spectacle of himself here. Brother Michael pressed Tom's hand gently, then took his place in his own stall.

In the morning, as soon as Mass and Chapter ended, Tom hurried up to the infirmary. He went in, and found Martin carrying a tray of drinks out to the old men who were sitting in the sun in the physic garden.

'Can I go in and see Father?'

Martin smiled at him cheerily. 'Yes, I don't see why not today. You'll have to wait a minute though, the brothers are washing him and whatnot just now. There's a bench there outside his room if you'd like to sit yourself down till they're finished. He's not so bad this morning. They think he's going to pull through. He's not like he was that first day—grey as a corpse he was, gave me the shivers! Brother John thinks he's all there and understanding us now, though I must say I can't see much sign of it. His eyes have righted themselves, but that's about all. Brother John says we have to keep talking to him, chatting like. "Chin up, never say die!" I say to him, and, "Look on the bright side!" Well, it's important to keep sick people happy, that's true enough. Sit you down then. They'll not be long.'

Tom went and sat on the bench outside the room. The door was ajar, and he could hear Brother John's voice talking quietly to Brother Michael. Years, those two had worked together now; they were a good team, understanding well the blend of hygiene, discipline, compassion and medicine that was needed to promote healing. He listened to the calmness of Brother John's voice.

'We'll leave the sheet for now. He may need a clean one

later anyway. Has he passed water this morning? Yes? Recently? Good. Bowels open? No? Still not? That's three days. Hmm. We'll have to do something about that then. I don't want to be messing him about with enemas. You dosed him, yes? But no luck. Let's have a look then, and clear out whatever's necessary. Pass me the jar of ointment there.'

Tom listened to the gentleness and kindness of his voice as he spoke to his patient, soothing.

'Father, we've to look and see if you need to relieve yourself, or you're going to be in pain. I won't hurt you. We'll roll you on your side over to Brother Michael, and I'll check if there's a stool formed needing removing, and take it out if there is.'

Silence.

'Ah, yes, I thought so. That's impacted there. He needs it out.'

Squelching. A whimpering moan.

'Oh God, will you never finish with this man?' Tom's spirit groaned. 'How much more are you going to put him through? How much more pain and infirmity and humiliation have you got in store for him?'

He leaned his head back against the cool stone of the wall behind him, and closed his eyes. 'It's not fair,' he whispered. 'It's not fair.'

Jesus, whom Peregrine worshipped and clung to as a suffering, broken Lord, was determined, it seemed, to make him bear the same grim cross, endure it to the bitter end. 'What a wonderful friend you are,' Tom muttered.

'There, that'll do for the moment. You should be more comfortable now, Father. Hold him like that a minute, Brother while I wash my hands, and I'll give him a quick wash, then we'll leave him in peace.'

Silence. Water splashing. A nailbrush. Silence.

'Good, that's done, then. There, we'll leave you alone now, Father. I'll come back later and see if you can manage something to eat at midday. I'll take the pot and empty it, Brother, if you'll take the water and towel and shaving things.'

They came out of the room.

'Hello, Brother Thomas! I didn't know you were here. I hope you haven't been waiting long. You can go in and see him if you like. He's not saying anything, but I think he's with us, taking it all in.'

Tom stood up and made himself smile at Brother John. 'Thank you,' he said, and went into the room.

It was cool and dim, a west-facing room that missed the morning sun. A table. A capacious wooden chair. Against the wall another chair, the jordan, with a circular hole cut in the seat and a chamber pot on a shelf below the hole. A low stool. The bed. Tom looked at the bed. He felt his throat constricting in the apprehension. You look small in that bed, he thought.

He went nearer, stood beside the bed looking down at Peregrine. Oh God, he thought; oh my God, what have you done to him?

Saturday morning, shaving morning; they had just shaved him, washed him, combed his hair. This was as good as he was going to look. The right side of his face with its disfiguring scar, sagged tonelessly. His eyes had righted themselves, but they had lost all their lustre of life, staring—no, not even staring, only gazing, blankly. Tom could not be sure that those eyes saw him at all. There was a mute, bleak, stillness about that face, except for the lips that vibrated and spluttered loosely and noisily with every outbreath. Every breath in grunted and rasped in his nose. Tom stood looking down at him. 'Oh God,' he whispered. 'Oh suffering Jesus...Father of mercy...oh my God...'

The door pushed open, and Brother Michael had returned, entering softly. He came and stood on the other side of the bed.

'Here's Brother Tom come to see you, Father,' he said lightly. 'He's been before, but now you're well enough to see him, and looking very clean and presentable. You put me to shame indeed! Your first visitor; and if you're very lucky, he might even say "Good morning" to you.'

Tom looked up at Brother Michael incredulously. What was the point in saying anything to this…?

Brother Michael returned his gaze with a challenge in his eyes. 'Please,' his lips mouthed silently.

Tom swallowed. He put out his hand and laid it gingerly on Peregrine's head, his thumb caressing his brow. 'Good day to you, Father,' he said. He looked up desperately at Brother Michael.

'Better not stay too long, not today.' That same light, easy tone, as if there was nothing wrong; as if he'd been visiting a man with no more than a cold in the head. How does he do it? Tom wondered. He let his hand drop to his side. Not a flicker of response from those dull, gazing eyes. Those eyes…such compassion, intelligence, laughter, anger he had seen burning in those eyes, dark grey brooding eyes. And now…now nothing, shallow emptiness; the bright lamp of the man's spirit snuffed out to a charred and smoking wick. He turned away, and walked to the door.

'Tom.' He looked back at the sound of Brother Michael's voice. Brother Michael indicated with a slight nod the still figure in the neat infirmary bed. Peregrine had turned his head. The lifeless grey eyes were following him. They bore no spark, the song of the spirit was extinguished, but they were watching him go. Tom looked back a long moment before he left the room.

Brother Michael followed him out, walked with him out onto the path, where the bright sunshine stabbed their sight.

'He's going to die, then?'

'No,' said Brother Michael, 'we don't think so. Not now.'

'You mean, he's going to live? Like that?'

Michael hesitated. 'It's impossible to say. He should improve—Brother John thinks he will improve, and so does Brother Edward. He should be able to get out of bed, sit in a chair.'

Tom looked at Brother Michael. 'That's wonderful,' he said bitterly.

'It may be better than that. He may recover his speech.'

'Speech? He'll have to recover his mind first!'

'We don't know that his mind is gone, Tom. It's better not to jump to hasty conclusions.'

'How long will he live, like this?'

'We don't know. It could be years, months, hours—we don't know.'

'But he's not going to die.'

'We don't think so: but it's impossible to say. We don't know.'

'Don't know much, really, do you?'

Brother Michael did not reply at once. He plucked a leaf from a bush of lemon balm that grew at the side of the path, and crushed it absently in his fingers. 'I love him too, Tom,' he said quietly. 'So does Brother John. It's not easy for any of us.'

'No. I don't suppose it is. I'm sure you look after him admirably. I won't hold you up any more.'

Brother Michael sighed as he watched Tom walk away. Which would I rather have, he wondered: the luxury of turning my back like that, or the privilege of facing it?

He went back into the building. The old men needed an opportunity to relieve themselves, and there were three men to be bathed before the end of the morning, and half the beds still to be made.

Brother Tom went straight up to the abbot's house, not seeing, not thinking, his memory harrowed by the vision of that empty, foolish, blowing face, like a derelict house with the shutters broken and the door swinging loose. He came in to Father Chad and requested bluntly to be transferred to the farm. He half-wished Father Chad had it in him to look at a man with shrewd compassion, 'Tell me about it;' but Father Chad was not one to probe too deep. Tom looked into amiable, accommodating brown eyes; not astute grey ones that saw through to the soul.

'It would make more sense for you to be on the farm than working in a job like this, wouldn't it?' asked Father Chad.

'Yes, Father. I'd like to be on the farm just now.'

And now he came into the farmyard, and stood listening for clues of Brother Stephen's whereabouts. The farm track wound up through the farm buildings—a barn, the cow byre, the milking shed with a dairy attached to the back of it.

This dairy was the occasion for many caustic remarks by the kitchen brothers, whose own dairy, at the back of the kitchen, was a spotless model of cool, scrubbed cleanliness, pleasingly stocked with wide bowls of cream set to rise, and dripping nets of curds destined to become soft, delicate white cheese, and pats of yellow butter, and stoneware pitchers of milk. The farm dairy, by contrast, was more or less swilled down each day and brushed through, but it was a comfortable haven for bats and spiders, and never scoured so viciously as to disturb the corners. A large, rough table stood in the centre, and that was well enough scrubbed. On it, the milk pails and water pails were stacked side by side, and the barrels in which the farm brothers transported the milk down to the kitchen, to be poured out for using fresh or making cheese, or left in the barrel to be churned for butter. Along one wall of the dairy ranged the capacious feed chests of grain and dried beet, which kept the cows happy during milking. Strictly speaking, these had no place in the dairy, but it was the most difficult building for the cows to plunder, so there they stayed.

On the far side of the milking shed was a foldyard and a byre. After milking, the beasts went through into the yard, where they stayed in colder nights, and daytimes as well in the depths of winter.

In the summer, they were released into the pasture

beyond the yard, but it was still useful to send them out through the foldyard, because any beast with mastitis or a cut leg could be kept back for treatment when the rest of the cows went out to pasture.

Past the milking shed, the track curved uphill still to an apple orchard enclosed by a stone wall. The pig sties formed part of the wall, and these apples grew mainly for the benefit of the pigs. They also fed on the beechmast and acorns that fell from a row of trees planted in a curve around the upper side of the orchard, sheltering the farm buildings from the north and east winds.

This year the two sows had fourteen piglets between them, and these Brother Stephen was nurturing carefully for the bishop's visit in the spring. He fed them on kitchen swill and wild plants, sow thistle, comfrey and dandelions, with the added luxury of a pail of milk thrown over their barley meal in the morning. The littler boys from the abbey school hunted snails on wet afternoons when lessons had finished. They took a gruesome pleasure in watching the pigs' eager, abandoned greed as they snuffled and crunched their way through a pail of them.

Beside the pig sties a stout stone shack with a thick, heavy oak door that fitted snug to the ground with no space beneath it, housed various of Brother Stephen's veterinary implements and animal medicines. From this shed there suddenly erupted the most appalling cacophony of noise; a deafening racket of screaming and squealing which Tom could attribute to only one thing. Brother Stephen was castrating the piglets. Brother Tom cast a nervous glance up towards the orchard. Where were the sows?

His question was answered the instant he looked. The two of them, in furious haste, came belting down the orchard to the gate in response to the screaming panic of their offspring.

Tom knew from experience that they could lift the orchard gate off its hinges as if it were no heavier than a milking stool. The pigs, if they could get their noses under the stone sinks in which they were fed, tossed them carelessly aside as though they weighed as little as a wooden pail.

Once in the farmyard, they would not be able to get at Brother Stephen about his bloody work: that was why the door had been so carefully fitted, too nicely seated to admit any pig's snout. Their enraged motherhood would therefore wreak its vengeance on whomever their small, livid eyes caught sight of. A full-grown pig provoked to wrath can crush a man's limb between its teeth with astonishing ease. Tom knew. He had witnessed it.

He stood frozen for one moment as the two sows thundered down the orchard to the gate, then, 'Sweet mother of God!' he gasped, and fled to the milking shed. He dragged the door shut behind him, sweating and cursing the accumulation of straw and cow dung that clogged around the foot of the door, and the rust that bound the hinges. The cows were staid old beasts, used to the routine of milking. They had no objection to it provided there was a manger of cereal in it for them, and they entered the shed in placid procession every morning and evening, each strolling peaceably to her own tethering ring, awaiting her pail of food. Those cows weren't going anywhere. No one had had need to close that door for years.

Brother Tom heard the orchard gate go with a crash. 'Oh, God, my God!'

He was shaking as he got the door to and dropped the heavy iron latch. Within seconds two dewy, whiskered pink snouts were snuffling and questing under the door. Tom watched in awe as the two of them heaved and the tall, wide door shifted a little. The hinges were made like those of all the farm buildings' doors, so that the doors could be lifted off if they were needed elsewhere or needed replacing.

'Dear heaven...' Tom murmured as he watched the hinges creak and shift. He didn't believe even the two sows together could take the weight of that door, and yet… 'Oh no, you're not having me for breakfast, sweetheart,' he said, and went through the milking parlour into the dairy. This time the door presented no problems, being always secured to keep the beasts out of the feed. Tom went in and shut it behind him. The latch was on the dairy side of the door, accessible from the milking parlour by a round hole cut in the wood of the door. Cattle had too much of an aptitude for mastering latches with their noses for a farmer with any sense to attach the latch where they could reach it.

On the table in the centre of the room a pail of milk and a pail of barley meal stood waiting. When Brother Stephen had finished with the piglets, he would release them out of the shed to their indignant mothers, wait until both piglets and sows had calmed down and wandered away, then restore their confidence in him and tempt them back to captivity with this extra feed.

Tom scrambled up onto one of the feed chests, and waited. Even after the ear-splitting discord of the terrified piglets had ceased, he did not dare move.

Eventually, he heard the scrape and creak of the milking shed door. Common sense told him it was Brother Stephen, but still he did not dare move. Pigs, after all, were intelligent and resourceful animals. Then unmistakably human fingers reached through to the latch of the dairy door and lifted it. Brother Stephen entered the dairy just in time to catch Brother Tom climbing down from the feed chest.

Brother Stephen stopped in his tracks, gazing at Tom in blank surprise. 'What on earth are you doing?' he enquired in amazement. Brother Tom found the question, and the foolish look on Brother Stephen's face, intensely irritating.

'I thought,' he replied with biting sarcasm, 'that the peaceful pastoral setting of this hillside would be an ideal environment for some private meditation. What do you think I'm doing, you fool? I got here just as you started work on the pigs.'

A slow grin spread over Brother Stephen's face, and he began to laugh. 'You were hiding from the pigs?' he chuckled.

'Is that so perishing funny? I only just got in here in time.'

'Well, well. What are you doing up here anyway?' Brother Stephen lifted the pail of milk and the pail of meal from the table. 'Come and show your face to the pigs.'

'I've permission to come and work on the farm now.'

'For good?' Brother Stephen looked at Tom in pleased surprise.

'For good.'

'How comes that, then?' asked Brother Stephen as they walked across the farmyard. 'Lift the gate back onto its hinges, will you? Here, pigs! Piggy, piggy! Here pigs!'

He tipped the meal and milk into one of the stone troughs that stood in the orchard, and banged the bucket on the side of it, calling. In a cloud of dust, the pigs came bustling up the farm track, and hurried greedily into their orchard, all trauma forgotten before the happy prospect of food.

Brother Stephen shut the gate on them, and he and Tom stood watching the grunting, hasty delight of their feeding.

'Father won't be out of the infirmary again,' said Tom. 'Father Chad is willing to have someone else for his attendant. Attendants. He wants two.'

'Yes, well that's sensible enough. It's a job for two men, for all so much of the time is employed in standing about.'

'Father didn't think so.'

Brother Stephen glanced at Tom's face, and decided against pursuing that conversation.

'So,' he said brightly, 'you're up here with us. Well I don't need to tell you how glad I am. One more day to dry that hay out, and we'll mow it tomorrow, God willing, if the fair weather holds. I need your hands, and I need your sense. We've Brother Germanus since he took his simple vows, but that's only been six weeks, and you wouldn't think he'd ever been within hailing distance of a cowshed, to watch him work. You couldn't have come at a better time. Wish we'd had you for shearing.'

Brother Tom did not reply for a moment. He leaned on the gate, staring gloomily at the pigs.

'Shall I milk tonight, then?' he said after a while, without enthusiasm.

'Yes, please. Brother...' Brother Stephen paused.

'What?'

'I know how you feel about Father Abbot—'

Brother Tom interrupted him savagely. 'Do you?'

Brother Stephen tried again, hesitantly, searching for the right words. 'I'm sorry about it. That's all I wanted to say. It's all I can say. We all know how close you are to him. It must be very painful for you.'

'Yes. Well, there's no point crying over spilt milk, is there? I'll do the cows, if you like, this evening. What about this afternoon?'

Brother Stephen sighed. It seemed Tom wanted his heartache kept private.

'Thank you. We'll start the hay first thing tomorrow, then, as soon as the dew's off the field. If you'll milk tonight I would be grateful, and in the morning, please. This afternoon I'm sharpening and greasing the scythes, and looking over the hay wagons. Then I'm going up to the hay field and the top barn to make sure all's ready. I'll have Brother Germanus with me, but you can come along if you like.'

Brother Tom pulled a face. 'No thanks. Don't fancy his company. I'll go and help Brother Paulinus get his beans in, and pod them tonight after Vespers. They've cropped well. He needs help. Oh, 'struth, there's the Office bell already.'

The two of them walked back down the hill in silence.

Tom did not spare a glance at the infirmary buildings as they passed them on their way to the cloister buildings and the abbey church.

The choir was full of sunbeams, and the whispering quiet of the movement of the brothers' robes and their sandals on the floor, the quiet undertow of sound that served only to emphasise the stillness of the river of light and peace that flowed at all times in the chapel.

Brother Tom was grateful for the silence as the brethren gathered to pray, each one motionless in his stall, his cowled head bent reverently.

Tom sat down in his own familiar place. Brother Francis, who had been close to him since novitiate days, took his place in his stall beside him. Brother Cormac had the stall on the other side, but his place was empty. The kitchen brothers rarely all made it to the Midday Office, occurring as it did during the preparations for the main meal of the day, any more than the infirmary brothers managed all three to attend the Office. Tom looked for the infirmary brothers. Old Brother Edward was there in his place, so bent and frail these days, he looked as though a puff of wind might blow him away; and Brother Michael, just slipping into his place now at the last minute, as the cantor rose to sing the versicle.

'*Deus in adjutorium meum intende.*'

Tom felt suddenly weary of the whole business as he rose to his feet with the rest of the community. '*Domine ad adjuvandum me festina.*'

He sang the words of the Office numbly, automatically; but the duty of worship, that usually sat so comfortably on him, today seemed too tedious to bear. Tom looked at Father Chad; the prior, but so naturally filling the abbot's place, sitting in his chair. It rankled. Why couldn't they have left his place empty, allowed his absence as the reminder of his presence, let his empty chair stand for a silent hope that he was not finished, not dead? I'm being unfair, Tom told himself. They have to fill the office. They don't pretend to replace the man. And besides, he is finished. Not dead maybe, but over, done with.

The Office ended, and the brothers filed out into the cloister to wash their hands at the lavatorium, then into the refectory to stand before their places for the long Latin grace. They sat down to eat: fish, beans (again), bread, fruit.

The reader stood at the lectern reading some interminable ramble from the Church Fathers. This could go on for ever, Tom thought. An endless, suffocating round of days; beans, porridge, bread, prayer, watered ale, silence. When I die, he thought, I shall go to heaven and St Peter will say, 'And what have you done with your life, my son?' and I shall say, 'I have been to chapel seven times a day, my Lord, every day for years and years and years. I have got up in the middle of the night to pray, every night, for years and years and years. I have choked down Brother Cormac's bread—uncomplaining, mark you my lord, give me credit at least for that—and I have eaten beans and pottage, pottage and beans, dried beans, fresh beans, stewed beans, boiled beans, baked beans till the thought of them turned my stomach.'

And St Peter will look at me in horrified pity and say, 'Is that true, my son? Is that what you did with the life you were given? Well, that's a shame, because you only have one. You won't get a night's sleep, or roast beef in heaven, you know. Ah well, chapel's along there. Have a nice eternity.'

Brother Francis, whose turn it was to wait at table, was removing Tom's dish from under his nose. It was not like Brother Tom to leave half his food, and Francis paused, looking questioningly at Brother Tom. Tom came out of his reverie, and looked at the dish of beans and bread sopped in fish juices. He shook his head. Francis smiled at him, and took the dish.

Brother Tom spent the afternoon in the vegetable garden, picking beans.

'I thought we'd take the haulm down and burn it today, but it's still going strong, isn't it?' he remarked to Brother Paulinus. 'We shall be in beans up to our necks all winter. Oh, joy. Here, I'll take this lot and shell them this evening after Vespers.'

As soon as Vespers was sung, Tom went swiftly up the hill to the farm, and brought the cows in, milked them, brought the milk down the hill on a hand barrow ('Whatever did you do that for?' asked Cormac in astonishment, in the kitchen. 'You'll kill yourself. Use the pony, for heaven's sake; that's what we keep it for.'). Then he went back to the garden and podded beans until the Compline bell rang as the sun was sinking.

After Compline, he went to his bed in its little cell, the wooden, partitioned cubicle in the dorter that had been allocated to him on moving out of the abbot's house. The air was lifeless and stuffy. He tossed and turned in his bed and could not sleep.

In the end, he sat on the edge of his bed with his head in his hands, and prayed, silently. 'I don't know what you want,' he prayed. 'I thought I knew you, but I don't understand you at all. Lord God, your loving kindness is supposed to be better than life. What have you done to my friend? He loves you. Don't you know that? Have you forgotten him? Well let me tell you something: you'd better remember him now, because I can't bear to think about him any more. I'm going to forget him. It hurts too much to see him like that, because I love him, God, and there's nothing I can do. Nothing. You're the almighty one, not me. If you love him too, you—you who know everything—then you do something about him. You know what to do. I don't. If I could make a miracle to make him well again, I'd do it; but there's nothing, nothing I can do. So it's up to you now. I can't stand any more. I'm out of it.'

After that, Tom had no more words, no more thoughts. He sat among the sounds of night; Brother Peter's whistling snore from the next cubicle mingling with Brother Thaddeus' awesome snoring from further down the dorter, Theodore's mutterings, and someone making a most extraordinary noise, rapidly smacking their lips, a sound like a dog chasing fleas in its fur.

Then the bell was ringing for the Night Office, and Tom got wearily to his feet. 'You heard me, God?' he whispered, just before he left his cell. 'You remember him, because I'm going to forget him. I can't bear to think about him any more.'

Morning came, and Chapter Mass, then Community Chapter, and Father Chad attempting to counsel the brethren on secret sins of the soul, how, according to the Rule, a brother must confess his secret sins to the abbot or a spiritual father, who could discreetly go about healing the wounds of others, seeing they knew how to heal their own wounds.

Do they, indeed? thought Tom bitterly. Does he know, my abbot, how to heal the wounds of his soul and mine too? Oh, shut up, Chad. What do you know about it?

Then the business of the day. Father Chad laying before the brethren the position now with their abbot. No improvement...serious condition...time going on...looking at permanent invalidity...time to consider election of a new man. And Brother John getting to his feet, 'May I speak?' Yes, assuredly.

'Brothers, please don't write him off. I have seen men before recover from seizures such as this, but they need time, and hope. Something to work for. I beg your patience. Father Chad can stand in for him very well. Give me till the spring to work with him. Let's elect a new superior at Easter-tide. Things will run smoothly enough till then. Give him his chance. Please.'

Idiot, thought Tom. Blind idiot. Wishful thinking. He's finished.

Then the community expressing doubt. They thought he was finished too; thought Brother John over-optimistic.

Father Chad overruling; 'Until Easter, Brother John. We know his amazing resilience, the power of his spirit. We grant him his chance.'

Tom shook his head in disbelief. Some people never knew when to let go.

He was glad to get out of the Chapter House and up to the farm. The weather was holding fair, no more than a lacy veiling of white cloud adorning an azure heaven. Tom stood in the hayfield in the sunshine, rolling and fastening back his sleeves, kilting up his habit into his belt. Every year of his life his spirit had lifted in joy at the blue and gold of harvest, but this year he was indifferent to its loveliness, lost in a dull misery that would not let him go, would not let him forget, would not let his soul out of its pain into the singing freedom.

The only hope and gladness in it was the opportunity the harvest offered to work himself into the oblivion of exhaustion, taking out his anger and unhappiness on the standing grass, slaying it in methodical sweeps of the scythe.

'All right,' he said to Brother Stephen, 'let's start. We'll have it mown and turned before dark.'

There were four of them to mow the hay; Brother Prudentius and Brother Germanus as well as Brother Stephen and Brother Tom. It was not many, but there was little hay still standing. They had no need to call on the rest of the community until the larger affair of the grain harvest. There was enough hay for the four of them to have their work cut out though, and they went at it at a gruelling pace, sweltering in the heat of the climbing sun. Brother Germanus, though he came of a farming family, was an aristocrat and had never laboured in the fields until he came to St Alcuin's. He handled the scythe clumsily, though he learned quickly, and he was left further and further behind the others as they mowed in a steady line along the meadow. By the time the bell rang across the hillside for the Midday Office, he was trembling with weariness, his palms bloody with broken blisters.

'Never mind,' said Brother Tom unsympathetically. 'You haven't held us up too much. We're three parts done. It'll be as hot as hell out there this afternoon. The grass'll be dry enough to turn before night. Bind your hands with a rag. They'll soon harden.'

'Easy, Brother,' protested Brother Prudentius. 'He's too young, and I'm too old. You work like a madman if you will, but don't forget, work here is supposed to be prayer, not frenzy. We can hardly keep up with you.'

'Let's not turn it yet, Brother,' said Brother Stephen. 'It needs to be well dry. We'll trust providence and leave it a day. There's no sense half-killing ourselves to rush it in, only to have the rick burst into flames a month from now because the hay wasn't dry when it was stacked.'

Tom shrugged his shoulders and grunted his assent.

The brothers went down the hill to eat their midday meal in the refectory. Once the cereal harvest had got underway, they would be given permission to dispense with this midday interruption, but this final day's mowing was a minor undertaking, and they had been given no dispensation from the Midday Office and meal. They finished the mowing in the afternoon, though it meant skipping Vespers, and stood leaning on the scythes, looking with satisfaction at the swatches of grass lying in neat lines along the meadow.

'Cows'll be up,' said Brother Tom. 'I'll milk again tonight.'

'Brother, you're a saint,' Brother Stephen responded warmly. 'My back's fit to break in half, and my legs are melting. I'll be hobbling down that hill like old Father Cyprian. Look at that sky now, coming crimson. Fair weather tomorrow. We shall get this last lot dry and stacked, God willing. Give me your scythe, then, Brother Thomas. I'll put it away for you. You can do the cows with my blessing.'

Tom gave Brother Stephen his scythe without a word, and set off down to the milking shed. The other men watched him go.

'What's eating him?' asked Brother Prudentius.

'What d'you think?' Brother Stephen replied.

'Aye, well...it's hit us all hard.'

'What has?' asked Brother Germanus curiously.

'He's breaking his heart for Father Abbot, is Brother Thomas,' said Brother Prudentius. 'He's taken it hard, poor lad.'

'Yes,' said Brother Stephen. 'Going to make life hard for all the rest of us too, by the looks of it. Still, he's more use working than he would be sitting about moping. Let's get these scythes away and grab a bite to eat before Compline.'

Brother Tom sat on the milking stool in the dusk of the milking shed, his forehead leaning into the hollow of a cow's flank, his hands wet and greasy with milk, rhythmically squeezing and pulling the teats. The whiskery hairs of the firm udder against his hand as he grasped the teat, the warm living bulk of the beast against his head, the gurgling of her belly, and the shifting of her flank as she moved her foot, the inquisitive blowing of her breath as she swung her nose round to inspect him, getting impatient as he stripped down the last of the milk; it made a world. He took refuge in the solid, living presence of her comfortable benevolence.

The milk was finished. Tom rubbed his face against the cow's warm rough flank, yearning for the comfort of her sensual, unquestioning being. Then he swore and fell back, knocked off his balance as she shifted impatiently, lifting her foot and planting it firmly in the pail of milk.

The sunset was fading by the time he had finished milking, turned the cows loose, swilled down the milking parlour and fed the pigs. He brought the milk down in the hand barrow, the muscles in his shoulders burning, his legs protesting with every weary step.

He ate a hasty meal of bread and cheese and ale in the kitchen as the Compline bell was ringing, tramped wearily to chapel, then fell into his bed and slept like the dead until the insistent clamour of the bell roused him for the Night Office.

After that, his days were a blur of work and weariness. They stacked the precious hay, and thatched the ricks with straw against the rain, the days still holding fine.

Brother Stephen and Brother Tom sweated to get the field shelter out on the hills repaired before the early plums needed harvesting.

Then the cherries were ripe and had to be picked before the birds had them all, and the last of the beans harvested and shelled, spread out to dry for the winter soups and stews, and some saved for sowing next time round.

Apart from that, there were all the little jobs; filling the water butts for the milking parlour, and the cattle troughs, from the spring above the orchard; teaching Brother Germanus to milk the cows, sharpening and greasing the scythes again ready for the corn harvest, clearing the ditches, mending the flails where the leather had perished, patching the hen-house where the fox had got in.

And every night and every morning the milking, and swilling down the shed, scrubbing out the pails, carting the milk, and checking that Brother Germanus had fastened the hens in securely at night, and the geese. Brother Stephen could be trusted not to forget his pigs.

'I don't know what we did without you,' said Brother Stephen with frank gratitude as he and Tom started work on the timbers for the second field shelter. 'You've done the work of three men. I never thought we'd get these done before harvest. At this rate we might attempt the dovecote ourselves before the cold weather comes. We shall have a breathing space before ploughing.'

And gradually, as he immersed himself in the work of the farm, Tom succeeded in blotting out the guilt and helplessness of his thoughts about Peregrine. He ceased to grieve, ceased to wonder if Father Peregrine knew enough to miss him, ceased to notice the ache of it. At first he had to force himself to think only of the farm, but now it came easily.

When he walked past the infirmary on his way down the farm track to chapel, he looked the other way at first; then, when that brought him the view of the back of the abbot's house, he walked with his head bent, setting himself to think of the milk yield, the egg yield, anything. And he did love the farm. Peregrine's absence, illness, became a familiar background ache, displaced from the fore of Tom's mind as he became involved in the work with the beasts and the land.

August passed in shimmering, coppery heat. Tom watched with satisfaction as the fields of grain turned redgold, white-gold in the sun, the fat ears rustling in the stirring of a breeze at evening. It would be a good harvest, providing the weather held.

The boys from the abbey school turned out to help harvest the plums, which was the usual noisy business of shrieking and laughter, as the boys did battle with the geese in the orchard, climbed the trees, fell out of them, ate the plums, gathered them in baskets, golden and green and purple, sweet and full, with Brother Prudentius fussing to and fro, beseeching the children to handle the fruit with care.

The fleeces from the June shearing all sold, and Brother Tom went with Brother Stephen to the Cistercian abbey higher up in the hills at Mount Hope, to buy some new ewes to replenish their flock.

'Thirty beauties,' said Brother Stephen happily, as they unloaded the sheep from the wagon. 'Beauties. And a good bargain too. Come with me again next time, Brother. You drive a harder bargain than I ever could. They always strip my purse to the lining.'

Tom shrugged. 'We should have waited and got them in lamb. We'd have paid more, but got a better bargain.'

'Oh, I don't know. Our ram's willing enough, and his seed comes cheap.'

Tom shook his head. 'Their pure stock's the best. You can't beat it. Still, never mind. We've not struck a bad bargain, as you say. Help me get the milking shed doors down before Vespers, if you will, to keep the cows out of the rick beside the farm track. They'll spoil it before we have any good of it at all, if we don't look out.'

'Get the shed doors down? That'll take some doing. The hinges are rusted. Don't you ever stop? I was looking for a rest in the sun, admiring these ewes, this afternoon.'

'They're not rusted solid. I oiled them and eased them before we went. They'll slide out easy.'

Brother Stephen sighed. 'Oh well, if you're doing the milking. But that's my last job today. That trip up to Mount Hope about rattles my bones loose. We usually take a week over it and drive them home. It was madness going in the wagon. Oh, I know, don't bother to say it; it saves time. For mercy's sake, will you slow down, Brother Thomas? You'll be the finish of me. I can't keep up this pace. You're like a man trying to run away from his own shadow.'

III

Picking up the Pieces

Brother Michael walked into the milking shed. The seven milk-cows that served the needs of the community had been brought in and tethered in their stalls for the morning milking. They were munching contentedly on the pail of oats and dried beet Tom had emptied into the feed trough that ran the length of the wall beneath the iron tethering rings.

The regular hiss and splash of milk squirting into the pail revealed Tom's presence in the shed.

'Brother Thomas.'

Tom leaned out from the flank of the fifth cow in the line.

'Hello,' he said, surprised. 'I mustn't stop now; can you wait while I've finished? They'll be restive if they've finished their food too long.'

'I'll wait.'

Tom stripped out the milk carefully, then appeared from behind the cow, with the pail in one hand and the low milking stool in the other. He went through into the dairy, and Brother Michael heard him pouring out the milk into a larger vessel. He returned with the pail rattling in his hand.

'Two more to go. I won't be long. Beautiful day, isn't it?'

'Lovely.' Brother Michael did not sound particularly communicative.

Tom picked up the pail of water that stood by the wall, and began to wash the sixth cow's udder with the cloth he fished out of the pail. 'Holy saints, this is filthy! Ugh! Did I say I wouldn't be long? I take it all back. You disgusting beast, you're crusted in it! Just a minute, I'll have to change this water.'

Brother Michael waited. He waited in silence, while Tom milked the last two cows and disappeared whistling into the dairy with the last pail of milk.

Tom unhitched the cows from their tethers, and slapped the first cow, the one nearest the door, on her rump.

'On your way, Petal,' he said affectionately. The cows lumbered slowly out of the shed, into the foldyard.

'Now then, I've to swill down in here and take them up to the top pasture, but that can wait five minutes. There's nothing wrong, is there?'

'I want to talk to you.'

Brother Tom looked at him. 'Come out into the sunshine. That sounds ominous. It's not—Father Peregrine's all right, is he?'

They walked across the foldyard and leaned on the gate, looking down the hillside towards the abbey buildings.'That's what I want to talk to you about.'

'What is it? Is he—?'

'Is he what? Dead? Worse? Better? Do you care?'

Brother Michael turned his head to look at Tom. 'Are you never coming to see him again?'

Tom plucked an ear of wild grass that grew high beside the gate. He twirled it in his fingers.

'I suppose I ought to. Would it make any difference?'

'Don't you *want* to see him any more?'

Tom stripped the little seeds from the stem, and broke it into tiny pieces with his fingernails.

'No. I don't. He...the thing I saw in the infirmary five weeks ago wasn't him. He'd gone. I wish he'd died. It was hideous.'

'He's got a lot better since you saw him. He's out of bed. He's still paralysed down his right side, but he's got a bit of tone back in his face. He's no longer so incontinent. He can speak, just a little; mainly "yes" and "no".

'He likes the kittens. He has a length of string tied to his chair, with a little piece of wood on the end. The kittens come and fight it and play with it. He likes to watch them. It makes him smile, and there's precious little that does. They climb into his lap and curl up to sleep there. He strokes them, broods over them. You know, I believe he prays for them, fleas and all.'

Tom couldn't speak. He stared at Brother Michael, appalled. That this man, with his intellect, his fire, the power of his spirit, should be reduced to playing with kittens, and find joy in it too. Brother Michael looked at his face, read his silence. He nodded.

'I know. But that's the infirmary work, Tom. To make the best of the circumstances. They bring us their own despair. Our job is to steal them a crumb of hope. Anything. Anything that will rouse a man from the profound grief of his infirmity is worthwhile. There is no healing without hope. Despair is life's direst enemy. Despair is living death. At the moment, he is entirely gripped by it. You know him. You will see. Humour, hope, interest in the day's events, the need to be with others—he's lost it all. The kittens help. They are a ray of sun in his prison. They don't sit in embarrassment wondering what to say to a man who gets angry because he can't reply. They don't remind him of the humiliation of his helplessness. They come to him, and they're glad of him, and it takes him out of himself a bit.

'Won't you come and see him?'

Tom threw the shredded pieces of stalk away, one by one.

'If you think I should.'

'Yes, I do think you should. He's very low in spirits. He's shattered, obviously he is, by what's happened to him—as anyone would be. After all, he's well nigh help-less. But there's something more than that.' Brother Michael paused, looking out across the hillside.

'When we open the door and come into the room—any of us—he looks up; and then...it's as though he's disap-pointed. He looks away again, listlessly. I think, Brother John thinks, he's looking for someone, waiting for some-one. Tom, I think he misses you terribly.'

'He didn't even recognise me when I came to see him before.'

'Didn't he? Didn't he? How do you know that?'

'His eyes. They were so blank and dead...'

'Oh, for pity's sake, man! He's *ill!* He's been dreadfully ill. What did you expect him to do? Get up and dance a jig?'

Tom said nothing.

'I'm sorry. I shouldn't have said that. It must have been upsetting for you. But if you can bring yourself to get over it a bit and consider his feelings as well as your own, will you come and see him?'

'I've said I'll come. I can't drop everything and come just right now. We've started to reap the corn now, we're halfway through the oats, I can't just vanish. Still, maybe if I put in most of the day here—we've plenty of help from the brethren and the neighbours, and the school, not that the boys are much use for reaping or stooking—I'll come this afternoon, after the Office.'

'Thank you. Thank you, Tom.'

Brother Michael put his hand on Tom's shoulder with a smile of real warmth. Tom managed a wry smile in return, then shook his head and looked away.

'You don't know what you're asking,' he said.

'Maybe. At least I'm not asking any more of you than I've asked of myself.'

'It's different for you. You do it every day.'

'Easier then, you think?'

'Yes. That is what I think.'

'In some respects, perhaps. There's nothing easy about watching someone you love eating his heart out because his friend's abandoned him.'

Tom sighed, impatiently. 'Don't start on me again. I've said I'll come. Is that all, then? The cows are standing waiting in the foldyard.'

'That's all.'

Brother Michael watched the defensive hunch of Tom's shoulders as he tramped back up to the milking shed. 'Help him out a bit, Lord God,' he prayed as he turned and walked back down the farm track to the infirmary. 'A bit of grace, and a bit more compassion. Help him find the Christ in himself.'

Brother Tom opened the foldyard gate and watched the cows stroll out to the pasture. Nothing hurried the stately, sensuous, matronly sway of their going; they had their own ponderous grace, from the great, luxurious curve of their bellies to the slender delicacy of their ankles, picking their way out of the foldyard into the open field.

He closed the gate behind them, and set off up the hill to the cornfields. The weather was set fair. The oats they had cut and stooked yesterday would be drying nicely. Three weeks of this and we shall be home and dry, Tom thought, with satisfaction. But not if I have to be spending half my time in the infirmary.

'You don't know what you're asking,' he had said to Brother Michael, but he could not fully admit, even to himself, the horror he felt at sickness and the decay of infirmity; at the memory of the vacant gazing of those empty, lustreless eyes. It was easier to bury it under resentment—call it a nuisance, an intrusion, a waste of time; anything but look steadily at the frightening, nauseous reality.

Up on the hill, Brother Stephen had already begun. The tenants of the abbey farms were too busy with their own harvest to spare hands to help, but all the monks he could beg or coerce to help him were out on the hill.

Brother Francis and Brother Peter; Fidelis, Paulinus, Prudentius, Mark, Walafrid, Germanus. Brother James was there too with some of the older boys from the abbey school. Oh, we shall get this in easy, if only the rain holds off; Brother Tom's spirits recovered as he put from him the disturbing encroachment of memories and fears, bringing the focus of his attention back onto his chosen course with relief.

He joined the men and boys coming behind the reapers, gathering the fallen corn and bunching it into orderly blond sheaves secured with oatstalks twisted together and bound about the waist of the sheaf. The stalks must all butt in neat conformity at the ends, and achieving this needed the skill of experience. Brother Germanus, his hands blistered from handling the scythe, was trying the sheaf-making, attracting covert smiles of derision from the older monks who worked alongside him, which burned his pride as much as the climbing sun burned the back of his neck and the top of his shaven head. Brother Tom, who was not in the mood for pity, shamed him even more by working twice as fast as his own very best attempts; shaping, fastening and stooking his sheaves with effortless precision and relentless rhythm.

The work was killing, worse than the hay harvest, because the hay, although it must be raked and turned, did not require this endless, back-breaking slog of stopping to gather the corn and standing to form the sheaf; endlessly stooping and standing.

Brother Germanus spat out the little prickles of chaff that had found their way into his mouth, gritted his teeth and narrowed his eyes against the dust and flying chaff. His ankles were scratched sore by the spears of stubble, and sweat poured down his back under the heavy, coarse fabric of his tunic. And I came here to pray, he thought incredulously, as he straightened up, dizzy in the heat, pressing a hand momentarily to his aching back.

The triple-pattern of the choir bell tolling for the midmorning Office of Terce carried up the hillside, and the brothers laid down their scythes, completed and propped their sheaves. This was the time for the schoolboys to have a break from work, hunting fieldmice nests and satisfying their thirst with the watered ale in stone bottles that was keeping cool in the stream which ran through the copse at the field's edge. There was bread and fruit for them too, wrapped in linen and hidden in the shade of the hedge.

With nods and smiles of farewell, the monks left them to their hour of play. After Terce and Mass and Chapter, the brothers would work through on the fields until Vespers, bringing food up with them for their midday meal, but there was no dispensation from Mass and Chapter. Brother Germanus marvelled that the day should have come when the Chapter meeting formed a cool oasis, a tranquil respite of grateful sitting.

Brother Tom walked down the hill beside Brother Stephen. 'I've to knock off at None,' he said, regretfully.

Brother Stephen glanced at him in surprise. 'Why so? Something amiss?'

'No. I've promised Brother Michael I'll come down to the infirmary to see Father.'

'Would not this evening have done?'

Tom was silent a minute. 'I dare say. I've promised him now though. I'm sorry. He wanted me to go this morning.'

Brother Stephen snorted indignantly. 'And whence comes the oatmeal for the infirmary if all the harvesters are visiting the sick? Do they stop and ask themselves that?'

'It's my fault, if I'm honest,' Tom said quietly. 'I should have been before. I'll milk, anyway. Don't you stop for that. I'll milk after I've been to the infirmary. I'll not be taking that much time out really.'

They came dusty and sweaty into chapel, some like Brother Germanus who was new to hard physical labour, and Brother Prudentius who was old, grateful for the opportunity to sit down in the coolness of the church. Others, like Brother Tom and Brother Stephen, found the interruption of the work a tedious discipline. Either way, after ten days' harvesting, it was not easy to keep awake during Chapter.

'This morning's Chapter exhorts us, "Do not be over-whelmed with dismay, and run away from the way of salvation," and promises us that as we persist in the life of faith and monastic observance, our hearts will be made larger, or opened up...'

Do I want my heart ripped open? Tom asked himself, as he listened to the beginning of Father Chad's homily. I've had a taste of that, and I don't like it. Faith and monastic observance are fine, but I don't want to have my heart torn open. What's Father Chad going to make of that, I wonder?

Tom could remember Father Peregrine speaking to the brethren on the same chapter of the Rule a few weeks before they had watched the cut hay ruined in the rain.

The rain had been streaming relentlessly outside the Chapter house that day, and he had begun with a smile, and some ironic quip about the patient suffering that this particular chapter recommended.

But then he had spoken to them about the sufferings of Christ that the chapter urged them to share, talking quietly about the necessary pain of having your heart ripped open that was part of following Jesus.

Tom frowned, remembering. What had he said? Something about the broken heart being the most intimate place of communion with God...and the psalm, the verses from the Miserere he talked about...about the sacrifice of God being a troubled spirit...the humiliated, aching heart a precious offering in his eyes. And it had carried conviction. When he had paused from time to time, the only sound had been the endless wet falling of the rain, not the ceaseless muted whisper of fidgeting that accompanied Father Chad's homilies.

He had told them that the road of God would of necessity bruise their feet, and sometimes have them on their
knees in the mud and the nettles. 'There are some hellish
deep potholes on the road our Lord has set us to walk,' he
had said with a smile, and he had added, 'That's why we
need each other. Sometimes we fall in.' Well, he had fallen
in now all right, up to his neck. Tom stirred, irritably. Oh
do get on with it, Father Chad, he thought, chafing to be
out, to get done what he could in what was left of the day.

Then came the business of the day. Brother James
would be going to university, at Oxford. Brother Francis
had a vocation to the priesthood, and would be going
away to the seminary for a while. All the piecemeal news
of the community. Is this really necessary? Tom wondered, tetchily.

At last they were through, and climbing the hill again,
carrying their packages of bread and cheese for the midday meal.

Brother Tom glanced in amused sympathy at Brother
Germanus plodding with stoical weariness along the farm
track beside him.

'Don't be discouraged,' he said, on a sudden impulse of
kindness. 'You'll feel just grand when it's all in and
stacked in the barn, and when you stand in the mill
watching sack after sack of grain pouring down the hop-
per, and the blisters have healed on your hands as you
break the bread.'

Brother Germanus looked at Tom in grateful surprise,
warmed by his friendliness.

'I'm sorry my work is so slow,' he said. Tom shook his
head. 'If we've made you feel bad about it, the fault is
ours. You're giving your best. It's me and Stephen, impatient, making hard work harder.'

Then, suddenly, he regretted opening himself to the
young man's need of friendship and approval. He did not

want a lad's dog-like affection tagging him, and he withdrew into his shell of uncommunicative silence the rest of the way up to the field.

In the grass beside the track, harebells grew, and purple vetch and wild scabious, and at the edge of the copse the blackberries were beginning to ripen, and the cob nuts forming green on the bushes. The smell of summer, the dusty fragrance of grass and the sharp scent of chamomile lay distilled on the arid air, too familiar to be remarked, but none the less part of the beauty of the morning. They worked through the heat of the day, stopping to eat the food they had brought and pass round the stone jar of watered ale at midday when the Office bell rang from the abbey. By the time the bell was ringing again, for None at four o'clock, most of the strip of oats was cut and stooked.

'You'll be through this patch by Vespers,' said Brother Tom as he gave his scythe to Brother Stephen. 'There, you can take a turn with the scythe again; I must be away.'

Time to face it, then. He walked down the hill alone, and the day with its larksong and nodding poppies, ripened fields and clear blue sky almost lifted his mood of uneasy apprehension; but not quite. He looked down on the abbey buildings as he walked, at the honey-coloured stone, gentle on the eye, and the lazy drifts of woodsmoke from the kitchen chimney. He could not find a way back into the satisfied contentment the scene usually brought him. He had a disturbing sense of having been pushed out of the nest; having left behind easy tranquillity and familiar peace; as though, like Brother Germanus, he was being required to break his back and bloody his blistered hands on a new, demanding task.

He went into chapel looking for courage, seeking peace in the daily round of the chant. Doubtless the founding fathers had never intended the Office to be treasured for the anaesthetic value of its familiarity, but it often was.

The Office of None ended at half-past four when the west end of the chapel was suffused with tawny light pouring through the tall, narrow windows. The choir, at the east end of the church, on the other side of the parish altar, was dim at this time of the day. Now, in early September, it was a warm, golden, dusty dimness, almost languorous in its tranquillity.

The chapel emptied gradually, the novices going to the novitiate Chapter meeting, and the fully professed brothers going about their afternoon work. Only Brother Tom sat in the luminous silence of the choir still; and he was sitting with his forearms resting on his knees, his back hunched and his head bowed, his hands clasped together. He had to admit it now. He was afraid.

'I don't want to see him,' he whispered into the stillness.

The silence of the chapel was never an empty silence. The air had a perpetual sense of hopeful expectancy, of radiant peace. 'I'm always expecting to catch a glimpse of wings, a shine of gold there,' Peregrine had said to Tom, smiling, one day in the early summer of the year. 'It is so pregnant with life and glory.'

'I don't want to see him,' Tom whispered in fear. 'God help me, I don't want to see him like he is.'

It was almost five o'clock before he finally gathered his courage and stood up to go. He stood for a moment, looking up at the great wooden crucifix that hung above the rood screen. 'You should do something about him,' Tom muttered. 'He's a friend of yours.'

Resolutely he tramped through the choir and the Lady chapel, out of the little door in the south wall into the afternoon sunshine, and up to the infirmary.

Outside the infirmary buildings, in the sheltered fragrance of the physic garden, four or five aged monks were tucked up in blankets, sitting in their chairs in the sun. Why do they live so damned long? Tom thought. Why don't they just die like people everywhere else? Brother John looks after them too well. He should let them die. Look at them. What have they got to live for?

He looked for Peregrine, but Peregrine was not among them. Brother Tom passed through them without speaking, into the cool peace of the infirmary. In the little anteroom, Martin Jonson was strewing fresh herbs on the floor. Their pungent, antiseptic aroma smelt clean and good.

'I've come to see Father Peregrine,' said Tom.

'Good, good, good! They like to have a visitor, cheer them up, tell them all the news. Brother Michael said you would be coming. Brother John wants a word with you first. I expect he wants to explain to you about Father— he's a bit peculiar you know. Temperamental, like. Not quite right in his head, between you and me, though Brother John won't have it said.'

'Where is Brother John?'

'Just along the way, in the linen room, Brother, folding the sheets.'

Tom went along the wide passage to the linen room and stood in the doorway.

'You wanted to see me,' he said.

'Yes.' Brother John laid the sheet he had folded into a neat square on the pile that lay on the table, and slipped two stems of lavender, from a bunch that lay alongside, between the folds of the sheet.

'Here I am.'

'Yes.' Brother John turned to face him. He folded his arms and stood looking at Tom. 'About time too, isn't it? You should be ashamed of yourself.'

Oh, here we go. I could do without this, Tom thought.

'I've already had this ticking-off from Brother Michael,' he said defensively.

'Is that so? Well now you've got it from me. Whatever have you been thinking of, never coming near the place all this time?'

'All right! I am ashamed of myself! I know what you're saying—it's written on my heart, as it so happens! I'm a coward, I couldn't face it, I was upset, I stayed away. It was selfish. I know. I know I should have been to see him before this. I know. I couldn't bear it, that's all. I don't want to see him witless and drooling. It twists me up inside. I can't…anyway, I'm here now. I'm sorry, and I've come. All right?'

Brother John regarded him thoughtfully.

'Who gave you the idea he was witless and drooling? Martin Jonson been talking to you? Yes?' Brother John snorted derisively. 'Witless he is not. He gets impatient— but then he always did, as I recall. He can't make himself understood. Can you not see the frustration of that? It's resulted in a few scenes, yes. He threw his dinner across the room on Tuesday and he bit Martin's finger this morning, but—why are you staring at me like that?'

'I'm sorry. Just for a moment I thought you said Father Peregrine bit Martin Jonson.'

'That is what I said. He did bite him. Will you give me a hand folding these sheets while you're here?'

'He *bit* him? His mind must be affected, then.'

'Why? There's nothing wrong with his mind so far as I can tell. You should never underestimate the frustration of being unable to communicate, Tom.

'Look what you're doing—take those two ends. Martin misjudged his man, that's all. You know what he is, all "there's a good lad" and "whoops-a-daisy". He patted Father on the cheek and chucked him under the chin once too often. He had hold of his chin and gave it a playful little shake. He's always doing it. He said, "How are we today, then?" and Father sank his teeth into his finger. Serves him right. I'm surprised nobody's bitten him before. I fancy he'll approach him with a little more respect in future. Well, caution at least.

'I'm particularly glad you agreed to come today. There's no one free here but Martin this afternoon to sit with him, and he needs someone, but not Martin. It's like a red rag to a bull.

'He can't read now, and the old men in here are too

senile to make the effort to converse with him. I've tried sitting him with them in the afternoons, but he doesn't like it. We ask him if he wants to sit outside with the others. "N-o," he says, like that, "n-o." So we leave him in peace.

'He needs some company though, he's that morose and miserable looking. It'll do him the world of good to see you. Read to him or something. Tell him what's going on. Thank you, I'll manage these on my own now. You know where he is?'

'Yes, I know where he is, but wait a minute: how can I talk with him if he can't speak?'

'He can speak. Who told you he couldn't speak?'

'You did. I thought you said...'

'He has very little predictable speech. He can say "yes" and "no" reliably. Other words are usually too difficult if he thinks too hard. But he says quite a lot really.'

'I misunderstood. I thought he could only say "yes" and "no", and the rest was all garbled.'

'Oh no; it's a struggle, but he can make himself understood if you'll be patient. Sometimes he comes out with something as clear as can be. In French usually.'

'In *French?*' Tom looked at Brother John in blank bewilderment.

'His family are French, aren't they? It will have been the language of his childhood. It's a strange thing, this kind of illness. I've seen it before. Memories, words, thoughts—they all jumble into a rag-bag mixture, and you never know what will come out; sense or nonsense, or a bit of both. Mostly "yes" and "no" are the only things he can say clearly, and he sometimes gets those the wrong way round, but just now and again the odd phrase comes through perfectly. This morning, he had his breakfast— I'd left him to get on with it—and he was muttering to himself as I went past the doorway. I stopped just outside to listen to him. I was intrigued. "Merde...incroyable..." he was saying to himself, and, "...dégueulasse," Cormac's porridge. I went in and tasted it. He was quite right, it was appalling. Grey and lumpy, and no salt that I could detect. But if I'd asked him, he couldn't have told me in English—nor in French either. Just sometimes the odd phrase slips through, that's all. I do mean odd, too. "Merci, chéri," he said to me last Saturday after I'd finished shaving him. I think he was as startled as I was. You can see why he doesn't want to sit with the others. It's embarrassing for him, and a bit frightening I think.

'Anyway, you'll see. Take him as you find him. He's in the same room as before. Thanks for your help with the sheets. I'm glad you've come.'

Brother Tom walked along the passage to the room where he had last seen Father Peregrine. He was still afraid. He stood outside the room with his hand raised to the door. Then he heard footsteps approaching further along the passage, so he pushed open the door and took two steps into the room. Peregrine was seated in the chair, near to the bed.

Tom had never seen him sitting like that; his left hand resting in his lap, idle; no books, no letters, doing nothing. Just himself, alone in the chair, the length of knotted string to amuse the kittens dangling forlornly to the floor.

The warmth and mellow light of the afternoon sun lit the room, but it had the lifeless air of a sickroom. There was no hope in that room. Even the wooden crutch, faithful companion, symbol of independence, was gone. He no longer needed it, of course.

His body sagged dispiritedly. As he raised his head and looked at Tom, his face was blank, shuttered. John's mistaken, Tom thought, his mind has gone.

They looked at each other in silence. Tom looked at Peregrine's face, the scarred right side of it still drooping slightly in paralysis. He was sitting askew in the chair, his useless right arm and hand awkwardly tucked into the side of the chair, pushed out of sight among the cushions. By himself, no doubt. Brother John would never have left him sitting like that. He liked his patients to look tidy.

What a mess, Tom thought. What an awful mess. He tried to think of words to say. Some news, Martin had said, to cheer him up. What news was there? Tell him maybe that most of the brethren felt he was finished for good now, and it was time to choose a new superior? No, not that news. 'Make him smile if you can,' Brother Michael had said. 'Try to rekindle some hope.' Hope. For God's sake, hope? There was nothing to say; nothing.

A moment later Tom wished he had thought of something, anything to say; because Peregrine spoke to him. It was just a jumble of sounds. Should I go and fetch Brother John? he wondered, nervously. Then Peregrine spoke to him again, urgently this time.

'I—I can't understand you...' Tom faltered. Anxiety clutched him. It was rubbish the man was talking; Tom had no idea how to respond, what to say. Inadequacy felt like fear, tightening his gut, making him want to leave, run away from this predicament. Peregrine was glaring at him, talking heatedly, beads of sweat on his face. He leaned forward, his eyes compelling Tom, willing him to understand; and Tom could not understand at all, stood dumb, uncomfortable, completely baffled. Peregrine raised his hand in desperate agitation, and crashed it down in frustration into his lap. Then, abruptly, he turned his face away. He held his head away from looking at Tom, in rigid misery.

'What? Whatever is it?' Stupid question, thought Tom, as soon as the words were out of his mouth. All he can say to me is more of the same. Then suddenly he saw the spreading, splashing puddle of urine under the chair. Maybe if I was Martin, he thought numbly, I could make a joke of this, ease his embarrassment. Then maybe if I was Martin, I'd be able to see something funny in it.

'I'll get Brother John,' he said. 'We need to clean you up. I'm sorry.'

Once outside the room, Brother Thomas stood, sick with the guilt and shame of his relief to be getting out of that room, finding someone else, not having to be left alone with Father Peregrine.

'Brother Michael!' Tom saw him passing the end of the corridor and hastened after him. 'Brother Michael, can you help!'

'Is something the matter?' Other people's agitation flowed off the infirmary brothers like water off a duck's back. It was too commonplace. In the infirmary, full of the sick, the infirm, the dying, occurrences that felt like emergencies were too numerous to count, and actual emergencies were almost unheard of.

'Father Peregrine's wet himself!'

Brother Michael smiled at Tom's appalled face.

'Has he? What do you want? Something to mop up with?'

Tom stared at him, aghast. 'Me? I...no...no! Please come and see to him. I can't deal with this. It's no use, the whole thing gives me the creeps. He doesn't need me. I'm no good at this sort of thing; I can't...I...I'm going.'

Brother Michael stood listening to him in mild surprise.

'There's no need to get upset. He's a bit incontinent— that's quite normal. Help me change his clothes, and then stay for a chat with him.'

'Oh, you're joking! Michael, I'm going.'

'All right, but hang on a minute, don't run away. When are you coming back? He might want to know.'

'I'm not. Don't look at me like that; I'm not like you are. I can't bear this sort of thing. I've simply got no stomach for it. He'll understand. Just give him my love— tell him I'll pray for him.'

'Tell him *what?* I'm sure he'll be really delighted to hear that! Don't be ridiculous, Tom—' But Tom shook his head, turned on his heel and left.

He strode up the track to the farm, where the cows were already queueing placidly outside the milking shed. He

called them in, rattling their cereal in the bucket, over-
whelmed with gratitude at the reassurance of their vac-
uous, undemanding stolidity.

His hands were trembling as he tethered the beasts in
their places; but as he went from one to the other, resting
his head against the warm, impassive bulk, moving his
hands in the rhythmic, sensuous physicality of the milking, the turmoil died away, and he was calm again.

After he had milked the cows and turned them out to
pasture once more, Tom walked the half-mile to the mill,
and spent an hour meticulously clearing out the millrace,
scraping all the accretions of moss and slime from the
wheel. He ignored the Vespers bell, and did not return to
the milking shed and take the milk down to the kitchen
until the sun was setting, having no wish to run into
Brother Michael or Brother John.

By that time the kitchen was deserted. Tom rolled the
barrels of milk into the dairy, and took out the empty ones
from the morning milking in solitary peace. He helped
himself to some bread and cheese and plums, then he
barrowed the empty barrels all the way back up the hill to
the farm again. The stars were coming out and the Compline bell ringing by the time he came down from the
farm. After Compline, the abbey would be folded into the
Great Silence, and all conversation of any kind forbidden.
Even if Brother John managed to get to Compline, there
would be nothing he could say.

Brother Tom had laboured too hard that day to lie
sleepless in his bed. He lay five minutes in the darkness,
wondering if the moon shone into Peregrine's room, and if
he slept or lay wakeful, but he could guess the answer to
that; then he turned his back on the whole thing and took
refuge in sleep.

In the morning, he slipped out of the choir and up to
the farm as soon as first Mass was ended. He breakfasted
on oats and barley-meal from the cattlefeed boxes, and
warm new milk from the cow.

'Take the milk down to the kitchen for me, will you? There's a good lad,' he hailed Brother Germanus as the men came up the hill to begin the day's work. 'I'll take your scythe.'

Delighted by this unexpected reprieve, Brother Germanus agreed readily, so Tom kept well clear of the cloister buildings until the bell rang for Terce and Chapter Mass. Brother John came into Chapter, but Tom refused to catch his eye, and concentrated on disciplining himself not to fidget through Father Chad's meandering discourse on Cenobites, Anchorites and Hermits. After the Chapter meeting ended, he slipped out as quickly as he could.

'Brother Thomas, wait a moment! I'd like to talk to you.' Brother John put a hand on Tom's shoulder as he was leaving the Chapter House. Tom scowled at him mutinously. He would gladly have knocked Brother John unconscious if it would have given him a way out of this conversation.

'I've no permission to talk.'

Brother John smiled at him. 'I've never known that to stop you. I've asked permission of Father Chad. He says we can talk in the little parlour.'

Tom shrugged his shoulders in ungracious assent, and the two of them walked in silence along the cloister, among the other silent monks who were going about their daily business. Away from the claustral buildings, the brothers were not so particular about silence, a certain amount of conversation being necessary on the farm, and good in the infirmary, though they were not permitted to stand in idle gossip anywhere; but here in the heart of the abbey, talking was kept to a bare minimum, and only in the abbot's house when a brother had come to seek counsel, or in the little parlour tucked away beside the day stairs, could any conversation of length take place, and that only with permission.

Brother John came into the gloomy little parlour after Brother Tom, and shut the door behind him.

'Sit down,' he said.

They both sat on the wooden chairs that were provided there—chairs, not stools, for visitors occasionally used this parlour too.

'Now then. What's this Brother Michael tells me, that you don't intend to come back and see Father Peregrine again?'

'That's right.'

Brother John sat in silence, looking at him.

'Oh, don't try your unnerving infirmary manner on me! I came, it was awful, and I'm not coming again. That's all there is to it. Is that all you want to know? Can I go? I'm supposed to be reaping the oats with Brother Stephen.'

'Tom, stop it! How long have we lived in community together? Can't you trust me? Tell me about it.'

Tom's head shot up, and he glared at Brother John furiously. 'Don't say that to me! Don't you *ever* say that to me!'

'Ssh now, peace.' Brother John held up his hands. He was not in the slightest perturbed by Tom's raised voice and furious face. He was too accustomed to the unpredictable moods of senility and the undermined emotions of sickness for that.

'What did I say to upset you? I didn't intend—oh, I see. That's one of Father Peregrine's sayings, isn't it? "Tell me about it." Yes.

'Brother Thomas...why are you making such a *fuss* about all this? It's like trying to get a nervous horse through a gate! He's your friend, he's sick, he needs you. Why isn't it simple for you, just to spend some time with him? A little while in the evenings would do, if you're needed on the farm in the day.'

'Oh...' Tom sat hunched and miserable, not wanting to talk. 'You don't understand.'

'Explain to me then! *Tell me about it!*'

Tom stared at him angrily. 'I told you...'

'Oh, never mind what you told me! You're behaving like a spoiled child! Come on. Talk.'

'He...I couldn't understand him, John. He tried to tell me, got angry with me; but it was all just rubbish, what he was saying. I don't know what to do. What could I say to him? I didn't know what he *is* now. He's destroyed, he's all different. If he'd died, I would have grieved, I would have cherished the memory of him, but...this—this is *horrible*. Can't you *see?*'

'Well, yes. I can see it from your point of view. Now, maybe you could try to look at it through his eyes?'

'He's been ill, it's taken a lot out of him. He desperately needs the comfort of familiarity to find his bearings again. He's lost his work, his status. He's helpless. He's stuck in the infirmary, can't go anywhere, can't read, write, talk. Tom, think about it. It's *horrific*, isn't it? And what's the one link that he could have with the way things used to be?'

Tom looked at him. 'I...I suppose I am.'

'Quite so. He would have wanted you anyway—he loves you, Tom. But having lost everything else, he needs you quite desperately. He's watched for you, waited for you, pinned his hopes on you coming, *all this time*. And then yesterday you came, and everything went wrong. Brother, have you no pity? Can't you imagine how he must have felt—the embarrassment, and the distress, and the pain when you walked out and didn't come back? The sickness hasn't destroyed him. Far from it, he's all there. It's you that's destroying him.'

'Ah, that's not fair!'

Brother John shrugged his shoulders. 'That depends how you look at it. Speech is not everything. Mobility is not everything. Besides, his speech will return if he will work on it. He has a little, it's not all gone—he can swear well enough! It's grief, despair, unhappiness that's making him an invalid. He won't even let us take him out of his room. He won't *try*. Tom...it's true, this has changed him.

You can't be this ill and it not change you, but he's still himself. At the moment, you're looking at the sickness, not at the man. If you can find enough grace, enough charity, to look past the paralysis and the muddled speech, you'll find him again.'

Brother Tom sat looking at the floor in a torment of indecision. He rubbed his hand nervously across his face.

'Oh God, Tom, is it so difficult? *Please*. I *beg* you to come. You've *got* to come back.'

'When?'

Brother John sat back in his chair with a sigh of relief. 'Today. Now!'

'Brother Stephen's waiting for me up at the farm.'

'Father Abbot's waited for you five weeks, and I can tell you he needs you more than the farm does. I dare say Stephen can wait an hour or two.'

'*An hour or two?* You want me to spend more than an hour with him? Saying what for mercy's sake?'

'Oh Tom, half an hour, ten minutes, anything. Just come.'

They walked along the cloister together. 'I wish Brother Bernard wouldn't hang the washing out in the cloister garth,' Tom muttered crossly. 'Makes the place look such a shambles.'

Brother John smiled, but did not reply. He had beseeched God to send Tom to see Peregrine; it seemed unreasonable to expect even the Almighty to send him in a good humour.

Brother John escorted Tom closely into the infirmary, and along the passage to Father Peregrine's room.

'Go in alone,' he said, very quietly. 'It would hurt him to know I had to fetch you.'

Tom nodded and put his hand to the latch. Brother John walked away, and Tom stood there summoning his courage a short eternity. He felt sick.

He lifted the latch and pushed open the door. For a moment, oddly, he had a sense of being given another chance; a sense that today was yesterday all over again, because in this room nothing had changed, except that the sun had not yet moved round to fill the room with golden light. Peregrine sat, just as yesterday, immobile, slumped uncomfortably awry in his chair, enduring the passing time.

He lifted his head a little at the sight of Brother Tom, something like interest lightening the leaden dullness of his eyes. But he did not speak.

'Father...' Tom came fully into the room, and stood; uneasy, tense. He hoped desperately that Peregrine would not say anything to him. Not just yet. He wondered what he would do if yesterday repeated itself. Suppose he needed to relieve himself again? Even if I managed to understand him, what would I do then? How does he do it? What should I do to help him? Why didn't I ask Brother John?

Why me? Tom asked it of God in silent panic. Why me?

He moistened his lips, became aware of his fingernails digging painfully into the palms of his hands. This is ridiculous, he thought.

Peregrine was saying nothing, watching him. He looks sad, Tom thought. Sad and...wary. Apprehensive. He's finding this as hard as I am. It's as though we were strangers. Worse. I've got to speak to him. He moistened his lips again.

'Please bear with me. I don't know what to say...'

He pulled the low stool over and sat down beside Peregrine, self-conscious under the silent, brooding gaze of his abbot's eyes. Shyly, he took his hand. He held it in between his own hands, gently rubbing it with his finger-tips. Peregrine suffered him to do it.

'I'm sorry about what happened yesterday.'

Peregrine said nothing. An unreasonable irritation seized Tom. He's not exactly making this easier for me, he thought resentfully. If he would only—only...what?

What could a man do with one crippled hand? He saw

then that Peregrine's silence was the best thing he could offer, the best he could do to ease the situation. He's not holding out on me, he's giving me time, Tom realised; time to come to terms with this...purgatory. There was a certain wonder in that insight for Tom, testing the ground of an unfamiliar form of communication, reaching in to the other man's wordless presence, groping for an understanding of the language of his silence, like a blind man's fingers exploring the surfaces of an unseen face.

What would he say if he could speak? Tom cast his mind back, pictured again the times he had come into the abbot's house, bringing his burdens, his perplexities to this man. Sometimes no doubt Peregrine had troubles and heartaches of his own, but he usually had time to listen. Tom remembered it so vividly; the man sitting at his table, the comfort there had been in his acceptance and affection, the amusement and penetration of his eyes— 'Tell me about it.' Maybe that's what he would say now, Tom thought.

It occurred to him that such disability had a terrible honesty. It left no possibility of social niceties, the smooth, conventional exchanges by which men assuaged their loneliness without ever compromising their isolation. In this silence and stark deprivation, a man was pared down to the bedrock of his humanity. There were no pretensions here. If there was to be any communication at all, it would have to begin at that level. It would have to be the truth.

'They want me to help you to smile again,' Tom said. His fingers moved lightly on the unresisting hand. 'But there's nothing to smile about, is there? This hand, this poor, broken hand is all you've got left. It chokes me. God alone knows what it does to you.'

There was a cautious answering pressure from Peregrine's hand.

'I'm thinking,' Tom said very quietly; 'I'm thinking it's like it was once before. Maybe you need to allow yourself to weep before you can think about laughing again.'

He looked into Peregrine's eyes, looking for the answer of his silence. He found his answer. It was like looking into a chasm of misery. No defence met him. He saw right in to the grey, barren hell of despair. It was overwhelming. Tom looked down, away from the intolerable unhappiness of those eyes, at the maimed hand he held in his. Peregrine's lack of speech meant that conversation was no longer a common ground. Tom also had to come in to the place of silence if they were to meet as equals. He had to find a way in silence to bring his friendship, his love, a crumb of comfort. He let the tentative shyness go from his touch as he held and caressed Peregrine's hand with uninhibited tenderness, trusting his love to be received, a human reality flowing from hand to hand.

'Do you?' he said softly, then. 'Do you weep?'

Peregrine nodded, slowly. The words came slow and muffled. 'Oh, y-es.'

Tom looked up into his face. Peregrine looked back at him a moment, then closed his eyes. He was silent. Then, 'Y-es,' he said again.

'Alone? At night?'

'Y-es.'

'And...does it ease things a bit?'

Another silence. Tom held his hand, waited.

'N-n...n-o.'

There was something very final about that. Tom cast about in his mind for something else to say.

'I've missed you,' he said in the end. He glanced up at Peregrine's face. The dark grey eyes were open again, watching him very intently. By my faith, Brother John was right, Tom thought. There is nothing wrong with your mind.

'Have you—have you missed me?'

The twisted hand gripped Tom's hand. 'Y-es. Oh, oh y-es.'

Tom looked down at Peregrine's hand, holding his tightly. 'That...um—that sounds like real heartache.'

'Y-es.'

Tom tried to look up at the grey eyes again, but could not. He felt too guilty. There was no backing out of this conversation now, though. That would be another evasion, another stealing away, and it would not do. Tom was in no doubt now that this was by no means a one-sided conversation, even if he had all the words and Peregrine had only 'yes' and 'no' at his disposal. His abbot was putting him on the spot as unerringly as ever.

'I—I've got no excuses. I was frightened. It was because you couldn't speak, and I didn't know what to say to you. I knew you'd be all churned up inside. It was too big for me to face. I felt so helpless—'

Peregrine snatched his hand out of Tom's, and Tom looked up, startled. Peregrine beat his hand against his chest, his face contorted with emotion. A stream of muddled words poured out, none of them intelligible, then he stopped, glaring indignantly at Tom, who tried not to smile, but couldn't help it.

'All right. I understood that. That was anger. And pain. Something like, "*You* felt helpless! What about *me?*" Yes?'

The misshapen hand came down onto Tom's hand again, and the fingers curled round his.

'Y-es.' The relief at being able to communicate some of the anger and hurt that tore at him was immense. Peregrine felt the sickening mass of despair that filled him, sometimes till he choked on it, faintly eased. Tom was aware of a slight relaxation of tension, and realised that some of it had been Peregrine's apprehension and fear, not his own.

'So! Do you forgive me?'

'N-o.'

Tom looked at him nonplussed. Peregrine smiled, an extraordinary, lopsided smile with the side of his face that had escaped paralysis. If you could see yourself, Tom thought.

'Why not?' he demanded.

Peregrine lifted his hand and beat it three times against his breast in the ritual gesture of the penitential rite from the mass—*mea culpa, mea culpa, mea maxima culpa;* my fault, my own fault, my own most grievous fault.

'*Your* fault? What's your fault?'

'N-o.'

'Then...' light dawned. 'You—are you asking me to apologise?'

A silence. The smile waning, a little bit shamefaced. 'Y-es,' very quietly.

'Oh, my Father—you'll make a good monk of me yet!'

Tom knelt on the ground beside his abbot, and took his hand again, his head bent.

'Father, I confess my fault,' he said. 'You needed me, and I knew you needed me, and I stayed away. I confess my fault of cowardice, and of hardheartedness, selfishness. I humbly beseech the Lord Jesus to restore the trust between us; and I ask your forgiveness, and God's.'

Father Peregrine blessed him, a jumbled sentence full of tenderness. 'Y-es,' he added, just to make sure.

Brother Tom sat back on his stool again, and looked again into Peregrine's eyes. 'So that's what was wanted,' he said softly, 'to rekindle a small flame of hope.'

He drew breath to speak again, then hesitated. Peregrine spoke to him. A question. Again, imperatively.

'What was I going to say? Yes? I'm not going to get away with much, talking to you, am I? You're worse than you were before. I was going to say, Brother John thinks—has he told you this?—he thinks you may recover your speech, at least in part. He says that the paralysis will probably be with you always, but you should expect to get quite a bit better. He thinks, by the spring—it's early to tell yet, but by the spring—you could be able to...well, at any rate to work again. Did he say this to you?'

'Y-es.'

'Well? What do you think?' Foolish question, thought Tom, as soon as he'd said it; as if he could tell me.

'N-o.'

'No what? Don't you believe him?'

'Y-es.'

'You don't think you'll work again?'

Peregrine held up his hand, broken, twisted, his left hand (and he was such a right-handed man, Tom thought). He shrugged his shoulder. 'N-o.'

The abbot's work: working with guests, important church officials, government officials, local dignitaries; entertaining; leading the brethren in pastoral counsel, spiritual direction, homilies; presiding over the Community Chapter, leading the Office; orchestrating the huge network of the community's business affairs: no, Brother Tom couldn't see it either. What else, then? Peregrine met his gaze, and nodded.

'Y-es,' he said slowly, and made a gesture of wiping clean with his hand. Finished.

Tom took a deep breath. Hope, Brother Michael had said; but this man was no fool. He was not going to be duped by false hopes or jollied along by shallow optimism. This was a time for honesty.

'No,' he said. 'I can't see it either.' Tom looked into Peregrine's eyes. Warmth. Gratitude. Affirmation. That man preferred the truth. He did not want to be patronised with kindness.

'All right,' Tom said. 'Let's look at the worst. You could be like this for years. Paralysed. No speech. Helpless. Just like now. That's the worst, yes?'

'Y-es.'

'Can you bear it?'

The briefest of pauses. 'N-o. N-o.'

'What then? Are you afraid of dying?'

'N-o.' No hesitation there.

'Have you thought about dying?'

'Y-es.'

'And is it...have you wished you might die?'

'Y-es. Y-es.'

'Do you want to go on living—like this?'

'N-n-o.'

'Father...shall I help you out?'

The abbot's eyes widened. He grew very still, looking at Tom. And I thought nothing would ever shock him, Tom thought.

Peregrine looked down, away from Tom's gaze. He was silent. When at last he raised his head and met Tom's eyes again, he looked so vulnerable, so wide open, that it hurt Tom almost physically.

'N-o,' he whispered.

'Because, when it comes to it, you fear death?' Tom hated himself for the brutality of the questioning, but he persisted.

'N-o.'

'What then? Do you really believe, deep down, that there's a chance you'll get better?'

'N-o.'

'Is it because it is forbidden to take life?'

Peregrine looked at him, unhappily. 'N-o,' he whispered.

'That makes you ashamed? That you would take your life, against the laws of the Church?'

'Y-es.'

'What then? You can't bear this shadow of living, but you don't want me to get you out of it, because...?'

Peregrine looked at Tom, waiting. Oh God, he wants to tell me, and I've run out of guesses. Help me. Help me to see.

'Maybe...is it just that life is sweet? That there are kittens, and sun, and the scent of rain in the morning. And maybe...having someone to talk to makes it a little bit worthwhile?'

'Y-es...T-om.'

So that was it. It shook Tom to the core to see the power that had been in his hands.

'Let me be sure of what you're saying. Do you mean...my coming to see you has made the difference between wanting to die...and wanting to live?'

A long, long pause. Even now it was terrifying to reveal his need of Tom's friendship, how he had ached for his company, wept at his absence. Like a man confessing a secret, shameful guilt, hanging his head he whispered, 'Y-es.'

Brother Tom sat in silence, looking down at the hand he held between his own.

'Do you know,' he said, 'it *hurts*, loving you. You turn me inside out.'

IV

Out of Silence

'You're very quiet today.'

Brother Stephen passed Brother Tom the stone jar of ale as they sat leaning against the hay rick, sheltering in its shadow from the midday sun.

'I'm supposed to be quiet. I'm a monk.'

Brother Stephen looked at him sideways.

'What are you looking at me like that for? You know, we really should have some mugs up here for this ale. Drinking it straight from the jar, all of us, and eating bread at the same time, it's like porridge before we're halfway down the jar.'

'Got something on your mind, have you?'

'Me? What makes you think so?'

'You're very quiet today.'

Tom rubbed his hand over his chin reflectively. 'I've been thinking about Father.'

'Peregrine?'

'Yes. Do you know, for all he can't converse, when Theodore came in to say Mass with him the other day—'

'Theodore?' interrupted Brother Stephen. 'Oh yes, *Father* Theodore! Sorry, go on.'

Theodore had been priested in the spring, and made Master of Novices when Father Matthew died, but it took the brethren a while to adjust to his new status. The notion of Father Theodore saying Mass and hearing confessions still had an aura of comical novelty about it.

Tom smiled. 'Yes,' he said, '*Father* Theodore. As soon as he said, *"Dominus vobiscum,"* Father responded, *"Et cum spirito tuo,"* as smoothly and easily as can be; never faltered. He said it without thinking, just automatically; *"Et cum spirito tuo."* I'm sure, you know, that all his speech is there locked away still...dammed up somehow.' Tom looked at Brother Stephen with a grin. 'Another thing, he swears faultlessly! Again, Brother John says that's because a man swears *before* he thinks, not afterwards.

'The words are there still, and the physical possibility of saying them. What's gone is the carry over from an idea to a sentence.

'I think...maybe it's a question of re-establishing a flow; you know, like a melody—so he can get the thoughts through to words again...'

'Can he not use the sign language of the Silence?'

Tom shook his head. 'Not really. He was never that good with it, because his hands are so inflexible. Before all this, he used to speak to me rather than sign if he had to tell me something in the night. But anyway, now, even when he tries to indicate something with his hand...it's funny, that comes out garbled too. He points to the wrong thing. Points to his mouth when he means his eye...it's as though—well, the problem is not speech, just. It's communication altogether. And yet...' Tom paused, frowning.

'What?'

'I don't know how to say it. He can't say anything much. He can't share his thoughts. Half a face and one mangled hand isn't much to communicate with, especially when what you want to put across comes out all muddled anyway, but...it's like a light shining in darkness instead of daylight...the light is all the brighter for the depth of the night. Himself...he can share himself—with absolute honesty and clarity too. Stephen, he's shown me—it's possible to have communion even without communication. If you don't hold back; if you don't withhold yourself.'

'Is that so?' Brother Stephen yawned and stretched his arms over his head. 'It's all a bit deep for me, I'm afraid. Time to stop withholding ourselves from that strip of rye, I should say. Brother Germanus will be thinking we've fallen asleep. You've answered my question, though: I can certainly see why you've been so quiet!' He got slowly to his feet. 'Ooh, my back! All this bending plays merry hell with it.' He rubbed his hands on the small of his back and stretched, to ease it. 'Come on, then; one last push.' He reached his hand down to Tom and pulled him to his feet. 'If we don't slack this afternoon, we'll have the whole field done, and tomorrow we can begin carting the oats home.'

The feeling at the end of the day, looking back along the strip they had cut, the golden stubble shining in the afternoon sun, the neat stooks of corn, was beyond words. Brother Tom put his arm goodnaturedly across Brother Germanus' shoulders, and waved his other hand expansively, taking in the broad sweep of the fields.

'Does your heart good, eh? The wind and the sun, and the good earth, and all that lot, bread and cattle fodder...beautiful.'

He clapped Brother Germanus on his aching back. 'How do you feel now?'

Brother Germanus smiled. 'Like you said,' he replied. 'Grand.'

'And tomorrow we can start bringing it in,' said Brother Stephen as they walked down the farmtrack to the abbey, the Vespers bell tolling across the fields, calling the brothers in at the end of the day. 'This makes up for the ruined hay.'

As he stood in his stall singing the responses at Vespers, Tom's mind wandered back to Father Peregrine. He shouldn't be in that stuffy room all day long, he thought. It isn't healthy for any man to be shut away from the fresh air and the sunshine. Not to see the grass on the hill blowing back in the breeze, and the lark tossing against a blue heaven, and the sun going down at evening; or the mist lying in the ditches of a morning, and the first sweet light of the day. I've got to get him out.

He sat when the others sat, stood when they stood, but his mind was on other things. If I could get his interest in something outside himself again...the farm maybe....

When Vespers had finished, Tom followed Father Chad along the cloister. 'Father Chad! Can you spare me a minute after supper?'

'Most certainly.' Father Chad was surprised, and pleased. it was the first time since Father Peregrine's illness that Brother Thomas had shown any inclination to talk to him at all. He received him with some curiosity in the abbot's house when the evening meal was over.

'Father Chad, can I borrow the maps of the farm that Father was using to plan the building work? I thought I might look at them with him in the morning; thought it might lift him out of himself a little, encourage him to go outside, take an interest.'

Father Chad smiled at him kindly. 'What a good idea! Yes, by all means take them. I have been more sorry than I can tell you that he had not the opportunity to let us know his scheme for the financing of the things we need to do. I'm no good at that sort of thing at all, I regret to say. Maybe it will come back to him. I haven't liked to trouble him about it, poor man.'

As he spoke, he got up to search in the heavy chest of documents that stood against the wall. Tom waited, looking round the familiar room. His heart was tugged with sadness for times irrecoverably gone. He put his hand out and stroked the surface of the great oak table. His eyes wandered over the ink, the seal, the box of sealing waxes, all of them clearly visible beside Father Chad's neat pile of letters waiting his attention.

Tom remembered with a smile Father Peregrine

searching irritably for his seal underneath a spilling riot of letters, accounts and books, accusing Tom of having lost it, and then snapping a rebuke at him for his indignant reply.

The scribe's table, under the window to catch the best light...Theodore had sat there so often, peaceful in Father Peregrine's company. The fireplace, not used since last winter: Tom had himself swept it clean and furnished it with a little pile of kindling: pine cones, dried rosemary and sage, knotted twists of dried grass. The times he had come into this room in the depths of winter, and Father Peregrine, embarrassed at the luxury, had asked him to light a fire; 'For my hands, Brother Thomas. They're so stiff in this cold.'

Apple logs; he had always asked for apple logs. Everyone else chose ash for firewood if they could get it, but Peregrine loved the smell of the applewood burning. There were one or two apple logs still, lying in the box at the side of the hearth.

Father Chad had the accounts and plans relating to the farm, and leaned on the open chest as he got up from his knees on the stone flags of the floor. 'Eh, it's a long way up! I must be growing old. Yes; here they are. I think you'll find they're all here in this bundle, though I must admit, his documents were not very orderly, especially the things he was working on. Let me know if there's anything else you need—and how you get on. No hurry to have them back; I shan't need them for a week or two.

'How about you, Brother? The harvest is coming in well ahead of time with your help, I hear.'

'Yes. Yes, we've done well. We start bringing it in to the barns tomorrow.'

'They've been glad to have you on the farm. How does it feel to be back in this room again?' He smiled, friendly.

Tom looked at him. 'Oh...well...' he said, and shrugged his shoulders. 'Thank you for the plans. I'll take them to him tomorrow.'

Tom was milking in the morning, and then busy with the preparations for carting home the corn. The first they had cut had stood more than two weeks in the fields now, with never a break in the weather. In the pouring heat of the afternoons and the breezes of the evening it had dried well, and needed to be in. Brother Stephen received Tom's request for time off to go down to the infirmary after Chapter with less than enthusiasm.

'Brother, you are needed here, you know. You have been going in to see him after Vespers. What's wrong with that?'

'I wanted him to get a look at the plans in daylight. I'm hoping I might persuade him out of doors. I—oh, please, Stephen.'

'You'll be back here after the midday break?'

'Yes; I promise.'

'You can tell Brother John I'll be needing another pair of hands for the farm if he's filching my men for the infirmary. No, go on, I'm pulling your leg. We'll manage. It's good to see you looking a bit less like a thundercloud than you have been. Greet Father for me.'

Brother Tom came down from the hill and collected the documents, taking them along to the infirmary. He paused and snapped off a sprig of rosemary, rubbing it between his fingers to release its fragrance as he strolled through the physic garden and into the low infirmary building. Peregrine raised his head and greeted him with a smile of surprised pleasure as he came through the door of the room with his bundle of plans, the smells of earth and air and herbs clinging about him. He had not expected to see Tom until evening.

'I've brought the farm plans. I thought I'd show you which bits we've been able to repair. Want to see them?'

'Y-es, s'il te plaît.'

'What? Oh, right.'

Peregrine looked up at him amiably, seemingly unaware he had said anything unusual. Tom suppressed a smile, and laid the plans on the table. Does he know, he wondered; does he know when he speaks French? Sometimes, maybe. Brother John had said Father was taken aback by saying, 'Merci, chéri.' But even then, had he known it was in French, or had he simply been embarrassed because he thought he'd said, 'Thank you, darling'?

Tom glanced down at the table which stood beside Peregrine's chair. Two books lay there already, a copy of John's Gospel, and a breviary.

'Brother John been saying the Office with you?' Tom asked, as he smoothed the plan on top of the books.

'N-o. B-Br-B…oh!…F-Fr…n…'

'Francis?'

'Y-es.'

'D'you know, I haven't spoken to him in an age. Dawn to dusk I've been up on the farm. And he's going away to be priested soon.'

'Y-es.'

'And Brother James off to Oxford.'

Peregrine reacted to this piece of news with an explosion of consternation, ending in an incomprehensible question.

'I beg your pardon?' Tom looked at him blankly. 'I didn't get any of that. Do you object to Brother James going to Oxford?'

'*Y-es.*'

'Why? I thought you set up for him to go to university.'

'Y-es.'

Tom frowned at him, puzzled, then his face cleared. 'Oh! Cambridge, wasn't it—for the cheaper accommodation? I suppose Father Chad forgot. Anyway, he's going to Oxford now.'

There followed a long muttered grumbling from Father Peregrine, which required all Tom's self-discipline to keep a straight face, then Peregrine sighed and dismissed it.

'Ainsi soit-il,' he said, and turned his attention resolutely to the farm plan.

Looking at the plans was not a success. Peregrine leaned over the map with interest at first, but his initial eagerness faltered as Tom pointed out to him the field shelter they had been working on, the harvest fields and the mill. He shifted restlessly, shadows of bafflement and unease gathering in his face as he studied the plan. He rubbed his hand over his eyes and looked at the map again, struggling to make sense of it. Tom, absorbed in his favourite object of thought, did not notice his disquiet at once.

'We've built the ricks here...and here. Brother Stephen wants to build a new shelter up here because of the stream; then we could pen the ewes in at lambing, and there'd be water on hand. It seems the ideal place to me; what do you think?'

Peregrine licked his lips. He was trembling. 'Y-es.'

'What's the matter? Are you all right?' Tom looked at him, concerned. 'Haven't you understood what I was saying?' he asked gently.

'Y-es,' said Peregrine hastily, frowning at the plan.

'Are you sure? You can remember when we looked at these to decide on the repairs and rebuilding?'

'Y-y-es.'

'Start here, then. This is the abbey. The chapel, look, and the cloister. Can you see the infirmary?'

The uneasiness was turning into outright fear in Peregrine's face. However hard he looked at the plan, it would not unlock its mysteries to him. Stalling for time, he rested his head on his hand, obscuring his face from Tom's gaze.

'Here's the infirmary. Look, trace your finger with mine. The infirmary here...and the path up to the farm. Do you remember?'

'Y-es,' Peregrine lied.

'All right. So this is the orchard where the pigs are, and

beyond that, the field of oats and rye. Now then...up here the pastures...Yes? You remember?'

'Y-es.'

'And the outlying buildings to the west, where the aisled barn is and the field shelter with a foldyard. Yes?'

'Y-es.'

'So then. You've got that?'

'Y-es.'

Tom looked at him, not at all sure he was telling the truth.

'Can you show me then, on the map, the place by the spinney, where Brother Stephen wants to build the new shelter? No, not there, it's north-east of that, above the long meadow. Do you see?'

'N-o,' Peregrine whispered hopelessly, his face shocked and ashen pale.

'Let me tell you about it then,' said Tom gently. He was not sure what had gone wrong, but judged this not the moment to ask, and tried to speak tactfully, wondering how to abandon the project without the total humiliation of conceding defeat.

'There's a spinney up there on the hill; lovely in the spring. The primroses grow there, and the bluebells. Violets too. It rings with birdsong on a May morning. Behind the wood is the source of the stream which runs down through the spinney, coming out beside the pasture. This is the lower pasture here, where we bring the ewes down when their time is coming in March. Up till now, we've brought them into the foldyard and the byre for lambing, because the cows are out to grass by then, but Brother Stephen wants to build a new shelter there, so we shall be able to take in the ewes that are about to give birth, without disturbing them too much. What do you think?'

Peregrine pondered the question. It was a relief to be released from the map, but he felt shaken still, his confidence undermined.

'Y-es, b-b-b...m...wh-wh...oh...' He sighed wearily.

'A good idea, but some reservations; yes?'

'Y-es.'

'What are the reservations? Too cold for the sheep?'

'N-o.'

'Unnecessary?'

Peregrine smiled. 'Y-es...N-o.'

'You mean yes, but that isn't what you meant?'

'Y-es.'

'What then? The expense?'

'N-o.'

'What then? It's a lovely sheltered spot. Perfect I would have thought.'

'Th-th...m...S-s-s...G...m..Sj...oh!' He strove desperately to shape the words, but the attempt was utterly futile, and Tom had run out of ideas to help him. Peregrine explained again, but Tom shook his head, helplessly. 'I'm sorry, Father, I'm stumped. I just can't make out what you're saying.'

Peregrine glared, exasperated at him, redoubled his efforts to make himself understood.

'I'm sorry, Father. I'm sorry. I can't make out head or tail of that. Try again.'

Peregrine waved his hand impatiently. 'Oh, n-o,' he said.

'Please. We'll get there in the end.'

'N-o.' His mouth was a grim line and his eyes were glowering as he looked at Tom.

'Come on, you'll never get anywhere if you don't try. Start again, slowly.'

'N-o.'

'Oh, you obstinate old man! Will you not just *try*?'

'N-o! N-o! N-o!' Peregrine lost his temper, shouted the words at him, beside himself with fury born of frustration and fear. He stopped himself, still breathing heavily, but the turmoil was too much to bear. He would not look at Tom and sat shaking his head from side to side like a wounded animal, then with a roar of anger and frustration he swept the plans and books from the table beside him with a violence that sent even the heavy Gospel flying. They crashed to the floor, scattering everywhere, and the binding of the Gospel split as it fell open and hit the wall. One or two of the pages were torn loose. Peregrine sat, trembling, his head bowed, refusing to look at Brother Tom.

Tom looked round as the latch clicked, and Martin Jonson appeared through the door. Martin viewed the scattered books and documents on the floor with alarm.

'Dear, dear me!' he said. 'What's been going on here? Are you all right, Father? I thought I heard some kind of a commotion. What happened? Has he been taken bad again, Brother? He looks bad.'

'He's all right,' said Brother Tom. 'I'll pick these things up. Don't worry yourself.'

'Well, if you're sure, Brother. Call me if you need help.' He looked apprehensively at Peregrine, who did not lift his head, did not move.

'N-o!' he ground out through clenched teeth, as Martin left the room.

'No what?'

'N-o! N-o!'

'Do you mean you don't want me to pick the things up?'

'N-o!'

'You do want me to pick them up?'

'Y-es.'

'No what then? What else did I say? Do you mean you're not all right?'

'Y-es! N-o!'

'Oh, for the love of God!' Tom ran his fingers wearily through his hair and across his tonsured scalp.

'I'm sorry. I didn't understand you. I can't promise to understand you. I'm sorry. Does it make me entirely a failure?'

'Y-es!'

'Thank you. So you hate me, yes?'

'Y-es!'

'Go to hell, Brother Thomas, is that it?'

'Y-es.'

'Get out of here, and never come back?'

'Y-es.'

'Would you do me the courtesy of looking me in the face when you say that?'

Peregrine didn't move for a moment. Then he lifted his hand and pressed it to his mouth; and Tom sat there an intolerable, harrowing eternity, listening to him trying to stifle the shuddering of his breath, watching the tears trickle down the back of his twisted hand; a painful, scalding grief of inadequacy and defeat, sparing nothing.

Eventually, Peregrine stole a glance across the room at the mess of plans and parchments, and raised a stricken face to Brother Tom.

'M...b-b...n-b-b...oh! merde!!...b-b-ook.' And he smoke his breast in the ritual gesture of penance, *mea culpa*. Tom looked at him, torn between pity and exasperation.

'Yes. As you say; book. Your nose is running and your face is a river of tears. Have you a handkerchief?'

'Y-es.'

'Use it then, while I gather up this shambles.'

He gave Peregrine enough time to recover some measure of composure, busying himself with the reassembling of the plans and letters. The intact Office book he placed with them on the table, and he took the torn Gospel onto his knee as he sat down again on the low stool.

'What did you say this was? Can you say it again?'

'N-o.'

'Try.'

'N-o.'

Tom sat with his elbow on his knee and his chin in his hand, regarding Father Peregrine in amused vexation. Peregrine blew his nose and looked back at him, shamefaced, but not giving an inch. Tom shook his head, and took the Gospel into his hands.

'You said that. You said "book". If you will at least try to say it again, I will take this Gospel *most discreetly* to Brother—oh, I beg his pardon, Father Theodore, and get him to mend it, no questions asked. If you will not even *try*, then I swear by this book I will tie it round your neck, and I will stack you on a barrow and take you to Chapter in the morning for you to make your confession there of your destructive tantrum; so help me, I will. Now then!'

Peregrine stared at him, incredulous, furious, horrified. 'Y…Y-y-ou…y-ou…b-aa…b-astard!'

Brother Tom dissolved into helpless laughter.

'Abbot Peregrine du Fayel, you are the most obstinate mule of a man God ever created. If you can say that, surely to goodness you can say "book". Say it! Try! Please.'

'Mm-b…b…b-ook! B-ook.'

'Yea!' Tom waved his fists in triumph, Peregrine watching him in an attempt at dignity which cracked up into a grin.

'Can you say it again? Book.'

'Boo-k. Boo-k.' He tried to look nonchalant, casual, but his eyes laughed at Tom in excitement.

'You can! If you can say that, you can say anything. Says it in the Scriptures, doesn't it? In the beginning; one word. I'll wager God's word cost him as much struggle and tantrums as yours did, too. Can you still say it? Book.'

'M…b-ook. Boo-k.'

'Ah, you're wonderful. I knew you could do it. Now I don't know how long I've been here, and I've promised Brother Stephen I'll be back up at the farm by midday, but I've been wondering, won't you come outside with me one of these mornings? It's beautiful out there, Father. You can smell the year turning, the ripening, joyful smell of the autumn, and the hills are just breathtaking in the morning light.'

Some of the laughter died out of Peregrine's eyes; he withdrew a little into himself again.

'N-o.'

'Don't you miss the trees, the dew...the sky?'

'Y-es. M...s-s-st—oh!' He shook his head irritably.

'The sunshine?'

'N-o.'

'What then? Won't you come outside, just for a while? It's a lovely morning!'

'N-o.'

'Why is it? Don't you want people to see you?'

'Y-es.'

'Who's to see? Old men in their second childhood— they can hardly see anyway, most of this lot.' Tom looked at him, encouraging, but Peregrine appeared quite adamant.

'You don't want to go out then?'

'Y-es.'

'You *do?*'

'Y-es. M...b...s-s-st—Ah!' He thumped the arm of the chair, angrily.

'All right, don't lose your temper again. There's something you want to do?'

'Y-es.'

'Something you want to see?'

'Y-es.'

'Outside?'

'Y-es. Y-es.'

'Shall I take you out now, then?'

'*N-o.*'

'Well...' Tom was perplexed. 'This afternoon?'

'N-o. *N-o!* N...n...s-s-st—oh, merde! s...' He waved his hand at the ceiling, gesturing all around.

'The sky?'

'Y-es. *Y-es.*'

'You want to see the sky?'

'Y-es.'

'So let's go out and see it then.'

'*N-O!!*' Peregrine screwed his eyes up, furious, grinding his teeth in helpless rage.

'Father, stop it! I can't help it. Don't be so impatient. You make me feel all harassed. You want to go out. Yes?'

'Y-es.'

'But now now.'

'Y-es. N-o.' Peregrine sat looking at him, his face twitching with impatience, the dark grey eyes burning with the words he couldn't say. Tom looked back, utterly baffled.

'Not this afternoon.'

'N-o.'

'Later?'

'Y-es. *Y-es. Y-es!* S-s-st...'

'You...oh, sweet heaven, you want to see the stars!'

Peregrine closed his eyes and relaxed in relief, nodding.

'*Y-es.* Y-es. Y-es!'

'Stars.'

'S-s-st-ars.'

Tom smiled at him. 'I'll take you. Tonight, I'll take you outside to see the stars.'

The infirmary had two contraptions, designed and built by Brother Peter, for moving its patients who could sit up but not walk. The design was a mutation of a barrow and a chair; either a barrow with no front and an upright back, the wheels being at the back and two legs at the front, like the opposite of a wheelbarrow: or a low chair with wheels instead of back legs—it depended how you looked at it.

Into one of these singular creations Brother Michael and Brother Tom lifted Father Peregrine after Compline had ended, and dusk descended into darkness. Brother Tom had begged permission of Father Chad to be late from his bed, and Brother Michael was up anyway, because the infirmary was never left unsupervised.

They padded the barrow with pillows, and lifted Peregrine into it, their hushed voices and the low-burning night-lights of the sleeping infirmary adding to the sense of adventure that attended the occasion. Brother Tom pushed the chair along the passage, carefully over the low sill of the threshold; Brother Michael closed the door behind them, and they were out in the aromatic darkness of the physic garden.

It was a fine night, the moon reigning proud and fair in the heavens, bathing the gardens in an unearthly beauty of light. A breeze freshened in the night air, but scarcely enough to stir the leaves of the herbs or the laburnham tree that grew beside the path. Peregrine gazed ravenously at the high, immense expanses of the moonlit sky and the silent brilliance of the stars.

What a relief it must be, Tom reflected, to be away from the geometry of man-made things, feeling the wild, anarchic beauty of the night wind's caress and seeing the random flung scattering of the stars, to a man who has lost the ability to interpret patterns, who has been baffled and defeated by codes and schemes these long, dismal weeks. It must have been like putting down a great burden to come out here where there was no pattern, no code, only the wordless immediacy of life. Tom thought on the times in his own life when everything had seemed to be disintegrating. There had been such a healing reassurance in the rhythm of natural things. Maybe, he pondered, maybe it was not that it had no pattern, but that human beings were part of the design, and couldn't look at it because it didn't exclude them, only restored them to themselves.

Day and night, the dance of the stars, the cool fingers of the breeze... it wove men into its purpose like single threads. Even the broken ones could be woven together with the others to make the whole thing beautiful. There had to be a pattern, surely, because it was not empty of meaning, all this. It made more sense than anything. It was just that the pattern was not so much of a code... more like a dear, familiar face.

'Are you all right?' Tom asked quietly, releasing his

hold on the handles of the barrow and resting his hands lightly on Peregrine's shoulders.

'Y-es. Oh…T-om…th-th-th…s-s-stars.' His voice was filled with the sweet agony of his yearning delight. 'I l-l-lo…m…'

'Yes. I know. You love the stars.'

In silent consummation Peregrine drank in the beauty of the night; the wide enchanting wilderness of stars, the close enfolding of the secret dark, losing himself in the music of loveliness. He closed his eyes and lifted his face hungrily against the exquisite kiss of the night air. 'Oh, le bien,' he sighed. 'Oh mon Dieu, comme c'est bien…'

Tom stood a long while, perfectly still, unwilling to intrude upon this silent communion. Then he took the handles of the chair again, and pushed it along the path, slowly, among the scented plants. He stopped beside a rosemary bush that had grown out across the path so that it brushed against them. Peregrine leaned over and buried his face among the thrusting young shoots.

'Oh, mon Dieu…' He breathed in the heady, resinous aroma; 'Oh le bien!' He reached out his hand and rubbed the fragrant leaves against his face until the air was suffused with the scent.

'Smells so clean and good, doesn't it?' said Brother Tom. 'It makes you feel more alive.'

'M…y-es. Oh y-es.' He righted himself in the chair, and they continued slowly through the fragrant paths of the physic garden.

'D'you think you can face the cobbles?' Tom asked him, as they came to the end of the flagged path that wound among the herb beds, and looked along the cobbled path that skirted the vegetable gardens and led to the cloister buildings.

'Y-es.'

'Here goes then, but it'll shake you up a bit. I'll go onto the grass where I can.'

The barrow, with its narrow metal-rimmed wooden

wheels, clattered and bounced along the path, and it was a
relief to reach the flagged passage that led from the back of
the cloister, between the Chapter House and the church to
the cloister. Tom pushed the chair through the passage,
and they stopped and looked at the deserted cloister garth
lit with white moonbeams. Nothing stirred there, sheltered as it was from the wind. Brother Fidelis' rose bushes
stood in immortal stillness, bathed in the silver light.

Tom hesitated. He wondered whether to walk round
the cloister, past the abbot's house. Deciding that the pain
of that might spoil the delight of the excursion, he turned
the chair round, and pushed it back into the passageway
towards the small door in the south wall of the church.

'I think this is not too wide to go through the Lady
Chapel door. Let's see.

'Oh, somebody's oiled the hinges. Wonders will never
cease. Now...yes, we can do it.'

He pushed the barrow past the vestry and sacristy
door, through the Lady Chapel and into the empty choir,
straining his eyes to see by the faint gleam of moonlight
that filtered through the windows.

Beside the altar, the perpetual light glowed in its lantern of ruby glass. Peregrine looked up, but it was too dark
to see the cross above the rood screen.

'He's hidden in the darkness,' Tom whispered, 'but
he's there.'

'Y-es. L-l-lum...'

'*Lumen Christi?*'

'Y-es.'

'*Deo Gratias.*' He pushed the chair up to the sanctuary
steps, the altar dimly discovered in the shadows by the
moonbeams and the warm, patient shining of the perpetual light. They rested without speaking in the holy
presence of the dark that bent over them and wrapped
them round.

'Have you missed being here?' whispered Brother Tom.
Then, when Peregrine did not reply he said quietly, 'I'm

sorry. That was thoughtless and stupid. Your absence has ached among us, too.' He paused. 'One day...one day, when you feel ready, I'll bring you to Mass. When you're ready.'

Peregrine said nothing, gazing at the dear familiarity of the altar, the silver cross, the rood screen, sick with loss.

'Come on then. I must take you back.'

And Tom wheeled the chair round, and found his way carefully through the Lady Chapel and out into the cloister passage.

'If we go through the kitchen, we can come round by the orchard and the vegetable gardens, and avoid the cobbles. What do you think?'

'Y-es.'

This proved less simple than it had sounded. Tom had forgotten the cobbles in the kitchen yard, and the chair nearly overturned in the uneven ground of the orchard, but he returned Peregrine in one piece to the infirmary, and with Brother Michael's help undressed him and got him back to bed.

'Goodnight, Father. I'll come tomorrow, after Vespers. Sleep well.'

'Y-es.'

Brother Michael went with Tom to the door.

'Was that a success?'

'Yes. Yes it was. We went into the chapel, and I think that made him feel a bit sad...but to be outside and see the stars, smell the herbs, yes, that was good. I'd like him to come out in the sunshine though.'

'So would we all. It'll come, now he's ventured out. Don't rush him. Thank you, Tom. Goodnight.'

Brother Michael closed the door, and Tom walked back through the herb garden, along the cobbled path to the cloister, where the night stairs led up out of the passageway between church and Chapter House to the dorter. Brother Peter, carrying the lantern round, nodded to him in greeting as he passed. Tom went into the little wooden cubicle where he slept, and sat on his bed to take off his sandals, his belt and knife.

'Father God...' he whispered, as he sat on the edge of the bed, feeling the coolness of the stone under his bare feet; 'just his speech. We can carry him, nurse him, dress him, but we can't speak for him. Because of your loving kindness, give him back his speech. And make him be able to hold his water long enough to get through Chapter. We can do the rest.'

He pulled back the covers on his bed and climbed in. He lay with his hands behind his head, gazing into the dark.

'Please,' he added, before he fell asleep.

Throughout the next day, Tom's mind teemed with the possibilities for developing Peregrine's speech, helping him to come out of his reclusive existence in the sanctuary of his infirmary room.

'How can I persuade him to really *try?*' he asked Brother Stephen, as they trudged up the hill after Chapter.

Stephen pondered a while. 'With animals,' he said at last, 'if you want to train them or persuade them to do something, you offer a reward—rattle a bucket of cereal, or tempt them with some corn. Maybe it's the same with people? Teachers sometimes reward children with sweetmeats for a lesson well done, don't they?'

Brother Tom turned over this idea in his mind. 'Yes,' he said finally; 'I think that might work. I've waited on his table long enough. I know better than the infirmary brothers what his likes are. I'll try a visit to the kitchen before Vespers and see what that turns up.'

He appeared in Father Peregrine's room after Vespers, carrying a tray with a bowl and spoon and a little jar. He had a very purposeful expression on his face.

Father Peregrine, sitting in the last warm light of the afternoon sun, absently stroking the tabby kitten that lay curled asleep on his lap, looked with interest at the tray;

then the interest in his face gave way to misgiving as he saw Tom's determined expression.

'Now I've some beautiful, sweet blackberries here for you, and I've wheedled my way round Brother Cormac to spare me a little pot of cream so thick you could stand the spoon up in it. You've got to earn them though. Brother John thinks that if we really work at it, you might get most of your speech back; all of it even.

'You said "book" yesterday, beautifully, and "stars"; you can say "yes" and "no" well enough, and the odd word here and there, and you can swear with great fluency in two languages; methinks it's time we developed your vocabulary. I want you to try repeating some words after me. Yes?'

Peregrine's eyes wandered to the fruit Tom had put on the table. He swallowed. His mouth was watering for it. He sighed. 'Y-es,' he said resignedly.

Let's try something you know really well; maybe the flow of it will help you remember: *"Pater noster qui es in caelis."* Try *"Pater"*. P-P.... Go on: P....'

'P-P-P-shlastr—oh, *merde!*'

'*Try!* P-P-P-Pater n-n-n-noster.'

'P-ater n-n-n-n NO!'

The kitten leapt down from his lap in alarm at his raised voice, its ears flattened back, scampering for safe shelter under the bed.

'Try. You did it. Just this one sentence. Try. Pater noster....'

'N...b...b...'

'P-P-P-'

'P...P...'

'P-a. P-a. P-ater'

'P-ater n...n...n...'

'Pater n-n-n-noster. Try.'

'N-os...n-os...oh! P-ater n-os-n-oster!'

'Very good. Try "qui"; qu-qu....'

'N-o.'

'Try. Just this one short sentence.'

'N-o. N-o. N-o-o.'

Peregrine glared at him defiantly, but Tom held the winning card. 'Don't then. But I'll take this fruit away and tell them not to bother, you didn't want it. Well?'

'N-o.'

Tom shrugged indifferently, and took the bowl of black-berries and the little pot of cream. As he reached the door, he couldn't resist a glance back to see Peregrine's reaction. He sat, the bitter disappointment and humiliation written plain on his face, his lips pressed tightly together to counter the treacherous trembling.

It was a moment not like any other in Tom's life. Without warning he was in the howling place of storm, the fearful meeting ground of the tortured and the torturer, the betrayer and the betrayed, the powerful and the powerless, those who have and those who have nothing; the still place of knowledge in the eye of the storm. The look on Peregrine's face filled that hateful, howling desert, assaulted Tom with the violence of a blow. In unendurable, stabbing accusation, Peregrine's eyes helplessly filled with tears. He bent his head, in a futile effort to hide his face, dismayed that Tom should see him so childishly upset over such a little thing.

But Tom was across the room in two quick strides, and dumping the fruit and cream on the table he fell on his knees by the chair and hugged Peregrine to him, his heart torn open in an agony of pity and shame.

'No, no, no,' he moaned. 'What was I thinking of? Oh, what was I thinking of? Father, forgive my cruelty...'

In that moment, Tom detested himself beyond bearing. He had never dreamed that he might play a part in driving home the nails, hoisting the cross, in this particular crucifixion.

He pressed his lips against Peregrine's face, tasting the salt of his tears as he drew back to look at him, his hands holding his shoulders, his eyes beseeching his forgiveness. 'Oh, my God, I'm sorry.'

Tom had known the blissful security of a mother's arms and the intoxication of being in love; but here, in the anguish of wounding and forgiveness, was a steep, austere intimacy; knowledge beyond ordinary loves. Such unconditional encounter demanded no lesser honesty than the humble, painful disclosure of his naked soul. He bent his head and closed his eyes, suffering the pain of it to sear through him and through him, a merciless, costly compassion.

'I haven't been much of a friend to you, have I?' he mumbled.

In the tenderest gentleness, he felt Peregrine's finger trace lightly across his cheek.

'Y-es. Oh y-es. Thank you, T-om.'

Tom lifted his head and looked at him in amazement. 'What did you say?'

'Th-ank you, T-om.'

The scarred, tear-stained, crooked face lit up suddenly in a most mischievous grin: 'Th-ank you, T-om.'

'You... terror! You can say that perfectly! Since when have you been able to say that? Ah well, it's a nicer thing than *"Pater noster qui es in caelis"*. Come on then; are you going to eat these blackberries?'

'Y-es.'

'I'll put the cream on. Can you manage the spoon if I hold the dish?'

'Th-ank you, T-om.'

'What *is* this? Have you been practising saying that?'

'Y-es.'

'You crazy fool! You let me go through all that *Pater noster* rigmarole and you never told me you'd been working on something else!'

'Y-ou d-did-d...n...m...'

'I didn't ask?'

'Y-es.'

'No. I didn't, did I? Well there you are. That's one more homily on courtesy you've notched up to your credit.'

Tom knelt beside him, holding the bowl. He watched Peregrine's awkward progress, carefully scraping with the spoon the dribbles of blackberry juice that escaped from his mouth, painfully anxious not to let the spoon twist in his clumsy hand.

Tom made no comment. Questions ached in his silence: why does it have to be him? God in heaven, couldn't you have found some slob who couldn't care less to strike down? Or would that have been less fun?

He smiled at Peregrine as the last scraping of blackberries disappeared. 'You've made a neat job of those. Good, aren't they? You know, blackberries make a beautiful sauce for roast pheasant. There should be some pheasants worth eating any time now—grouse too. Yes, my mother used to roast them with honey, and serve them in gravy and blackberry sauce, with parsnips and turnips...it was good, that. We used to eat two each.'

Peregrine lifted his hand and wiped away a dribble of saliva from the side of his mouth that still drooped in paralysis. Tom grinned at him. 'I'm sorry. Am I setting your digestive juices flowing? Is that what you'd like, some roast pheasant in blackberry sauce?'

'Oh, mon Dieu...y-es.'

Tom laughed. 'I'll see what I can do. I'll talk to Brother Cormac. He'd do anything for you anyway. Now then, I'm sorry to go so soon, but I need to have a word with Brother John before Compline, so I'd better be moving. I'll leave this bowl here if you don't mind it. It can go back to the kitchen with the things from here in the morning.'

He stood up to go. 'Goodnight, Father. I'll see you tomorrow.'

'Y-es. Th-ank y-ou, T-om. G-G-G...m..G-o...m...b-ble...Oh!'

'God bless you too. Goodnight.'

Tom closed the door behind him, but did not walk away at once. He felt upset and ashamed still, that he should have pushed Peregrine to the point of tears. Two months ago, if he had hurt someone that much, he would have gone to Peregrine and knelt before him, and confessed it; but now...who? He had no intention of telling Father Chad about the incident. Brother John, then. Tom walked slowly down the passage. So much turmoil, he thought. I get so exasperated with him, and I feel so sorry for him, and I need him still; his faith and wisdom. I'm so angry with him for being ill and needing me, when I still need him.

Brother John would likely be setting out the medication for the night at this time of day, while Martin and Brother Michael made the old men comfortable in their beds. Tom walked along to the little room where the medicines were kept, a small room full of the fragrance of aromatic oils and herbs, furnished with a stout workbench and two stools, and lined with shelves full of innumerable jars and pots and phials.

Tom stood hesitantly in the doorway.

'Have you a moment to spare, Brother?'

Brother John was preparing the evening medicines; sedatives, sleeping draughts and pain relief. He had several bottles of physic on the workbench in front of him, and three pots of liquid heating slowly on a tiny brazier raised on wooden feet on a block of stone. He looked round at Brother Tom standing in the doorway holding the doorhandle.

'No, not really. Not if I'm to get done in time for Compline. I've skipped Chapel so many times this week I shall be earning a scolding if I'm not careful.

'However,' he added, looking again at Tom's face, 'I might make a free minute, provided you can help me give out these doses?'

'Yes. Yes, of course.'

'Sit down then. Excuse me if I carry on with this. What's troubling you?'

Brother Tom sat on the stool without speaking. Brother John finished his medicines in silence. He was familiar with this kind of communication. It came with the infirmary work. He had learned by now to understand as much from men's silences as he did from their words. It was time-consuming though; he privately resigned himself to missing Compline for the third time that week. He swivelled round on his stool and sat opposite Brother Tom, his hands loosely clasped in his lap. He waited until Tom was ready to speak, and in the end Tom asked him, 'You taught Father Peregrine to say, "Thank you, Tom"?'

'Almost. I taught him to say "thank you". He could already say "Tom".'

'Why did you teach him to say that? How did you go about it? Was it a struggle to get him to do it?'

Brother John smiled. 'Been arguing with him, have you?'

'Not exactly.' Tom hesitated. 'I think it would be fairer to say I've been bullying him. I didn't intend to...at least...oh, I don't know. I thought I'd try and build on his speech, teach him some words. Brother Michael said you told him that could be done. I tried him with *"Pater noster qui es in caelis"*, because of it being so familiar. He managed *"Pater noster"* and point-blank refused even to try further than that. I'd brought him some blackberries. I told him I'd take them away if he wouldn't try. I made to take them away, but...his face—he looked so...reduced. Degraded, stripped—I can't put it into words. He looked like a child. As though I'd robbed him of his adulthood. Such power, such abuse of power. I'm afraid to have such power. He wept, John. For blackberries and cream. Wept.'

Brother John looked down at his hands, sensitive to the uncertainty and dismay in Tom's voice.

'Not quite for blackberries and cream, I would think,'

he said, speaking with the same reasonable calmness he used on his patients when they were anxious or distressed. 'The humiliation of powerlessness like that is very hard to bear.

'It is not easy for us who can choose and determine so many basic things—feeding ourselves, relieving ourselves, talking, walking freely—to appreciate at all what it must be like, such broad deprivation. His emotional balance seems, to us, rather precarious, until you remind yourself of how the world looks from where he is. Blackberries and cream—well, you were able to go and get them, weren't you? And you could just as easily go and get some more. Him, he might as well long for the moon. Unless someone takes the trouble to decipher what he wants, and bring it, he has to do without. Don't be too hard on yourself, though. Be content to learn from it.

'As to the speech, I think no one could teach him better than you, but a few tips might help you do it better. "Thank you" is two words of one syllable each; an easy and rewarding target. Also, it's something he desperately wanted to say to you. He wanted me to say it actually, but I said no. It's taken him two days to learn to say, "Thank you, Tom," reliably. Two days. *Pater noster qui es in caelis* is a bit of a mouthful, and it may not be something he really wants to say himself. If he does, he'd probably sing it more easily than say it, incidentally.'

'I thought—Brother Stephen suggested it—I thought it might be possible to teach him by rewarding him; like you do with children and animals.'

Brother John could not help the broad grin that spread across his face, in spite of the crestfallen tone of Tom's confession.

'You didn't tell him that? No, I should think not. Sancta Maria, that would have made him spit!

'You have to bear in mind, Tom, he's very afraid of failure, of making a fool of himself. His sense of humour only takes him so far. He needs to feel that he's being treated with respect, courtesy—his watchword! Did you say sorry to him?'

'Yes. Yes, I did.'

'I'm glad you did that. That goes a long way. Is that all, then?'

'Yes. Thank you. It's a relief you don't think what I did was too cruel.'

'Did I say that? It was cruel indeed. I think it would have reduced me to tears if I'd been in his place. The look you saw on his face was your best guide to how cruel it was. The degradation of punishment, you know. Brother, I'm not blaming you, because I've done the same kind of thing myself, too often. There is the most terrible power attached to this job, and I don't always use it wisely myself on days when I'm tired or distracted. A sharp word, a hasty rebuke from me sears them to the soul. I've learned to say sorry, and say it humbly. It helps to rebuild some of the fragile structures I so thoughtlessly destroy.

'Now Tom, I really must get these medicines out.' He strained some of the steaming liquid infusing in the pots into small beakers as he spoke. 'Can you take this for Brother Denis, and this for Brother Cyprian—there's hyssop, coltsfoot and honeysuckle in it for his wheezy chest.'

'What's in Brother Denis'?'

'Sleeping draught. Chamomile and limeblossom. Take Brother Cyprian's first—he ought to have it hot. When you've done that, would you come and help me turn Father Aelred, please?'

Tom took the two beakers and went into the dorter. The rooms were smaller here than in the main body of the abbey, to allow for a man to be isolated in cases of infection or insanity, or if it seemed better for any reason that he should be alone.

Brother Cyprian and Brother Denis shared a room, and there was also one empty bed in with them. When Brother Tom came into the room, he found them both neatly tucked into their beds, ready for the night. He set down

Brother Denis' beaker by his bed, and moved round to Brother Cyprian, who was already asleep. Tom stood looking down at him. 'Brother Cyprian,' he said, quietly.

Brother Cyprian's eyes opened instantly, and Tom found himself met by a gaze of the most piercing wisdom. They looked at each other for a moment.

'Have they mended it yet?' asked Brother Cyprian irritably in his broad Yorkshire accent. Tom blinked at him, taken aback. 'Mended it?' he echoed. The shrewd old eyes continued to watch him. Clearly an answer was required. 'I don't think so,' he said. 'They're terribly behind with the repairs.'

Brother Cyprian clicked his tongue impatiently. 'Aye well, that's nowt fresh, is it? Where are we off then? Into town?'

'Um...no, it's bedtime, Brother. I've brought you your medicine.'

'Bed? Have I to stay in bed? I don't want to go to bed. I have to stay here hours and hours and hours. Don't be like that, lad. Let me get up.'

'But Brother, it's night-time.'

'Nay, don't say that to me. What's that you've got there?'

'It's your medicine.'

'Oh, I can't have that, lad.'

'But, Brother John said...'

'Nay, nay...I should never have done it. I let them poison me, and I died last Monday, and I've to do it all backwards now, if you catch my drift; to get back again. Why are you looking like that at me? Is it some kind of wizard or necromancer you are?'

'I'm a monk, Brother Cyprian.'

'A what?'

'Oh, glory be to God—a *monk!* Same as you. Please drink this medicine, or I shall catch it from Brother John. You've to have it while it's hot. Let me help you sit up.'

Brother John came into the room. 'Aren't you done yet?

Being awkward, is he? All right I'll do it. Give Brother Denis his. Come on, Brother Cyprian, sit up.' He slipped his arm under the old man's shoulders and raised him up to a semi-sitting position, holding the cup to his lips.

'Nay! Nay, Cedric, I don't want that, it tastes nasty!' the old man protested.

'Behave yourself, Brother! Get this down you!' retorted Brother John sharply. 'There, that's right. All of it now. That's better. You'll breathe easier now. Go to sleep.'

'You'll not put the light out, will you, Cedric? Leave me a light—please. I hate the dark.'

'Ssh, go to sleep. When have I ever left you in the dark? The night light is burning here. Hush now.' Brother John stood with the beaker in one hand, smoothing the old man's brow with his other hand. 'Ssh, ssh...go to sleep. Be at peace. Ssh.'

Then he turned quietly away from the bed and joined Brother Tom who was waiting for him at the door. He glanced back across the room, which was darkening now, the small flame of the night light beginning to glow in the shadows. He held out the empty beaker to Tom, tiptoed back to Brother Denis, and tucked his blankets in firmly.

'God give you goodnight,' he whispered. Then, satisfied that his charges were comfortable, he was content to leave them.

'How came it Brother Cyprian drank that stuff for you when he wouldn't for me?' said Tom as they left the room, leaving the door ajar.

'Ssh, don't disturb them now, for mercy's sake. He's a naughty old man, that's why. Half his mind doesn't work, and the other half works all too well, the old devil.'

In the next room four men were settled in their beds. Brother John put his head round the door to see that all was well with them, then Tom followed him along the passage past the linen room to the little room where Father Aelred slept.

'Why is he all alone here?' asked Tom.

'You'll see. Light the candles from the night light, will you, so we can see what we're doing. That's right. You go that side of the bed. We have to turn him so he doesn't get bed sores. We'll check if he's wet, and if not it's just a matter of turning him onto his other side.'

The old man was sound asleep, his face peaceful with the rapt innocence of a child. John looked at him, smiling. ''Tis pity to disturb him,' he said softly, 'but it has to be done.' As Brother John lifted back the blanket and sheet, Tom was assaulted by a nauseating, overpowering reek of sweat; the sickly stench of a body that was old and unwell and needing a wash. He grimaced, revolted. Brother John glanced at his face.

'We'll bath him tomorrow,' he said quietly. 'He's not well. It's a job to keep him fresh. He's wet, look. On the chest over there are some pads of sheeting and a pillowcase stuffed with sphagnum moss. Two pads please, and the pillowcase. That's right. Put them ready here. Now, roll him over to you.'

As Tom took hold of the shrunken, bony old body clothed in the standard infirmary issue of an undershirt and grey woollen socks, Father Aelred let out a high, wavering shriek of pain or distress so wild and piercing it made Tom's flesh crawl. 'Aaagh! No! No! No!' he cried. 'Oh please, no! Oh leave me alone! Please, please! Aaaagh! No! Aaaaagh!'

'Hush, Father Aelred,' said John soothingly. 'We won't take long.' He looked up at Tom's appalled face with a grin. 'That's why he sleeps on his own.'

The loud quavering protest continued unceasingly as they changed his bed and turned him and repositioned his pillows. It only diminished as Brother John rubbed his hip and shoulder with ointment to guard against sores, talking to him gently for a while.

Then John tucked the blanket in firmly, whispering, 'Goodnight, Father Aelred.'

'Goodnight,' replied the high, loud voice with startling,

hysterical clarity. They gathered up the wet sheets, blew out the candles and left him. He had not once opened his eyes in all the time they were in the room.

'I'll wager you thought we were negligent not bathing him oftener until you heard that,' said Brother John as he pulled the door to behind him. 'We'll take those along to soak until the morning; there's a tub out at the back. I'll show you.'

Outside the building in the yard, where the washing hung drying in the dusk, a thrush was singing, the outpouring glory of sound filling the twilight. Tom paused to look for the bird while Brother John took the sheets from him and pushed them with a stick into a vat of soaking sheets waiting to be washed in the morning.

'Beautiful, isn't it? Will you take the pad with the moss, and empty the moss out on the heap yonder for burning? Thank you. The pillowcase can go in soak. There. We can wash our hands here—we've our own lavatorium.

'Brother...' John hesitated, rubbing his hands dry on the linen towel. Tom looked at him enquiringly, shaking the drips from his hands.

'Brother, you should never look at a sick man with disgust on your face. Even someone like Father Aelred whose stink makes your gorge rise, and whose mind is gone. You can't be sure how much they know, how much they understand. Never let them see if the care of them revolts you. It fills them with shame, confirms their worst fears, seals them into their distress. It's important to look at a sick man with love in your eyes. Always.

'There's the Compline bell now, and I thought we'd miss chapel. Brother Michael will be on his way over. I'll walk along with you.'

He laid the damp towel over a bush of lavender that grew in the bed bordering the yard.

'It dries smelling of lavender there if the dew falls on it and then the heat from the sun dries it out.'

Tom spread his towel on the next bush in the border,

sweet-smelling southernwood, and the two of them went round the back of the infirmary building to the cobbled path.

'I'd like to get Father out into the sunshine before the days turn chill,' Tom said to Brother John as they walked along the path.

'You will. Now he's begun to master his speech, he'll get it back quickly. That's what'll give him the confidence to go out. It won't be long now. Ah—there's Brother Michael. God give you good evening, Brother. All's well. I'll be in after the morrow Mass, so you can go to Office and Chapter Mass as soon as we've got them up.'

Michael smiled, and nodded a greeting to Brother Tom.

'Thank you. Father Theodore said to tell you he will be coming after Chapter to say Mass with Father Peregrine and bring the others the sacrament. Goodnight, then.'

'Goodnight.'

The bell ceased tolling as they took their leave of Brother Michael, and they quickened their footsteps, hastening into the choir just before Father Chad gave the knock and the men rose to begin the last Office of the day.

V

A Promise

Still in September the days continued fair. The blazing heat of summer had faded and the dusk came earlier, the sunrise born in low-lying mist and heavy dews. The apples had almost ripened, the trees bowed under their load of fruit, and the grain was nearly all into the barns, a few strips still waiting the reapers, and some corn still standing in stooks, drying in the fields.

It was the busiest season of all on the farm, and Brother Tom had had little time to spare for the infirmary. He called in every evening, but only for a brief while, to bring news of the harvest, and to let Peregrine know he had not been forgotten. He did not sit down to talk, and sometimes, if he managed only to snatch ten minutes before Compline, Peregrine would already have been put to bed.

'When the harvest is all in,' he said to Peregrine, 'I'll come and see you properly, I promise. You—you do understand, don't you? I'm not running away, it's just…'

'Y-es,' Peregrine had said, and smiled for him, to set him at his ease. 'Y-es.'

And now the grain was in, and the weather could do what it liked, and Tom had a little more time until the ploughing began.

So he came into the infirmary after Vespers on the evening they had seen the last of the grain under cover, and found Brother John preparing to put Peregrine to bed.

He had undressed him and washed him, and he sat in his nightshirt and drawers, and his grey wool socks, while Brother John folded his habit neatly for the morning and cleared away the washing things.

'Hello, stranger,' said Brother John, as Tom entered the room. 'It must be near on a week since last we saw your face here for more than five minutes at a time. Still, I told Father, all I've seen you do in the Office and Chapter Meetings this week is sleep, so I reckoned you'd been working hard.'

Tom smiled. 'You were right. The barns are full. We've a good harvest. The rain can come now. But I've missed you, Father. I've been thinking of ways we might work on your speech while I've been breaking my back in the fields. Am I intruding? Can I stay for a while? You're early with bedtime, aren't you?'

'Y-es,' said Peregrine, and Brother John laughed.

'You're intruding if you're here to make him more rebellious than he already is, Brother Thomas. Maybe I'm a quarter of an hour early, but no more than that. I've had more grumbling than a quarter of an hour deserves though, you may take my word for it. No, it's just that I have to trim the toenails of one or two men tonight. It's easier to do it at bedtime than any other time, so this poor soul has missed his usual privilege of being last to bed; and left me in no doubt of his objections.

'You should be tired, anyway, Father. You've been working all day and every day to get your speech back under control; I'm surprised you're not glad to go to bed.'

'Have you?' said Tom. 'You've been working on it? What have you done?'

'I think you found Father Theodore's pictures helpful, didn't you, Father?' said Brother John, as he pulled back the blanket on the bed.

'Father Theodore's pictures?' Tom felt a sudden stab of resentment. He really had been too busy to call in during the last few days, but he felt put out that Theodore had taken his place, and irritated with himself for his own unreasonable resentment.

'Yes. Father Theodore spends a lot of time here with Father.'

'*Theodore* does? Why?'

Brother John chuckled at Tom's defensive tone. 'Maybe you thought you were the infirmary's only visitor? Father Theodore came every day when Father was first ill. Just to spend time with him, talk to him, hold his hand. Good thing somebody came, wasn't it, Tom?'

Brother Tom said nothing.

'T-om. A-a-re y-ou j-eal-ous?' The slow, blurred voice was full of affectionate amusement. Tom flushed.

'That was a very advanced sentence for someone of your disability,' he said acidly.

Peregrine grinned at him, happily. 'I'v-ve b-een pr-a-ac-tis-ing w-ith F-a-th-er Th-e-o.'

Tom stared at him. '*Have* you?'

'M...y-es.'

'You didn't tell me.'

'N-o. I w-w-anted t-o s-urpr-ise y-ou. *A-a-re* y-ou jeal-ous?'

'No! Of course I'm not! Why should I be?'

Tom looked from Peregrine to Brother John. They were both laughing at him.

'Hmm...' Brother John considered him critically. 'Not only jealous, but too proud to admit it, I should say, wouldn't you, Father?'

'N...n-o...n-ose d-ef-in-ite-ly ou-t of j-oint.'

'All right! Have you two had enough? What pictures, anyway?'

Peregrine started to tell him, but his speech scrambled hopelessly. After one or two attempts he waved his hand in a gesture of defeat: 'I...I...oh...t-ti-r...ed...J-ohn.'

'I'm not surprised you're tired. You've done very, very well.

'The pictures, Brother, were some illuminated Gospels

and books of Hours that Father Theodore had done. He brought them to show Father, and then thought he might use them to help him communicate the things he wanted to talk about, or that he'd been thinking about, by finding and pointing out the pictures. Then they practised the words and sounds that seemed relevant to the picture, and the related thoughts it inspired.'

Tom digested this information in silence.

'T-om? T-t-ell m-e.'

Tell me about it. The relief and emotion that flooded Tom's heart at hearing those words again were inexpressible.

'Tell you about it? I was just wondering how it was that Theodore had thought of that and I didn't.'

'Th-at's ea-ea-s-sy.' The dark grey eyes were smiling at him, teasing. 'H-e's-s b-b-ri-ight-er th-an y-ou a-re.'

Tom looked at Brother John. 'We'll get this rascal into bed, shall we, before he heaps any more insults on my head?'

'Yes, indeed. I must get Brother Denis' toenails pared. He'll be wondering what's become of me. Yes, if you'll lend a hand, Brother Thomas, it'll save Brother Michael a job.'

Brother John plumped the pillows on the bed, and arranged them to provide the right support. He came and stood behind Peregrine, his hands on his shoulders.

'Are you ready, then, my lord?'

'H-ave I a ch-ch-oice?'

'No.' He squeezed his shoulders gently. 'No. I'm sorry. Brother Thomas, if you can take his legs, please.' Brother John moved his hands down to a firm grip under Peregrine's arms. 'Lift, then. On his right side.'

'N-o. On m-y b-b-ack.'

Tom looked questioningly at Brother John. 'Yes, Tom, if he wants.' They laid him on his back on the bed. 'I can see,' said Brother John, as he deftly stripped Peregrine of his drawers, pulled up the sheet and blanket and tucked them in with firm precision, 'that I'm going to have nothing but trouble with you now you can speak to us!

'There now, are you comfortable? Good. I must get on. I'll bring your night light. It's almost too dark to see in here already. Are you staying a while, Tom?'

'Just a few minutes, yes.'

'Good. I'll bid you goodnight then, Father. I'll call in to you before you go to sleep. Here's your jar, and your bell.'

'G-oodn-n-ight.' Peregrine watched Brother John as he gathered up the washcloth and bowl and dirty linen, casting a quick glance round the room to check that all was in order before he left.

'H-e...h-e's a g-ood m-an,' commented Peregrine as Brother John left them.

'Yes.' Tom fetched Peregrine's chair over to the bedside and sat down beside him. 'Father...now that I have a bit more time, will you let me take you out of doors, while the fair weather lasts? Please.'

'Wh-ere?' Peregrine sounded doubtful.

'Not in the thick of everything. Up to the farm, maybe. Up to the field below the burial ground; it's quiet there, and sheltered by the beech trees.'

'Mmm.' Peregrine considered this. 'I'm n-n-ot s-sure. H-ave y-ou as-ked Br-oth-er J-ohn?'

'Yes, he thinks it's a good idea. What are you worried about?'

'N-oth-ing.'

'Then will you let me take you?'

Peregrine hesitated. 'Y-es,' he said finally.

Tom smiled at him. 'You'll enjoy it, you wait and see. I'll come for you in the morning, before you have time to change your mind.'

Peregrine returned his smile, but Tom thought he looked anxious.

'I'll leave you to go to sleep,' he said. 'Father, I'm amazed at the way your speech has come on. I think it's wonderful.'

Peregrine's smile this time was genuine, happy. 'Th-ank y-ou, T-om. G-oodn-ight.'

Before he left the infirmary, Tom sought out Brother John again. He found him just setting out with his tray of medicines.

'Brother, I won't keep you but a moment. I've talked Father into coming out of doors with me for a while in the morning.'

'Oh, *good*. After all this time! If you come after Chapter, that would be a good time.'

'He seems worried about it. I said I'd take him to a quiet place, away from everybody, but he seemed...anxious. Said had I asked you. What is it he's worried about? Do you know?'

'Yes: almost certainly, I should say, he's afraid of wetting himself.'

'Oh.' Brother Tom looked taken aback. 'I hadn't thought about that.'

'No. Well, of course, that's just what he's worried about. On the one occasion when his incontinence intruded on your life, you fled the building, if I remember rightly.'

'I don't know how to help him. I can push him around in a chair, but...it's a bit beyond me, this infirmary stuff. What do you do with them?'

'Tom, it's common sense, more or less. They simply need whatever help is appropriate to do what anyone else does. If it goes wrong, and there's a mess, we clear it up. What else would anyone do with them? What else would you do?'

Tom grinned at him. 'Me? That's easy. I'd bring them to you.'

'How kind. No, all you need to do for him is take a water jar with you, and don't delay if he needs help with it. He can manage it on his own with a bit of fumbling, but obviously it's no easy task with that crippled hand of his.

Once he sees you feel comfortable about it, I think his worries will be laid to rest too.

'My guess is, that's all that's bothering him. I'll tell him I've talked to you about it, if you like.'

Tom nodded. 'And that's all I'll need? A water jar?'

'Well…not quite. A water jar and a sense of humour. All right? See you in the morning, then.'

Every day after that, Tom took Peregrine out in the sun and breeze, sharing his delight in the freedom and space, the clean, good scent of the air. The warm dry days continued unbroken, and they spent long afternoons out on the farm, or in the field on the hillside below the burial ground enjoying the sunshine, and talking. As Peregrine talked, his speech improved. As he struggled to put into words the store of thoughts that had burdened his heart during the past weeks, he gained more confidence, and won his way back to coherent, articulate communication. Each word was slurred and slow, every sentence had to be fought for, but it was there. He had overcome the barrier, and the words came with more facility every day.

One evening, after they had put him to bed, Brother John commented to Tom how much good it had done Peregrine to go out, to find an interest in life again, to be able to talk.

Tom nodded. 'It has been good,' he said. 'Good for me too. It hasn't just been a case of me doing him a favour. I thought I'd lost him, thought it was a death within a life; grotesque. But now I'm wondering, you know, wondering if I ever really knew him. Whatever's happened to him has closed some doors—that's plain enough to see—but it's opened some too, somehow; windows into his thinking and into his heart. As if we'd mourned the loss of the sun when the night came down, but without the darkness we'd have never discovered the stars.'

Brother John smiled at him. 'That was very lyrical for Brother Thomas!' he said. 'I think some of his poetry's rubbing off on you.'

'Wouldn't surprise me. He's talked enough this last week to make up for the six weeks that went before it twenty times over. I meant it though. It really is like that.'

'Yes. Yes, I know. I've thought it myself. *"Et dabo tibi thesauros absconditos et arcana secretorum; ut scias quia ego Dominus, qui voco nomen tuum."* '

Tom looked at Brother John in surprise. A smile curved his lips as he softly translated the words, as if he had glimpsed something very precious. ' "I will give you the treasures of darkness, riches hidden in mystery, so that you may know that I am the Lord, who calls you by name." Oh John...that...where's that from?'

'Isaiah.'

'Isaiah? Well, if this has made a poet of me and a theologian of you, there must be some strange, divine workings in it somewhere!'

Brother John hesitated. 'Yes...Tom—be ready. You're right in what you say, more right than you know. Be ready. The work of God...all his paths lead through the cross.'

Tom nodded. 'True; but this is resurrection. Father's had his crucifixion.'

John was silent a moment. 'Maybe. But I didn't mean him. I meant you.'

The hills cradled the abbey buildings so that the porter at the abbey gate, or the faithful leaving the west door of the church, looked out across the valley, the road winding down from the abbey to the village nestled below at the foot of the hills; but the back of the abbey was sheltered by the protective curve of the hills. Behind the abbey buildings to the east a track curved up to the farm, and to the north another path led up beyond the church to the burial ground within its low stone wall.

A drift of woodland, a patch of ground which had been allowed to remain a wilderness, protected the burial ground from rough weather. Beyond the wood, the abbey farm spread out over the curve of the hills, petering out eventually as the upper ground gave way to the moors. Below the burial ground a row of beech trees lined its approach, and a sweep of greensward sloped down to the abbey school and church.

It was here on this field below the burial ground that Tom and Peregrine had been sitting talking together one afternoon in the second half of September. The wood behind the graveyard was a haven for birds and wild creatures, and the two men had listened to the birds singing when there was a lull in the cawing of the rooks that nestled in the taller trees, and amused themselves watching the antics of squirrels and rabbits that strayed out of the cover of the trees.

Tom had lifted Peregrine out of the wheeled chair and helped him down onto the grass. That was not too hard. It was getting him back in again that presented the difficulties. But for the moment they were peaceful in each other's company, each quiet in his own thoughts, Peregrine lying on his back gazing at the slow drift of clouds across the evening sky, and Tom sitting beside him, looking down on the abbey spread out below them, basking in the rays of the sun.

'It's a ted-iou-s busin-ess...d-ying.'

Tom looked down at him startled, his own ruminations forgotten.

'Dying? What d'you want to talk about dying for? You're not going to die.'

'Oh, T-om. L-ove gives l-ife, b-but not f-or ever. Brother J-ohn said...'

Tom felt a sudden chill of foreboding. 'Yes? What did Brother John say?'

'He said tha-at sei-s-sei-zures like th-is come ag-ain, soon-er or l-ater. Th-is ti-me is a br-ief gr-ace. Sw-eet, though.'

Tom sat very still, gazing into the distance across the sprawl of buildings. Above him were the yellowing leaves of the beech trees and the clouds fanning out across a sky tinged now with the gold and pink of evening. The beauty of the day shone all around him, but its glory was blighted by those words.

'Is that true? You could be ill again the same, and all this...all this be undone?'

'Y-es.'

'Oh...God.'

'Y-es.'

'And...I suppose you might even die, then—if you were ill like that again.'

'I h-ope so.'

'I don't. When you were ill, at first...I wished you'd died. I...I wanted you to die. It was too horrible. But now, no. The...I...oh, what shall I say? It's meant so much, taught me so much, these weeks. If you did have another seizure and went right back again, even to incontinence and not being able to speak and blank gazing, I'd want to start again.'

'O-h, th-ank you v-ery m-uch! T-om, I c-ouldn't d-o it. Being p-aral-ysed l-ike th-is is...h-ell. I h-ate it. This is wh-at I said, a gr-ace, but...en-ough is en-ough, *non?* I mean, is-n't it?'

Tom said nothing. Overhead the beech tree stirred and rustled in the warm breeze. A few leaves loosened by the movement floated down. Higher up the hill, a sheep called mournfully. The sun, low in the sky now, slanted across through the branches of the trees above them. Tom moved his hand restlessly, tugging at the grass, absently uprooting and throwing aside some of the wiry little stalks. Then his hand ceased to move.

'I don't think I could bear to lose you, that's all,' he said quietly. It was an admission of the very core of his heart, belonging to the same place of silence in which he had first learned to communicate in total honesty. It came clothed in the overwhelming silence of that honesty, and Peregrine accepted it in the same way, in the truth from the place beyond words. The sky, the fields, the light, the very air became a bowl of silence, cupped hands receiving the breaking pain of love.

'I don't know how you can talk about it like that, anyway,' said Tom eventually.

'L-ike wh-at?'

'Matter of fact. "Dying is a tedious business." You sound as though you're talking about the weather.'

'Wh-at sh-ould I s-ay? Th-at I c-contempl-ate th-e f-uture and th-e earth op-ens out in a ch-asm of terr-or in fr-ont of m-e? Th-at I cl-utch fr-antically f-or cour-age l-ike a lunatic tr-ying to gr-asp a wr-aith of m-ist? Th-at panic rises up unt-il it is ch-oking m-y th-thr-oat? Wh-at?'

Tom shifted irritably. 'Was that a poem or a speech? There's no need to make a three act tragedy of it. All I meant was—'

'Th-th-thr-ee a-a-act...T-om! I am n-ot dr-ama-tis-ing it. I am s-erious. M-ust I coll-apse in t-ears bef-ore y-ou ev-ery *day* bef-ore y-y-ou w-ill...w-ill...oh, n-ever m-ind it. Dr-ead also h-as a c-ertain tedium if it g-goes on l-ong en-ough. The m-ost appall-ing r-ealities ev-entually l-ose th-eir n-ovelty. Th-ere is a time of dr-ab gr-ey horr-or wh-en y-ou acc-ept that th-is r-eally is h-appen-ing to y-ou. It is pr-ecisel-y wh-at you s-aid: a m-atter of f-act.

'Th-at m-oment of acc-eptance turns y-ou to ice, T-om. It's l-ike dead m-en's f-ingers str-oking y-our s-oul. Th-e w-ay out of th-e pl-ace I am in is a sev-ere, n-arrow pass-age.'

'*Stop it!* You're making my flesh creep. "Dead men's fingers"! You...stop it!'

'Y-ou w-on't all-ow m-e ev-en th-e indulg-ence of a l-ittle m-orbid s-elf-pity th-en?' He grinned at Tom, but Tom, looking into his eyes, saw no laughter there. Death was teasing him like a cat with a mouse, playing with his life, a mirthless, taunting game. He was weary of it.

The day had begun to turn chill. The warmth of the afternoons no longer burned with the heat of summer. The

lazy golden length of sunbeams belonged to colder evenings, longer nights. The shadows of the trees lay across
the meadow, and the pink sky began to deepen into a wash
of rose. A little cloud of gnats danced their incessant
aimless ritual on the evening air. In the tall trees behind
the burial ground the rooks were cawing and flapping,
their racket suddenly loud in the stillness that steals upon
the day and draws it down into dusk, silence, night.

The two men lingered in the waning day, the afternoon
warmth prolonged here in the shelter of the low wall that
separated them from the burial ground.

'T-om.'

'Mm?'

'I w-ant y-ou to p-p-romise me s-om...um...so-...oh!'

'Something. What?'

Tom turned his head to look at Peregrine. He had
mastered speech well enough not to get stuck on a word
these days, unless he was very tired, or under some sort of
emotional pressure.

'Y-ou s-s-aid once th-at...if I w-w-ant-ed...y-ou wou-
would he-lp m-e out.'

'Yes. I said that. But...'

'If...whe-en i-t h-ha-hap-pens ag-ain...d-on't l-eave
m-e in it. I c-ould-n't, T-om, c-ouldn't go th-thr-ough it
a-gain.'

Tom said nothing. He had deliberately not thought
about the future. The present had seemed daunting
enough. He chewed his lip anxiously, the months to come
opening out ominously ahead of him now.

'Th-ere are h-h-ard time-s ahea-d. N-o sh-ort-cut-s on
th-is r-r-oad. I am n-not af-raid to d-ie, and...en-ough is
en-ough. P-rom-ise me, T-om.'

'Help you out? How?'

'H-em-lock...a p-ill-ow o-n m-y f-ace...I d-on't m-ind.
B-ut if y-ou lo-ve m-e, d-on't m-ake m-e end-ure it ag-ain.

'T-om?'

'I'm listening. Believe me, I'm listening. Do you know

what you're asking? This is mortal sin you're talking about—um—hell. For both of us.'

'There is n-o such th-thing as h-ell for-r two people.'

'What?'

'Hell is f-ull of p-eople who a-re p-p-pur-suing th-eir p-pers-onal gain. Ev-en person-al s-alvation. L-ove anti-dotes hell. If y-our f-ear of h-ell ou-ts-trips y-our com-pa-assion, th-en y-ou have r-un to m-eet h-ell. M-ake hell w-ait; forg-et you-rself.'

'I hope the bishop hasn't checked up on your theology lately.'

'T-om. Pr-omise me.'

Tom shifted uneasily. Until now, the shadows of this level of reality had never lengthened over his life. Their chill carried a sense of gathering dark. When he finally replied, his voice shook in spite of himself. 'If you're sure it's what you want.'

'P-romise me.'

'I will.'

'S-ay it.'

'I promise that if you have another seizure, and you are as helpless as you were before, I will...finish it.'

'Th-ank you, T-om.'

'I hope you don't regret this when it's too late, that's all.'

'If I d-id, the c-consequ-ences wo-uld be no bl-eaker.'

Tom blew out his breath in a long sigh. 'Well, no. I suppose not. Look, I'm not easy about this, Father. It seems...it seems such a pity to risk forfeiting heaven when you're...well...knocking on the door, more or less. God is patient and merciful, but he has his rules, doesn't he?'

'God. Wh-ere is this G-od of y-ours, T-om?'

'Where is he? What do you mean, where is he? He...well, he's enthroned in heaven, isn't he? With Jesus at his right hand.'

'V-er-y p-retty an-d c-lean. Wh-at does he do?'

'What are you getting at? What do you mean, what

does he do? God keeps everything going, neither slumbers nor sleeps.'

'In a w-orking d-ay, th-ough; h-ow does your God s-pend his t-ime? S-ending men to h-ell, b-urning the ones who w-ere too af-raid to s-ee their nightm-ares th-rough?'

'Well, no, not all the time, but...I suppose that's part of what God does.'

'And th-is is the God in wh-ose image y-ou h-ope to be perf-ected, y-es? Th-e butchers in I-taly wh-o are b-urning the F-ranciscans...are they antic-ipating heaven then, or h-ell? If the G-od of h-eav-en b-urns people...a-nd people burn in h-ell...h-ow will you kn-ow the dif-ference?'

'Father! That's *heresy!*'

'M-y-es, I kn-ow. I h-ave stud-ied th-e Ch-urch F-athers t-oo.'

'I don't know...I don't know about God.'

'Sh-ould do. You're a m-onk.'

'Tell me what you think then, about God. Where do you think he is?'

Peregrine did not speak for a minute. He drew breath, then paused. 'I...'

'Well?'

'Th-is m-ight h-urt you.'

'Go on.'

'When I w-as first sick, a-nd you d-idn't come to s-ee me, I w-as s-o w-wound-ed. As e-ach day ende-d...V-esp-ers, C-ompline, night, I t-urned my f-ace to the w-all and w-ept. I was l-onely and afr-aid. I n-eeded y-ou. After a wh-ile, I re-alised y-ou really w-ere not c-oming. When I f-aced th-at, someth-ing d-ied in m-e. It w-as tr-uly m-ore than I c-ould bear.'

'I'm sorry.' Tom's voice was husky with sadness and shame. 'I'm sorry.'

'N-o; w-ait. I w-ept before G-od, and I s-aid to him, "Where are you? Wh-y have y-ou aba-ndoned m-e?" I s-aid to h-im, "Y-ou have p-ermitted th-is. Y-ou s-uffer-ed me to be cr-ippled. Y-ou suffered me t-o b-e s-tripped of all dignit-y. Y-ou suffer-ed me to b-e p-aralysed and dumb a-a-and t-ortured. Could y-ou n-ot…God, in whose h-hand is th-e g-ift of all our d-ays…could y-ou not h-ave left me my friend? Wh-ere is your mercy? If it is true y-our v-ery be-ing is love, *where a-a-are you?*" T-om, I h-ad p-lenty of t-ime to th-think.'

'And?'

'I r-emembered the creat-ion s-tory. G-od m-ade Adam f-rom the d-ust of th-e earth. God the artist, s-tooping, kneeling in the dust, tend-erly, absorb-ed, h-is h-ands f-orming A-dam. W-e make th-em t-oo. Statues, im-ages fashioned with a-artistry and love, but G-od wanted more th-an that.

'H-e st-ooped and p-ut his mouth on Adam's mouth, a-nd closed his eyes, a-nd b-r-eathed in-to Ada-m l-ife. S-o Adam became a living being; not w-ith the dumb l-ife of the flesh, d-ust th-at g-oes down to d-ust, but with the breath of God.'

Peregrine struggled up onto his elbow to look at Tom, the spark of eagerness rekindled in his eyes.

'The thing—Holy Sp-irit—that m-akes God divine, is the same as th-e th-ing th-at makes m-an h-uman. H-umanity and deity share one br-eath. Just as man and w-oman are th-e s-ame b-ut d-ifferent, a-nd it is th-e d-ifference in th-eir unity wh-ich is th-e secret delight o-f th-eir love; "At last! Fl-esh of my fl-esh, b-one of m-y bone"—rememb-er? So it is th-at G-od's r-eality is found in our human-ity. D-o y-ou f-ollow m-e?'

'Um…no.'

Peregrine sighed in exasperation. 'It's my f-ault, I don't th-ink so cl-early n-ow. L-ook; God did not *w-atch* m-e w-eep, watch p-art of me die in m-isery. We sh-are one br-eath, he and I. G-od also w-ept, g-roaned, d-ied. He carries my w-ounds in h-is body. M-y gut clenched in s-obbing, a-nd it w-as the h-eartache o-f G-od. All my fear and d-efeat are s-cars that he w-ears on h-is breast.'

'But…God lives in eternal bliss. God can't die. Surely

that was the point about Jesus; he came so we could have life—to put an end to death. God's supposed to lift us up! It's a poor do if our miseries drag God down in the dirt too, isn't it?'

Peregrine smiled. 'Oh, T-om; don't tr-ample on all m-y th-eories w-ith your common s-ense. Wh-y do you h-ave to be r-ight all the t-ime? Y-ou'll n-ever m-ake a poet.'

'You don't think I am right though, do you? Don't smile at me like that. I want you to explain it. I don't understand the way you see it. Talk to me about it. After all, you might drop dead next week, and then I would never have understood. The dying bit. Tell me what you mean.'

'W-ell... th-e soul of us; our hum-anity, is th-e breath of God. If y-ou expose a h-uman being to too m-uch h-orror, too much agon-y, h-is spirit is w-ounded; s-omething in him dies. If a ch-ild is bullied a-nd beaten, h-as nowh-ere to turn, n-o refuge, his h-umanity is murdered. He becomes h-imself cruel, inh-uman. The im-age of God in him is s-oured: th-e v-ery breath of G-od in part dies in h-im. In m-e, p-art of m-y humanity is def-aced...des-troyed. Speech, th-ought, movement: I am not c-omplete an-y m-ore.'

Tom shook his head, protesting his denial.

'N-o, *w-ait*, T-om. 'Tis tr-ue. I h-ope th-e part of m-e that l-oves, tr-usts, forgiv-es, is still f-unctioning, but not even a f-ool would pretend th-at all of m-e is. And I conf-ess it to y-ou; h-ope has died in m-e a little; terror h-as advanced, and h-ope retreated. I th-ink th-at might be a s-in, but I can't h-elp it. I am v-ery afr-aid, n-ot of death, but of l-ife. But, our f-aith is n-ot in immortality; n-ot th-e immortality of h-uman endeavour, or of th-e hum-an s-pirit. We die: s-ome in sw-ift r-acking agony, l-ike Jes-us, some piecemeal, like me: but all of us en-tirely die. Wh-at I believe in is th-e resurrection of th-e dead. Th-e m-an whose childh-ood innocence h-as b-een wrung, str-angled, he w-ill see it r-isen. Th-ose like m-e, for whom h-ope is n-o longer realistic, we will f-ind a r-isen hope, bec-ause God is bound up w-ith us. H-e h-as thrown his l-ot in w-ith us; desc-ended into h-ell for us; h-arrowed hell ev-en m-ore thoroughly th-an hell has harr-owed us.'

'You're not entirely a heretic, then; you do believe there is a hell.'

'M-e? T-om, how c-an y-ou s-ay...I *kn-ow* it. I have tas-ted in m-y own b-ody th-e ag-ony of th-e d-eath o-f God. Sw-eating in f-ear I h-ave cried out to h-im, oh l-ose me n-ot utterly; do n-ot l-et go of m-y hand. He is with m-e. Odd, isn't it? God wh-o is l-ife, he is f-ound in death. It is th-e cr-oss, not th-e empty tomb wh-ich is th-e symbol of our f-aith. Th-e empty t-omb is tom-orrow's story. Th-e cross is the ch-apter of our day.'

'So where is all this leading?'

'The l-ove of G-od is not s-omething that stands over agains-t us. Th-ere is a j-udgement, b-ut it does not look on our despair d-is-passion-ately, w-eighing righteous-ness in the b-alance, and r-ecking no-thing of our an-guish. Th-e justice of G-od holds us in h-is arms in in-timate em-brace.

'What i-s G-od? Well, wh-at is it th-at makes h-umanity precious? What is th-e love by wh-ich I w-ept for you, and y-ou h-eld me c-lose wh-en I w-as in ang-uish, if it is n-ot the b-reath of God?'

'Human life is sacred.'

'Y-es.'

'Even so, you aren't God! It's not for you to take life until it's yours to give it.'

'N-o. I u-nderstand. B-ut, if wh-at m-akes m-e a l-iving be-ing is the b-reath of God, then what will he s-end to h-ell? T-om...I asked it of you n-ot as the p-roduct of th-eologic-al logic ch-chopping, but because m-my c-ourage f-ails at the pr-ospect of end-uring it ag-ain. By what c-razy, cr-uel ethic is it r-ight to s-end a lad of ei-ghteen to d-eath in b-attle, but needful to d-eny a t-errif-ied, c-rip-pled old m-an rel-ease?'

'Don't ask me. You're the theologian. You're making my head ache. It's getting cold, and Brother John will cut my liver out if I let one of his little chicks catch a chill. Let's get you home to bed. Don't worry about it any more. I've promised you. I don't like it, but I've promised. You can rest easy.

'Do you need to use this jar before we go? Yes? Go on then, while I get the chair turned round and sort out your pillows.

'Faith, there's quite a breeze when you stand up where it blows above the wall.

'I'll empty that, shall I?

'Here we go then, I've got your chair ready.'

It was a difficult manoeuvre, and it required all Tom's strength to heave him without help into the chair. The procedure was not always completed without mishap, but today it went smoothly enough.

'I don't know about you dying, you'll be the death of me. I'm sure you're putting on weight.

'Nay, not really,' he added quickly, seeing the discomfiture in Peregrine's face. 'Come, let's see what they've got for your supper.'

That day proved to be the last of the summer warmth. In the night that followed it, the wind got up, bringing rain in the morning, and there were no more days mild enough to sit outside. The rain came in squalls and the wind tossed the trees, tearing down the dying leaves and laying about the last of the summer flowers, except for Brother Fidelis' roses in the security of the cloister garth.

Occasionally, when the rain held off, one or other of the hardier inhabitants of the infirmary would be loaded into a wheeled chair and trundled around the paths for a short walk, but they felt the cold more quickly than active men, and such excursions had to be short and rare now.

'We'll be lighting fires in the rooms not much after Michaelmas if this gloom doesn't lift,' said Brother John.

'The place is as damp and dreary as a vault. It's taken me three days to dry Monday's washing.'

Michaelmas Day dawned in grey clouds and puddles, depressingly chill, the wind blowing from the east, discovering every chink in doors and windows and aggravating every ache of rheumatic old age, in spite of the shelter of the hills ranged about the abbey to the north and east. The rain fell in showers, depressing deluges that eased off after a few minutes to a blowing mist of drizzle. The summer was gone.

On that day every year, the daily rhythm of the abbey altered. The central section of the day, incorporating the Office of Terce, Chapter Mass, Chapter, work, the Office of Sext and the midday meal remained the same, and the brothers still rose for Matins and Lauds at midnight: but None, Vespers, and Compline were said earlier, they ate supper earlier, and they rose later for Prime and first Mass, which gave them an extra hour's sleep before midnight, and an extra two hours after midnight.

The morning after Michaelmas Day was a blissful lie-in, as the brothers, used to the brutal clamour of the bell shattering sleep in time for Prime at five o'clock, slept on for two hours, and rose with a comfortable sense of having rested well.

Brother Tom felt well-disposed towards everyone on the day after Michaelmas Day. He was never sure whether Brother Cormac's cooking tasted better on that day because of his own good humour, or whether in fact Cormac cooked better for being well-rested and relatively cheerful. This year, as always, Tom felt contented on Michaelmas Day, in spite of the rain and wind.

His spirits were slightly dampened by the day's reading from the Rule at the Chapter meeting. It was not the most encouraging Chapter in the Rule in any case, being a stern warning against the harbouring of forbidden lust and desire, with a reminder that death lurks near to the gate of delight, and that the deeds of the brethren were at regular intervals reported in humourless detail to a God who was already keeping a strict eye on them.

On that particular day Father Chad, who had chanced to overhear Brother Thaddeus remark to Father Theodore that Father Chad's sermons sent him to sleep, took it upon himself to rub the brothers' noses thoroughly in the shameful depths of their own inescapable original sin. He chastised them in what for him were extraordinarily savage terms for the slothful, perilous indulgence with which they, like all men, were inclined to regard the stirrings and yearnings of the flesh.

He urged them passionately to root out every thought which offended against holy chastity, and every immodest word or look, adding that they must no more wink at such evil in others than did Christ in his purity who held the keys of death and hell. The brothers were slightly startled at this uncharacteristic outburst, but in the main received his exhortation with due humility and resolved to try harder in case the severity of their superior might be Christ in his purity giving the keys of death and hell a little rattle for their benefit, rather than a mere recurrence of Father Chad's chronic indigestion.

After Chapter, Brother John overtook Brother Tom as he was trudging through the rain along the track that led past the infirmary, on his way up to the farm.

'Have you time this afternoon to spend an hour with Father Peregrine?' he asked, squinting at Tom from under his cowl in the blowing rain, his shoulders hunched against the weather.

'Yes, it would be no trouble at all. I'm not especially busy today. Why? Is something amiss?'

'No. But the nights are long and often wakeful for him with his disabled body and active mind. Michaelmas Day is not as welcome to him as it is to the rest of us; even longer nights to lie alone with his thoughts. He'd be pleased to see you...delighted even.

'Also, he bade me tell you his friend Père Guillaume in

France has sent him a cask of good wine, and he wants you to share a cup of wine with him before he does as he should and surrenders it to the abbot's table. It *is* good wine too—he gave me some this morning. Father Chad'll be wringing out the dregs, I fear, by the time we've all begged a sample.

'I'll tell him you'll come, then? After the midday meal?'

'That would suit me well, yes; I'll come then.'

'Thank you kindly, he'll be grateful. That Chapter took the skin off our souls, did it not? Whatever do you suppose brought that on? We haven't had a going over like that since you ran off with a woman in the novitiate.

'I wonder if he's planning to terrify the novices with it in their Chapter this afternoon? Theodore will need to pick up the pieces of a few stricken consciences if he does.'

Tom smiled. 'He's right, though. We are inclined to get slack. I'll see you after dinner, then,' and he raised his hand in farewell as their ways parted.

Tom spent the morning threshing oats with Brother Stephen, showing Brother Germanus how to use a flail. It was hard work, and cold, the barn doors propped back to allow the chaff to fly in the wind.

He was ready for his dinner by midday, and applied himself with pleasure to a large helping of roast capon and green salad, followed by plum tart and cream.

He felt on good terms with life as he strolled over to the infirmary, looking forward to a beaker of first-class French wine.

Peregrine greeted him with a smile. 'It's g-ood of y-ou t-o c-ome, T-om. W-ill y-ou sh-are s-ome w-ine w-ith m-e?'

Tom could not help but notice the slightly glazed look of his eyes, and judged that Peregrine had probably had enough already, especially in view of the fact that his dinner lay untouched beside him on the table.

Tom felt some sympathy for him in the rejection of his dinner. It seemed likely that it had been concocted from the same ingredients as his own meal, but that it had been macerated with milk into a broth-like substance, and the bread that had accompanied it torn up and put to soak in the liquid. The kitchen staff had, it seemed, grasped only too well that most of the residents of the infirmary had dim sight, aging tastebuds and no teeth. Beside the unappetising savoury dish stood another bowl bearing well-stewed greengages that had been vigorously mixed with custard to a pale green curdled pulp. This offering Peregrine had also ignored.

'I'd love to share some wine with you,' said Brother Tom, and he poured himself a beaker.

'D-on't g-ive m-e an-y m-ore,' said Peregrine, to Tom's relief. 'I've h-ad m-ore th-an w-ill b-en-efit j-udgem-ent or discr-etion.'

The atmosphere in the room was not entirely happy. The day scarcely lifted the light in the room above a damp grey dusk. Peregrine's face sagged in lines of despondency, his eyes fogged with wine.

'Aren't you hungry?'

Peregrine glanced in contempt at the meal on the table beside him. 'I w-as unt-il I s-aw th-at.'

Tom could think of no answer to this. He sipped his wine. 'This is good, at any rate. I'll wager you've enjoyed it.'

'Y-es. T-oo m-uch.'

They both looked up at the click of the latch, and Martin put his head round the door.

'Have you finished with those crocks? Oh, for shame, Father, you bad lad! You haven't touched your meal at all! Whyever not, now? They went to no end of trouble to mix it up for you. It should have been just what an invalid needs—hot and soft and wet.'

Peregrine looked down at the mess of shredded bread soaked in broth. It had long gone cold, and globules of yellow grease floated on the liquid and washed up on the surfaces of bread.

He looked up at Martin and contemplated his wagging finger of disapproval for a moment. Then, leaning forward in his chair with an expression of bland, almost empty-headed, innocence, he said to him, 'Th-e o-only th-th-ing th-at i-s h-h-ot a-nd s-s-oft a-a-nd w-w-et I ev-e-er h-ad a l-l-iking f-or, I l-e-eft beh-h-ind wh-en I e-nt-ered th-e cl-oist-er.'

Brother Tom choked on his wine and put it down, coughing and spluttering. Martin smiled tolerantly at Peregrine.

'And what was that, Father? Perhaps we could get you some if there's something you fancy? Tut-tut, that *has* gone down the wrong way, Brother Thomas. Let me clap you on the back—that's better. Now then, what was it you fancied, Father?'

'No!' said Tom hastily, when he could speak. 'No, Martin, he'll be all right. You be getting on. I'll find him some supper.'

'Oh, very well then. Thank you very much, Brother; if you're sure. I'll take this bowl with me. That's a naughty lad though, wasting good food when it's given to you!'

Peregrine blinked slowly, like a disdainful, rather befuddled bird of prey; he did not reply.

When they were alone again, Tom sat looking at Peregrine, waiting for him to meet his eyes, which eventually rather shamefacedly he did.

'Father!' said Tom. 'I'm surprised at you.'

'H-e pr-ov-okes m-e bey-ond end-ur-ance,' Peregrine muttered guiltily.

'Even so, that was a most distasteful remark.'

Peregrine flushed, and looked away from Tom's disapproval.

''Tis tr-ue th-ough,' he mumbled, mutinous, and he added, 'I *h-ate* th-is inf-f-irm-ary sl-op. I h-ate be-ing p-atr-onised. I h-ate th-e w-eath-er. I th-ink I ev-en h-ate b-eing a m-m-onk. I w-ant a d-ec-ent d-inner a-nd s-ome g-ood c-omp-any.'

'Thank you, Father. You're so appreciative.'

Peregrine glowered at him. 'Wh-y do y-ou h-ave to b-e s-o self-r-r-ighteous?'

'I'm not! I—'

'Y-es y-ou are! Y-ou r-em-ind m-e of F-Fath-er M-atthew.'

Tom stared at him in astonished indignation, but Peregrine was not looking at him. ' "Oh, f-or sh-a-ame, F-ather, y-ou b-ad l-ad," ' he mimicked Martin to ludicrous effect in his slow, difficult speech. 'D-on't l-augh at m-e, h-e m-akes m-e s-ick. Wh-o does h-e th-ink I am?'

'I wonder,' Tom replied. 'Why? Who do you think you are? Or is that the trouble? Aren't you sure any more?'

Peregrine glanced up at him with a quick frown of pain. The question had touched surely on a wound.

'M-e? I know wh-at I am n-ow. Wh-at h-e s-aid; in-valid. I'm a cr-ipple, an obj-ect of p-ity. I sp-ent y-ears f-ighting n-ot to b-e, b-ut n-ow...' He shrugged impatiently and turned his face away. 'It s-ticks in m-y thr-oat, th-at's all,' he muttered.

'And taunting Martin with lewd remarks? That restores your self-esteem?'

Peregrine's mouth twitched in irritation. He lifted his head and glared hopelessly at Tom. '*A-all r-ight I'm s-s-orry!*' he shouted at him. 'B-ut d-o y-ou h-h-ave t-o be s-o s-s-sanct...um...s-sa-a...*oh merde!*'

'Sanctimonious?'

'Y-es.'

'You think I should just indulge your lapses of propriety, do you? On account of you being an object of pity, maybe?'

Peregrine did not reply. Tom leaned forward and encased Peregrine's hand in his own grip. 'It is not my pity you have earned, but my respect, my fealty, my love. I will tell you who you are, in case you have forgotten. You are my lord Abbot, and I depend on you still, for your counsel, your wisdom, your example.

'So please don't say anything like that again, because it made me laugh—and I ought not to have—the angels are watching.

'Now, my Father, put it behind you, and tell me what you'd like for your dinner. Let me see…if I can lay my hands on some cold roast capon and a little salad…maybe a large slice of plum tart and some cream…something of that order? Yes? A man after my own heart! Wait for me—I'll see what I can do!'

Tom begged a laden tray of food from the kitchen.

'Cormac, why do you send him that repulsive mush?' he asked.

'It's what Martin asks for. Isn't it right?'

'Oh, come on—you know what kind of food Father likes. He's still the same person. The only good thing about that slush is that it makes life easier for Martin. He doesn't have to cut it up, and Father's less likely to drop bits.'

Brother Cormac looked thoughtfully at Tom.

'Yes, I can do that. I can send him over anything he likes. You're upset about this, aren't you?'

Tom held the tray as Cormac filled it with plates of food. 'Yes,' he said. 'It seems such a little thing to do, and it means so much. All the while he hasn't complained, no one's thought of it. It…it's not fair. It's like forgetting he's a person.'

Cormac nodded. 'All right. I won't forget. I'll see he gets what he likes.'

Tom carried the tray back to the infirmary room where Peregrine's eyes brightened at the sight of it. Tom cut it into manageable pieces and set it on his table within reach.

'Now I'm going to tread on the toes of Holy Poverty by finding some candles to wage war on this gloom,' he said.

'It n-ever f-ails t-o am-aze m-e,' Peregrine said to Tom, as they sat together contentedly by candlelight in the satisfied companionship that follows good food and good wine, 'th-at a m-an, m-ade b-y G-od t-o b-e l-ittle l-ower th-an th-e ang-els and cr-owned w-ith gl-ory and hon-our, c-an b-e br-ought d-own to th-e l-ev-el of a b-east, s-unk in d-espair and s-elf pity, by d-isappointm-ent, or h-unger, or l-oneliness.

'I h-ardly kn-ow wh-ether t-o be ash-amed or m-oved to w-onder, b-ut y-ou h-ave f-ed m-y *s-oul* w-ith th-is g-ood f-ood...and w-ith y-our c-ompany.'

'If you ask me,' said Brother Tom, 'it's not such a bad thing to be a little lower than the angels. I wouldn't swap with the angels for love nor money if they have the job Father Chad said they did today. Roast capon...Père Guillaume's wine...Mother of God, the angels don't know what they're missing!'

VI

Sore

Brother Tom woke up on the third of October with a feeling of well-being that he could not at first account for. His soul was happy in anticipation of a good day, and he could not remember why.

Then, as he sat on the edge of his bed, fastening his boots and buckling on his belt and knife in the murderous clangour of Brother Thaddeus ringing the handbell to rouse the brothers for Prime, he remembered. Today saw the beginning of the ploughing.

The sense of well-being swelled into a blithe melody of joy as he came down the daystairs into a morning clear of rain, the dawn promising well for a fine day after so many days of wet.

Tom loved the ploughing better than anything else on the farm. The sight of the neat rows of earth, good dark earth, well manured, turned back in straight, true furrows, was deeply satisfying. The steady purposeful work of following the plough, maintaining the rhythm by singing the chants of the psalms and the Mass, expressed for Tom as perfectly as anything could, his faith; a simple glad rejoicing in the earth and its Creator, a grateful fusion of adoration and hard, satisfying work. And all of it under the wide, happy skies of a fine October day, bracing and blowy; the exhilaration of a light fall frost without the biting stone-cold of winter.

Gladly, wide-awake for once, he joined in the Morning Office and the morrow Mass. Happy and hungry, the breakfast of a hunk of yesterday's bread and a beaker of well-water seemed almost appetising.

After breakfast, the Great Silence ended, and the absolute prohibition of speech lifted. It was now permissible for brothers to indulge in necessary conversation, though idle chatter and gossip still had no place in their lives.

Brother Tom stood with the others, stooping to wash his face and hands in the icy water of the lavatorium. He rubbed himself dry vigorously with a towel from the pile there, and combed his hair after a moment of indecision. I'll look like I've been dragged through the hedge anyway after a day on the farm, he thought. Still, may as well start out beautiful.

As he left the cloister buildings and set off for the farm, Tom saw Brother Josephus walking down from the infirmary. Only Brother Edward of the infirmary brothers had managed to get to Mass, a sure sign of a difficult night and a busy morning. Sometimes, if one of them was sitting up through the night with a sick man, the infirmary brothers would be given permission to sleep through the night and miss the Night Office and morning chapel to enable them to work shifts and catch up on sleep. Brother Josephus had not been in chapel either. Probably he had been conscripted to help with getting the old men out of bed and feeding them their breakfast.

'Brother! Can you spare a minute?' Brother Josephus hailed him as Tom waved cheerfully from the path that led to the farm.

Josephus broke into a run across the grass and joined Tom on the path.

'Tom, Brother Michael sent me to ask you, could you give them half an hour in the infirmary? Please.'

Tom looked at him, dismayed. 'Not really. We're starting the ploughing today. I've promised Brother Stephen. We'll be busy all day.'

Brother Josephus looked more harassed than normal. 'I can't give them any more time. Father Chad has people in after Chapter; I've to clean his house and get some refreshments sorted out for his guests. Just half an hour, Brother.'

In Tom's experience, there was no such thing as just half an hour. He resigned himself to saying goodbye to a whole morning with the best grace he could muster. Brother Stephen, he knew, could manage perfectly well for a morning without him. He could get started with Brother Germanus to help him; everything was ready to go. It was only.... 'Oh, all right then. What's wrong?'

Brother Josephus looked relieved. 'Brother Michael said that if you could just come in and spend half an hour with Father, he'd be so grateful. He needs someone to talk to, and Brother Michael just hasn't time. Oh, thank you, Brother Thomas. I know he'll be so grateful.'

Tom nodded, and walked slowly across the grass to the infirmary path, as Brother Josephus hurried away to his chores in the abbot's house.

Still struggling with resentment, he came into the infirmary and found Brother Michael renewing the dressings on Father Denis' purple, ulcerated legs. He glanced up and, seeing Tom, straightened up and smiled.

'Oh, it's a relief to see you, Tom. Did Brother Josephus tell you? Thank you for sparing the time. I know you're busy. We're all walking on egg-shells this morning. You'll find his lordship *very* much on his dignity—what's left of it.'

'Why's that then?'

'Brother John has told him he's got to spend two weeks lying on his belly in bed, to let the sores on his behind heal. They all get them, sitting in the same position all the time. This he rebelled against, and they had a right old ding-dong this morning. I just kept out of the way. Brother John walked out in the end and left him—he hadn't the patience to reason with him. Poor John, he's exhausted; been working all day yesterday, up all last night with Father Anselm, and now it's Martin's day off. Brother Thaddeus will come in this afternoon to help Brother Edward, but we're a bit stuck at the moment. Anyway, there's been nothing but scowls and short answers from Brother John since he fell out with Father Peregrine this morning, and Father I haven't been near. I'll come in later to put him on the jordan before the midday meal, but I thought I'd leave him a while to calm down.'

'What's the matter with Father Anselm?'

'Oh, it's his chest, nothing new; he's wheezy. Most of them get like it when they're in bed or sat in a chair all day. But it flares up in an infection every now and then. One day we'll lose him that way, and Brother John's fond of him. He sits up nights with him when he's bad, feverish, like this.'

'So I'm to pour oil on troubled waters with Father Peregrine, is that it?'

Brother Michael smiled. 'If you can! Do your best to talk him round to the idea of lying on his front a few days. We could do a lot for him if only he'd let us. So much of this black melancholy can be shifted with simply a bit of comfort; the reassurance of discovering that his body can be eased of its aches and sores. It's not just a question of falling down and down into worsening disintegration and helplessness—which is what he thinks at the moment. Poor soul, you can't blame him, he's fallen far enough, but there's no need for him to be quite so uncomfortable. Bleeding sores do nothing for anyone's temper, do they Brother Denis? No, that's right. You could tell him, couldn't you? He needs to get off them till they're healed up, then he can sit in his chair all day until he grows some new ones if he likes.'

Brother Tom grimaced apprehensively. 'I see. So I've to convince him of the need for common sense. I shall expect a hundred and fifty days off purgatory for this mission. I know this man's temper! I shall walk into that room feeling exactly like Daniel walking into the lions' den saying, "Here Pussy, Pussy," waiting to be shredded.'

Brother Michael laughed. 'I wish you all the best of it. Now then, I must get on with this. If Brother John finds me here talking in his present humour, I shall be gaining an extra day of purgatory, starting now.'

Although Tom would rather have been out helping Brother Stephen and Brother Peter with the ploughing on this windy October day, the infirmary was a pleasant place to spend time, being one of the few places in the abbey that were heated. As he entered Father Peregrine's room, the pleasant sight of a fire glowing on the hearth met him.

Brother Tom had spent some time the previous spring raising that hearth, because it had smoked badly and could only be used when the wind blew from the south and they had least need of a fire. Tom had built the hearth up to two feet off the floor, and fashioned a hood to fit in the chimney, and it served well now. Today, the little logs from the smaller branches of an old, diseased pear tree that had come down in the spring gales were burning on the hearth, warming and scenting the air. He glanced appreciatively at his handiwork as he came into the room, then braced himself to encounter Father Peregrine's state of mind.

'Oh, those smouldering eyes!' The words were out and Tom was laughing before he could stop himself. 'Is it as bad as all that?'

Peregrine looked at him without speaking. Angry falcon, feathers ruffled. Don't go too near it, Tom thought. 'Haven't you even a "Good day, Brother" for me? Really, anyone who didn't know you could be forgiven for thinking you were insane. You look like Saul brooding in his tent, plotting to kill King David.'

'It would be a c-omfort to Father Matthew to know

you'd learned your Old Testam-ent history so w-ell.' Per-egrine roused himself to speak, his voice as morose as the expression on his face.

'H-ave you come here s-imply to unburden yours-elf of your impertin-ent wit at my expense, or is there s-omething I can do for y-ou?' he added, acidly.

Tom sighed. The prospect of gently persuading Per-egrine into a more amenable outlook seemed suddenly too wearisome. He spoke with less patience than he had intended: 'Outside, the wind is blowing, the sun is shining and Brother Peter is taking the oxen out to start the ploughing. In here it is dark and stuffy, with you glower-ing in the corner like a bad-tempered owl perched in the roof of a barn. No, there is absolutely nothing you can do for me. By the sound of you, there's not much I can do for you today either.'

He could have bitten his tongue off as soon as he'd said it. No apology would serve to mend it. Peregrine looked away, his mouth twisting in bitterness.

Tom fetched the stool and sat down beside him, waiting for Peregrine's wounded pride to recover sufficiently for it to be possible to have a conversation with him.

'Y-ou don't have to st-ay.'

'No.'

'Y-ou were looking forw-ard to the pl-oughing.'

'Yes.'

Peregrine forced himself to look at Tom; sore, offended, hurt. He knew that if he said the words that naturally followed ("Go then"), Tom would get up without a word and go. He had to say it if he wanted to preserve his self-esteem, but he couldn't bring himself to say it, so he dropped his gaze again, saying nothing.

He wanted Tom to help him out, make a way forward for him, but Tom, longing to be out of doors, disinclined to spend a morning coaxing Peregrine out of a foul temper, decided against smoothing the path for him. He allowed the silence to continue, feeling a certain callous desire to see how Peregrine would go about climbing down, asking him to stay, and he felt shame too at his own merciless waiting.

'W-ould y-ou pr-efer to g-o, then?' asked Peregrine, icily, at last.

'Yes.' Tom stood up promptly and picked up the stool. Just because you're having a bad day, he thought, justifying himself, it doesn't give you the right to wreck everyone else's day. He replaced the stool, very precisely, and walked to the door.

'T-om.' Even now that his speech had almost perfectly returned, Peregrine had never reverted to the formality of address, 'Brother Thomas', that he had insisted on before. 'Tom' he called him, always, still; a frank admission of his intimate dependence. It was also an acknowledgement of the no man's land in which he lived; outside status, peripheral to the life of the community, a marginalised limbo life.

Tom looked back enquiringly, his hand on the door.

Peregrine met his gaze, reluctant, mortified. 'Will y-ou h-ave me m...beg y-ou?' he asked stiffly.

'No. Civility will be adequate for me.'

Peregrine nodded. It was hard to say it. 'Pl-ease. Will y-ou st-ay?'

Tom came back into the room, laid another log on the fire, brought the stool again and sat down resignedly.

'Out of sorts, then?' he said, mustering his patience, aware that his unwillingness was all too apparent to Peregrine, which would not help.

'Y-es.'

'What's biting you? Tell me about it.' What a long, ignominious fall, Tom thought, that he should need to tell his troubles to me, as once I used to tell mine to him.

'I h-ave been pond-ering.'

'On what?' He did his best to sound interested, without much success.

Time was that Peregrine would not have spent two

minutes sharing his private thoughts with someone who had no inclination to listen. His abhorrence of scrounging other men's time burned him, but his need outstripped his pride. Today found him clinging with his fingertips to faith and rationality. He was desperate for someone to talk to. He would not look at Tom's face; had no wish to see his longsuffering boredom.

'Have y-ou time to l-isten?' he asked quietly, 'I c-an hardly...I'm s-orry to b-e a nuisance.'

'Father,' said Tom, penitent, 'I have as much time as ever you had for me. As much time as you need. Tell me.'

'When a m-an c-omes here...' Peregrine paused, searching for words. 'When he j-oins th-is commun-ity, he l-earns a discipline o-f silence, and it is s-ilence in the f-ace of th-e presence of G-od. That w-ill b-e what Father M-atth-ew t-old y-ou in the nov-itiate, non? I mean, isn't it? Th-at all our l-ife here in the cl-oister is prayer, a self-offering lived out in the f-ace of God's presence. He said th-at to y-ou?'

'More or less. It wasn't quite so poetic the way Father Matthew put it, but yes, he said something like that.'

'M...y-es. Now, here am I, f-ound m-yself d-umb. Sh-ould th-at not have b-een a p-erfect silence, a f-inal self-offering, true prayer at l-ast?

'And y-et, Br-other John and Th-Theo-d-Theodo...oh! Theo, and y-ou, have all d-one your b-est to help m-e speak again. There is l-ess silence in m-y life than before, wh-en I c-ould speak w-ell. Don't y-ou f-ind that amus-ing?'

No, thought Tom, and nor do you. He waited in silence for Peregrine to continue.

'Wh-why is it? Wh-y do we always dem-and of ours-elves the difficult, p-ainful things; espe-cially in the n-ame of God? To speak wh-en we are dumb, to be d-umb when we c-an speak.

'I h-ave wondered if G-od is p-unishing me. M-aybe my words bef-ore had s-ome worth, and he h-as silenced m-e, th-at I may not r-aise the head of m-y hum-anity in pr-ide before his deity. Has he cr-ushed my human-ity so that my words w-ill be inv-alid…m…inva-alidated, like m-e?'

Tom smiled. 'Sounds like a bad attack of self-pity to me. You might be confined to bed, but there's nothing crushed about your humanity. Besides, God—well, isn't it a bit arrogant to suppose that your humanity posed a threat to *God?*'

'Y-es; very arrog-ant.'

'As for being told to be silent when you could speak, and to speak when you had only silence, well that's life, isn't it? Ironic, but not significant. You're brooding, that's your trouble.'

'Oh, is th-at all? Why didn't s-s-someb-body t-ell m-e?' retaliated Peregrine angrily. 'I th-ought there was m-more to it th-an th-at. S-ince I was tw-enty-four I h-ave s-erved God in the cl-oister. How l-ong is that? Th-irty-six years, non? All those years I h-ave s-erved him, y-earned f-or him, hunted him down, and now that he has f-inally turned and sh-own me his f-ace, I am t-errified. M-y Jesus, the Lord of Misf-fortune, the King of th-ose who are sn-apped in two, th-ose whose grotesque rem-ains enact a pitif-ul surv-ival of disease, abuse, tr-agedy. I offered h-im m-y homage, and now he has taken m-e f-ully as his subject. I vowed him I w-ould live in poverty, and oh, m-y God, this is p-poverty. I said I w-ould l-ive in ch-astity, and wh-at w-oman—forg-ive me, but what w-oman would w-ant me n-ow, this th-ing I have bec-ome? I prom-ised obedience, and h-ere I am: I cannot eat or def-ecate or even get fr-om the chair to the b-b-bed without h-elp, permission. "T-ake all of m-e," I said to h-im, and I approached w-ith my head held high, m-eaning to kneel gracefully, lay down m-y life at his f-eet. Instead of th-at, he h-as reached d-own and t-aken it out of my hands.' He laughed, bitterly. 'Damn it, he has *t-aken* my hands! He h-as taken my gift w-ithout ceremony, an-nd thro-wn it aside. I am a n-aked soul, abased before him, stripped of m-y offering. I have n-o life to offer h-im any m-ore, and his thr-one which gl-glowed so invitingly fr-om far away is a bl-aze of terror, scorching m-y face now. The pr-esence of God, surely it should bring deep peace, home-coming, comf-ort; n-ot an agon-y of bitter tears and an endless des-ert of despair.

'T-om! I am afraid of God! Has he n-no pity? M-y sacrifice is not l-ike the s-acrifice of Jesus. Th-at bought r-redemption for mankind. M-ine is empt-y, v-alueless. My life was w-orth something to *me*. Of wh-at use c-ould it be to G-od, that he sh-ould snatch it fr-om me l-ike this? He has taken my life, heedlessly, and cr-ushed it und-er his heel in the mud, gone on his w-ay. He has l-eft me. M-y Lord ... he has rejected m-e.'

'Father, you're not making sense,' said Tom gently. 'You're saying God has rejected you, left you; and you're also saying he has made you fully his subject. You're not being sensible about it—'

'Oh *God,* T-om, *help me!* I am in despair! I c-an't lift up this weight of bl-ackness. I f-eel as though there is n-othing left of m-y soul but a split, sw-ollen br-uise ... oh G-od ... help me ... T-om ...'

Tom looked at him. Plainly this was not an agony that could be placated with kindness. I suppose I should feel honoured, he thought, that he trusts me with his heart-ache. Honour apart, what can I say to him? God help me! For Christ's sake, don't abandon both of us!

'Can you not use your theology now to fight this despair?'

'*Theology?* Th-eology is n-o use to anyone! It is an intellectual's t-oy, an elegant f-encing f-oil, a usel-ess courtly g-ame.'

'All right. Forget theology. What about God?'

'Well, y-es; wh-at about G-od? I don't know. I th-ink I must h-ave off-ended him. Wh-ere is he in all th-is ... mess?'

He waved his maimed hand in a gesture of hopelessness

and disgust, baffled by the tangle of pain and doubt. Tom tried again.

'Father, do you remember talking to me earlier this fall, out in the field below the burial ground, about God's breath? Yes? And you said that God is not outside, watching, but in the middle of all the sweat and turmoil, with you. Remember?'

'Y-es.'

'Do you still believe that?'

'It is st-ill m-y the-ology, y-es. It remains th-e only w-ay I can m-ake sense of anyth-ing.'

'Will you tell me more about it?'

'About wh-at?'

'About God being with us, in us. I'm not sure I properly understood.'

Peregrine looked at Tom very carefully. He felt fairly sure this was nothing more than a ploy to draw him out of himself, but Tom's face was giving nothing away.

'It is only basic incarn-ational theology. Y-ou should have it by h-eart from your novitiate studies. Th-e Christian religion p-pivots around a b-elief in incarna-tion. Its central ten-ets f-orm a dual st-atement about G-od and about man, s-pringing fr-om the person of J-esus. Th-ere are various things to b-e l-earned fr-om that. F-irstly, v-ery important, is th-at tr-uth is essentially p-ersonal. Tr-uth does not exist in the abstr-act: y-ou could s-ay, truth has to be inca-arnate. Jesus said it b-etter, m...''I am the way, th-e truth a-nd the l-ife.'' G-od is tr-uth, and truth is pers-onal because the v-ery *heart* of God, his c-entral r-reality, th-at he is love, is to d-o w-ith r-elating, giving of h-imself, embr-acing.

'I th-ink the reason God forb-ade the making of idols, gr-aven images, is th-at the image of God is personhood in intim-ate relation; m...Adam and Eve, to y-ou. M-ust be breathing, loving, vulnerable to pain, ar-oused to life, to b-e the image of G-od. Everything a statue is n-ot. Statues are the image of everyth-ing that is not God. They are f-orm without personhood. He is personhood without f-orm. I hope I...tell me tr-uth, Tom; am I boring y-ou?'

'Go on.' Tom smiled. He was none too sure that he knew what Peregrine was talking about, but there were signs of eagerness in the man's face, a flicker of something better than misery. You need your job back, Tom thought sadly. Your faith would burn as bright as ever if you had to teach in Chapter again.

'So, truth is p-ersonal. That is why h-ypocrisy is so great a s-in, because it is anti-truth. It is the statement of truth without the body of truth, so to sp-eak. It is m-ore important to *be* truth than to t-ell truth.'

Tom listened, fascinated to hear the impediment in Peregrine's voice lessen as his distress lessened and he grew absorbed in thought.

'Wh-en God cast Adam and Eve out of the garden, his image was l-ost, defaced. There was no way through to him any m-ore. Truth was all bottled up in God again, and nowhere could fl-ow out cl-early, until Jesus.

'Jesus showed us God again; b-ut also, Jesus, because he is the true likeness of the F-ather, showed us for the f-irst time since Adam, hum-anity. Je-sus is wh-at he s-aid he was: the revelat-ion of the Fath-er. We don't take h-im s-eriously. H-e als-o is th-e revela-tion of hum-anity. B-efore Jesus came, we h-ad not s-een God, a-nd we had n-not seen man either. We th-ought we kn-ew man, but...u-tter humanity, br-eathed by the mouth of G-od...we s-ee tha-at in Jesus.

'Man, the living image, had been lost in sin. Jesus r-estored to us a vision of God and a vision of humanity. Better than that even, he gave us a w-ay back; to our God, and als-o to our humanity.

'B-ut what an awesome vision, non? We w-ere used to the tradition of God as power and m-ight, glory and m-ajesty. But remember, the only images we h-ad were defaced images; sin-distorted, abased. Therefore our conc-ept of pow-er and majesty, learned from what we s-aw of earthly kings, was also corrupt. W-e th-ought power and majesty were self-protective, comfortable, luxurious, remote. That is because we saw their reflection in images all burdened with sin. Then J-esus, startling Messiah, the first true man—I mean true like a line is true or an arr-ow speeding to the target—showed us a true p-icture of m-ajesty and glory. Remember his words: "Father, the hour has c-ome. Glorify your Son." What an hour of glory…flogged and derided, n-ailed up…oh…G-od…

'He showed us that the shekinah of G-od, his radiance in creation, does n-ot rest where we looked for it, in pomp and pr-ocessional, in riches and state and inv-estiture of power. N-o, the fragrance of his presence is f-ound in the broken, suffering ones. The beggar at the r-oadside, we have to kneel to see his f-ace. The newborn child and the torn, exhausted body of the labouring w-oman, the mid-wife m-ust kneel to deliver. Brother Michael describes to m-e how he kneels at Brother Cyprian's side, helping the old man l-ost in his dementia to eat his oatmeal, sw-allow his m-edicine. 'Tis true, we still kneel before his glory. But we do not recognise it, least of all wh-en our own hour comes and his gl-ory is agonisingly born in our selves. F-ather, the hour has come. Glorify your Son. Oh the torture of Geths-emane, the prospect of his inheritance, the gl-ory of God…' Peregrine shook his head, his face stilled with sorrow.

'Father, that day…that day…you remember that awful day with the blackberries and cream, when you were just starting to speak again? Is it like that, you mean? Remember? I knelt and…took you in my arms. The glory of God in your…weeping and…humiliation.'

Tom felt his gut writhe with embarrassment to speak such words; to expose to scrutiny that humiliation and grief. Silence, those things belonged to silence; not to conversation.

Peregrine looked at him, intrigued by his shyness. 'Y-

es,' he said. 'Y-ou, and I, at that mom-ent, found ourselves reduced to the raw m-aterials of our humanity.' He
smiled. 'V-ery raw. It w-as a painful m-oment, as I recall.
But for the angels, what did th-ey see? Perhaps a m-an
kneeling in homage to God who is love, expressing the true
f-ealty of his heart, that he will serve love and gentleness,
not indiff-erence, detachm-ent. M-aybe to th-em, a man
whose heart is wrenched with pity does not appear
qualitatively diff-erent from a m-an whose heart is m-oved
to adore the Most High...and, maybe it is n-ot.'

'Father...' Tom hesitated. Now for the difficult bit.

'Mm?'

'If that's true, then...we owe it to each other to allow
ourselves to be comforted, nursed—even when it feels
humiliating. If what you say is right, then to let other
people help us allows the glory of God to shine in our
helplessness, and lets them pay homage to his presence.
Doesn't it?'

Peregrine looked at Tom suspiciously, waited for what
was coming next.

'Doesn't it make you ache, sitting in your chair, not
able to move?' Tom met Peregrine's gaze with what he
hoped looked like a kind of artless candour. He was rely-
ing on Peregrine's gratitude for company and conversation lowering his defences enough to make him open to
persuasion.

'M...y-es.' He sounded wary, but he was not disposed
to shut Tom out completely. 'It w-ouldn't be so bad if I
could get some lever-age with m-y leg, but one being paralysed and the other l-ame...this elbow is n-ot enough to
shift my weight. I...straight answer is y-es; I f-eel as
though I've been beaten.'

Tom looked down, innocently examining his fingernails. He knew he could not steal a march on Peregrine
and look into his eyes at the same time.

'Couldn't you ease it a bit by shifting your position in
the chair?' he asked, with childlike, ingenuous concern.

Peregrine looked very hard at Tom. He was not sure how loaded this question was.

'No,' he said shortly. 'I...I've s-ores from s-itting. They hurt. I...it m-akes my eyes w-ater to sh-ift the tiniest bit.'

Tom met his gaze levelly then. That admission would have eroded Peregrine's resistance almost entirely. A little gentleness now should disarm him completely.

'Well then...will you not lie on your belly awhile and let them heal?' he asked softly. 'Someone could rub your back and your legs, ease them a bit of the aching. Give those sores a chance to heal up.'

'Oh y-ou w-ily tr-aitor! Who told y-ou?'

'Brother Michael. Come on now. Have some sense.'

'S-o, I am r-educed in the end to comm-on sense. Ah w-ell, I have av-oided it l-ong enough, I suppose.' He was fencing, delaying the mortifying capitulation. But Brother Tom would not release him, waiting relentlessly. Peregrine looked down, away from Tom's eyes.

'To s-it upr-ight...it's all th-e dignity I h-ave left.' It was a mumbled, wretched confession, and the pain of it raged in Tom as if it were his own so that for a moment he could not speak.

'Father,' he said then, gently, 'think of all you've just told me. Nobody, nothing, can rob a human being of his dignity. A man on his belly, aching and sore, is the house of the dignity of God. It's only our corrupt understanding, our *tradition* of dignity you stand to lose. No one can take real dignity away from you.'

If all this had taught me only one thing, Tom reflected as he waited for Peregrine to reply, it would be that silence has many qualities. It is not colourless and plain. It has all the richness and variety of a stained-glass window. Silence is full of speech. This one is a battlefield.

Eventually, Peregrine spoke to him out of that struggling silence. His voice was almost inaudible, he could hardly bring himself to say it. 'I expect Br-other J-ohn would be busy now,' he muttered, beaten.

'Man...you don't need to sound so utterly defeated. Look at me. You've fought your pride and won; and as you well know, you've more pride than most of us. Oh, thank God; I do believe that was almost a smile!

'Let me go and find Brother John then. I'll not be long.'

Tom vanished hastily from the room before Peregrine had a chance to change his mind.

He found Brother Michael taking Father Denis outside to sit in the physic garden. 'You can take your little bell with you, and if you feel too cold, ring it and I will come, or tell Brother Edward and he will fetch me. It is chill, but we shan't have much sunshine now. You might as well make the most of it. Hello, Brother Tom. Success?'

'Yes. He's had enough. He consents to be given a rub over and take to his bed with his tail in the air. Grudgingly.'

'Ah, bless you, you master of tact and diplomacy! Will you bring Father Denis' blanket off his bed—the thick, soft one; no—yes, that's it. Thank you. And his water jar. No, no I don't mean water to drink, the other one. That's it. Bring it outside for me if you will. Oh, and he'll need the pillow from his bed I think—bring it in case.'

Outside in the garden, two or three old monks sat dozing in their chairs, well tucked in with blankets, and wearing woollen bonnets under the hoods of their winter cloaks. A picture of cleanliness and tranquillity, they were Brother Michael's *opus Dei*, the means by which he expressed his faith and devotion. He came to chapel when he could, and attended reverently at Mass, but the infirmary was the place of his true worship, and he made his communion with Christ in his dealings with the senile and helpless men who had been entrusted to his care.

The end and object of his devotion was to produce the result he had now, an expression of peace and contentment on the face of the man he was tending. He patted

Brother Denis on the shoulder. 'There you are then. I won't leave you so very long. Here's your little bell, look, and your jar. You'll have to have help if you need that, you're that wound up with woollies. Happy? See you later.

'Come and speak to Brother John with me, Tom. Oh, sorry, were you hoping to go?'

Tom shook his head. 'It doesn't matter,' he said. 'Let's spend the whole day persuading crabbit monks out of their sulks. Why not?'

Brother Michael smiled. 'It's worth it in the end. You stay long enough to see the change we can bring about in Father Peregrine once we get him comfortable. It's the most satisfying thing in the world. Brother John should be in here doing the medicine. Ah, yes. Brother—'

Brother John looked up from the workbench where he was grinding a pile of slim, shiny leaves into a hideous green pulp with his pestle and mortar.

'Good day, Brother Thomas. Are you through with washing and feeding yet, Brother Michael?'

'Yes. Um…Father Peregrine is willing to allow you to dress that sore for him, and take his weight off it.'

Brother John grunted irritably and added another leaf to the mush in the mortar. 'How gracious of him. Right now, I suppose?'

'It might be wise, Brother, since he's asked.'

Another irritable grunt.

'Oh, come on,' said Brother Tom. 'I've given up this morning to wheedle him into complying. Strike while the iron's hot, for mercy's sake.'

'It so happens,' Brother John inspected the mess he had ground, poked at it with the pestle, and put it down satisfied, 'that I have just finished pulping this heal-all for a green poultice for him. I had an idea from his temper this morning that he'd about reached the end of what he could bear. But he'd better not try any more nonsense with me, because I've had enough too. Let's get him back onto his bed then.'

It struck Brother Tom as he looked at Brother John standing, arms folded, glaring down formidably at Peregrine in his chair, that Brother John's authority created the supportive structure which made Brother Michael's kindness possible. It could be no easy task trying to nurse Father Peregrine, but he looked suitably chastened under Brother John's unswerving, intimidating gaze.

'You'll consent to lie on your bed and let this thing heal then? Sure?' He turned to Brother Michael. 'Very well, let's have his clothes off. I'll clean the sore, anoint it with some of Brother Walafrid's marigold ointment, and lay a green poultice on it for today. Tomorrow morning we can wash it and paint it with egg white.' He knelt down as he spoke, unfastening Peregrine's sandals, unbuckling his belt. Tom thought how crumpled and fatigued John's face looked as he glanced up at Brother Michael. 'Should heal rapidly, but he will need to lie on his side or his belly, day and night for several days—two weeks maybe—because the flesh will be fragile there even after it heals.'

'H-ow is F-ather Ans-elm?' Peregrine asked the question timidly, aware that his own conflicts and unaccommodating behaviour had contributed to Brother John's weariness this morning. He could not quite bring himself to apologise, but he wanted to make amends.

'Twice as ill as you are, and half the trouble,' Brother John dismissed his question shortly. 'Do you need to pass water? No? Open your bowels? No? Tell me *now* if you do, because I'm dead on my feet. I need some sleep, and once I've gone to my bed there's only Brother Michael and Brother Edward here today. No? Thank God for that.'

He pulled Peregrine's tunic up to his thighs. 'Lean forward on my arm then. Brother Michael, take this habit up over his head. There, that can go to the wash, he'll not be needing it for a few days. He can keep his shirt and stockings on. You take his legs, Michael. All right? Lift. On his right side for now. That's fine.'

He leaned over Peregrine's body and undid the string of

his drawers. 'Now then, let's see.' He clicked his tongue impatiently. 'I'm not going to be able to get these drawers off easily, there's that much blood and serous fluid glueing them to the flesh. Oh, Sancta Maria, this is going to take for ever.'

Brother Tom watched Brother John's face, dark with weariness, but careful, attentive still, as he tugged experimentally at the fabric, glancing up quickly at Peregrine's sharp, shuddering, hastily suppressed intake of breath as the cloth pulled at the sore. 'Did that hurt you? Brother Michael, this will have to be soaked off. Warm water, with a little salt in it. I'll need some oil too, and aromatics—lavender and rose—to ease out the general aches. Snap to it, come on! I'm all about worn out.'

'Brother John,' Michael was shaking his head at him in a mild, smiling rebuke. 'Go to your bed. I can finish this. I'll clean the sore place, dry it, anoint it, poultice it, dress it. I'll rub him over with oils, and he'll be as right as rain by the time I've finished with him. Brother Thomas can help me if I'm short of a pair of hands. You go and get some rest. Father Anselm may need you again tonight. Please.'

Brother John stood in hesitation, and Michael took his elbow, propelling him gently towards the door.

'I'll stay till you're back,' volunteered Tom.

'Thank you. Thank you. All right.'

Brother Michael closed the door behind Brother John, then came and stood by Peregrine's bed, looking down at him lying on his side in his undershirt and socks, and the drawers caked in sticky blood and serum. Michael considered him for a brief moment, then sat on the edge of the bed beside him and laid his hand on Peregrine's head, stroking over it as he spoke to him.

'You,' he said quietly, 'have a look on your face like a child who's been whipped. I think you feel thoroughly scolded...and confused...and afraid of the way your body keeps betraying you. Am I right? I think the thought of lying on your belly in nothing but an undershirt, smeared with ointments, exposed to whoever walks in, is more appalling to you than pain. Yes? I also think you probably do need to use the jordan, make yourself comfortable, and there's plenty of time for that.' He sat, observing Peregrine quietly, stroking his head all the while.

'Father...you know the weight and weariness of responsibility. You know how tired John is. This morning, you've been frightened and in pain, and he's been extremely tired. He'll probably want to apologise to you himself later on, and you were none too civil to him yourself in the way you spoke to him earlier. Maybe you'll want to say sorry to him. Anyway, that's up to you. But whatever, it's nothing to get upset over. It's easily enough put right.

'I think I'll cut these drawers off that you're wearing, so you can sit on the jordan a while, relieve yourself if you can. Then I'll soak free the cloth that's stuck to you and do something about the sore place. How about that? Does that sound good?'

'Th-ank y-ou.' Peregrine sounded relieved, but he still spoke stiffly, and Brother Tom, looking at him, thought how old he looked. Old and bewildered and defeated, his spirit withdrawn somewhere deep inside him in an ineffectual evasion of indignity and loss of privacy. Tom looked down at his own hands and arms, muscular and browned by the sun and wind, resting on his knees as he sat on the low stool. I don't want to grow old, he thought. Nobody can take the terror out of this kind of stuff, not even Brother Michael. I don't ever want to see the day when I can't walk or hold my water, sit mumbling milky oatmeal and talking rubbish, humoured and coddled by young men, a toothless bundle of sores and creaky old bones.

'Brother Tom?' Michael had cut away the drawers with his knife, and was ready to move Peregrine. 'You were a thousand miles away then. Help me move him, would you? It might be easier if you bring the jordan over by the bed. So, what were you thinking about?'

'I was thinking that I don't want to grow old. It doesn't look easy.'

'Different for different people,' said Brother Michael.

Peregrine said nothing.

'You take his legs, Tom, under the knees. Lift when I say. Ready? Lift.'

'Now then, Father, you just sit here and see if you can go. We'll go and get the things you need and be back in a while. No rush. There, I'll put the blanket over your legs so you're covered. See you in a while.'

Brother Michael came out of the room after Brother Tom, and closed the door.

'Poor soul, these bed sores are the final indignity. Excruciatingly painful, too. Did you see him bite his lip when Brother John moved him forward in the chair? No? It was all he could do not to cry out. It's no good being impatient with him. He's at the end of his rope I think. Let's check on the old men and have a look at Father Anselm, give Father Peregrine a chance to use the pot, then we'll collect the things we need and have him back to bed. Did you get to first Mass? Would you mind if I go to Chapter Mass, or I'll not get to Mass at all today. Thank you. I won't stay for Chapter. You can go if you like.'

'Father Chad on the fifth degree of humility, confessing our evil thoughts to the abbot? Thanks all the same, I think you need me here.'

Brother Michael frowned at him reprovingly. 'Tom, that's not the attitude. The work here sometimes detains us, but it's not to be used as an excuse.'

'Fine. You go to Chapter then. Do you good. I expect you have more evil thoughts than I do. This morning's Chapter will be just what you need. I've already had one homily this morning, from Father Peregrine. That'll do me.'

'Hush, Tom. Come in quietly to Father Anselm.

Yes...no different, look. We'll turn him over, I think; don't want *him* getting sores. You take the legs again. One, two, over. Faith, he's hot. Bed's not wet though, and it should be by now. Mmm. Not long with us, I fear, poor soul. I'll ask Father Chad to come to him this evening. Dip the cloth there into his drinking water and trickle a little into his mouth. Moisten his lips. That's right. Distressing, that wheezing, isn't it?'

Brother Michael tucked the sheet into the bed and laid the blanket over the shrunken old body. He stood with his hand on Anselm's shoulder, quietly looking down at him; took the damp washcloth that hung on a nail on the bedhead, and wiped the old man's brow, watched him a moment more. Then he replaced the cloth and turned to go.

'We'll look in on the men in bed, then the men outside. Father should be ready for us by then.'

There were only two old men left in the infirmary dorter, and both of those had to be turned over and given a sip of water.

'Oh, Father Paul, you're sodden—we'll have to change this bed, Tom.'

That took time, and then the three old men in the garden all wanted to pass water.

'I'm surprised this work doesn't drive you up the wall,' said Tom. 'Some days it must be next to impossible to get anything finished.'

'Well...you know. Anyway, we're done now. I'll get the ointments and such if you'll get some warm salted water and a few rags. He's got a towel in his room. Meet you there. He should have performed for us by now.'

Brother Michael was just before Tom into the room, carrying a tray of oils and salves.

'Oh, you've used the pot; I'm glad of that.' He put his tray down on the table, and took the bowl and rags from Tom's hands, placing them beside the tray.

'You'll be more comfortable soon; get a bit of sleep

maybe.' Brother Michael chatted amiably as he soaked a rag and wrung it out. 'There, let Brother Tom take your weight forward while I clean you; that's it.'

Tom loved Michael for his quickness of compassion, the comfortable, reassuring monologue drawing a veil over the undignified, distressing ugliness of helplessness, its smells and pain and unsightliness. It dawned on him that Martin Jonson intended to achieve the same result with his aggravating patter. The difference was one of insight, sensitivity. Brother Michael was acutely aware of the moods and dispositions of his charges; to Martin they were all sick and senile, and that was it.

'That's fine now. Ready to lift him back on the bed, Brother? On his side, as he was. Lift. Good, that's lovely. Empty that pot please, Tom. Now then, let me see; a towel to catch the drips, a bowl of water...let's soak this off and clean up the sore...eh, dear, we've let this get bad; that's poor nursing. You must have felt as though someone was sticking knives in you. Never mind, we'll soon have it healed up.' The quiet discourse continued all the while Tom was in the room removing the pot with its stinking contents from the shelf of the chair, gently counteracting the faint atmosphere of uneasiness, embarrassment.

When Tom returned, Brother Michael was carefully lifting free the clinging fabric.

'There, that's off. Thanks, Tom. Now I'll clean it as gently as I can. So...that's good...and dry it. Finished with the bowl and rags, thank you, Tom. Ointment...this is wonderful stuff for healing...wonderful. And a poultice now.'

He laid on the place the green mush Brother John had prepared, covering it with a square of fine linen, pressing the edges of the linen onto the greasy ointment so that it stuck down well.

'There now. How are you feeling?'

'Th-ank y-ou,' Peregrine replied.

Brother Michael smiled. 'No, no; I said, "How are you

feeling?" Indescribable, is it? I can believe it. All right, let me see what I can do. Let's have you on your belly then...that's it. See my hands? Full of the peace of God they are. Some oil—doesn't it smell beautiful? Peace to you then, while I rub this into your back and legs. Lavender; for soothing, and against infection. Rose; for comfort...peace to you. Let the fear and misery go out of you. Easier said than done, well I know it, but try not to hold on to it. Feel my hands on you, rubbing the peace of Jesus in. There...on my life, Father, your shoulders feel as though they're carved in wood! Put some of it down, now. Let it go. Feel those aches easing out...there...it's the love of God soothing you now...a place to put burdens down. There now...peace to you. Be at peace...let it all go...yes...It's all right; don't hold it in...that's the way. It doesn't matter if it has you weeping. Don't try to stop it; there's no one here to see but me and Tom, and I think we know you well enough for that. There, there; that's better. Let go of it now...so...make some room for peace...and faith...again.'

He reached over and dipped his hand in the oil, carrying it deftly back without dripping any. 'Another log on the fire, Tom. It's chill to be naked. See how these knots of muscle ease out wonderfully now he's not hanging on to his woe. That's soft up here now. It was Brother Edward taught us this skill—a beautiful thing—bringing the peace of God...the peace of God to you.'

Brother Michael worked on in silence once his words had achieved their purpose, and Tom sat watching him. Although the day was bright enough outside, it was as gloomy as evening in this west-facing side of the infirmary through the early part of the day until the sun moved round. The fire on the raised hearth-stone acted as a lantern for the room. Its kindly glow reflected on Brother Michael's hands gleaming with oil as they worked methodically, firmly over Peregrine's back and buttocks and legs; slowly, carefully on the area around the sore at the base of his spine, so as not to pull at the fragile connection of skin.

The room had filled with the scent of rose and lavender oils, mingled with the heavier, earthier smell of the base oil and the fragrance of fruitwood smoke. Tom felt the silence settle around him like a mantle, a silence full of the most delicate tenderness, interwoven with primaeval, ancient strength.

Quietly, in the silence, the fear and misery that had haunted the room like shadows seeped away, displaced by a slow, deep peace; a peace of such solid personality that it arose among them with as much presence and conviction as if it had been a human face.

There was no sound in the room but quiet breathing, the occasional settling of the fire, sometimes a sound of Michael's oiled hands moving on Peregrine's skin; and two deep, shaky sighs from Peregrine as the peace that had come there breathed into him, penetrated the very depths of him, and he let go of the last drains of his anguish.

'There now.' Brother Michael had finished. 'How does that feel?'

'C-omfortable. W-onderfully comf-ortable. I...th-ank y-ou.' He sighed again, a long, slow sigh of contentment. 'Oh, th-at feels g-ood.'

'And on the inside? What's happened to all that misery? Mm?'

Peregrine looked across the room at the fireglow. The hard, enduring set of his face had relaxed into quietness. 'C-omforted,' he said.

Brother Michael smiled at him, pleased. 'You have a little sleep then, Father. I'll come in to you later. I'll cover you with this sheet—save anyone who comes in from the sin of Ham! Sweet dreams. Bring the things would you, Tom? I'll not touch anything with my hands this oily. Can you shut the door behind us? Lovely.

'When I've washed my hands I'll be off to chapel, if

you're happy to be left here. Oh yes, there's the Office bell now. Never mind that, I'll put the oils and so forth away. It's Mass I don't want to miss. You can leave the three in bed. If you'll just take the others a drink and see to their needs. I won't stay for Chapter. Thank you, Tom.'

Brother Tom became conscious of a rising sense of panic as he heard the door close behind Brother Michael. He would not have admitted this to anyone, and he mentally shook himself and administered a sharp rebuke. 'Don't be such a womanish fool, Brother Thomas,' he scolded himself. 'A handful of old men in your care— what's to be afraid of in that?' It also occurred to him that 'womanish' was probably not the word for it, since any woman would have faced the prospect with equanimity; but this reflection tended to make him feel worse rather than better. He went to look for Brother Edward.

'Ah, Brother, are you managing?' he asked with an air of what he hoped sounded like purposeful briskness when he finally tracked down Brother Edward, who had begun the task of measuring out the morning beakers of rich red wine that the residents of the infirmary took each day to promote their health.

Brother Edward, eighty-one years old, dim of sight and hearing, but otherwise possessed of all his faculties and as canny as ever, did not bother to hide his amusement: 'Gives you the jitters, does it, having to care for this lot?'

Brother Tom blushed. 'No,' he said, carelessly, 'I think I should be equal to an hour's nursing. It's not that difficult, is it?'

Brother Edward smiled. 'That depends,' he said. 'Ah, that's Brother Denis' bell ringing now. I expect he needs the jordan. Will you go or shall I?'

Their eyes met and the glint of good-humoured mockery needled Tom's pride. When he opened his mouth to speak, the 'Please come with me, I haven't a clue what to do' that he intended, came out as, 'Oh, I'll go, Brother. There's plenty here to keep you busy.'

Brother Edward smiled. 'As you wish, Brother Thomas. I'll finish these drinks and take them round then. Call me if you need me.'

The little bell tinkled again, rather more frantically this time, and Tom hastened out to the physic garden and Brother Denis.

'Can you help me, young man?' he asked. 'I need to relieve myself. I have a jar here, but I'm that bundled up with scarves and mittens and such, I don't think I can manage without help.'

Tom smiled brightly; a nurse's smile—the smile of a man who has the situation in hand.

'Fine,' he said, and began to extricate Brother Denis from his wrappings.

As he did so, muffled by the infirmary walls came the faint but unmistakable wavering shriek of Father Aelred: 'Aaaaagh! Aaagh! Aaaaaaagh!'

He squatted down beside Brother Denis, burrowing through the mountain of woollies, and began to lift aside the folds of his habit.

'What are you doing, Brother?' enquired Brother Denis with interest.

'You want to pass water, don't you?' Brother Tom felt instantly ashamed of the note of irritation in his voice. The continuing distant commotion ('Aaagh! Aaaagh! Aaaaaaagh!') was beginning to worry him slightly. What if he's fallen out of bed? Tom thought in alarm. What if he's dying?

'Yes, but we have a slit cut in the front of our habits in the infirmary, Brother. Saves time you know.'

'AAAAAAAAAAAAAGH!' Then silence. Why silence? Perhaps he is dead.

'Well, why didn't you say so?' Tom sounded more impatient than he had intended.

'I'm sorry, Brother,' replied Brother Denis humbly. 'I thought you knew what you were doing. I—ooh, I'm piddling! I'm piddling!'

'Have you a handkerchief, Brother?' The educated, aristocratic voice of Father Gerald in the next chair scarcely penetrated Tom's panic. 'I don't like to distract you from your work, but I have rather a bad cold, and I can't find my handkerchief. I have a mouthful of rather nasty sputum, and I aa-a-aa-aaaSHOO!...I'm awfully sorry to trouble you, Brother, but I really *do* need a handkerchief.'

Brother Tom glanced up at the old man, the woolly rug round his knees hideously spattered with grey-green phlegm, and a long string of the same dangling trembling from his nose.

'Brother Thomas!' It was Brother Edward's voice in the doorway. 'I wonder if you might give me a hand with Brother Aelred. He's messed his bed, and he's absolutely plastered. Got the runs, I think. I've got his shirt off and cleaned up the worst, but it'll take two of us to change his bed.

'What's the matter? Is Brother Denis wet? That's not like him. Oh dear me, look at Father Gerald. He needs a hanky! Whatever have you been doing, Brother Thomas?'

Tom rose wearily to his feet. 'What am I to do about Brother Denis? I can't change him out here, he'll catch cold.'

'Put his rug back for the minute and help me with Father Aelred. I've left him naked, and if he does any more...well, he is inclined to play with it and get in a bit of a mess if he hasn't got his hands tucked outside the sheet. You'll be all right a minute, won't you, Denis? Yes, that's right—don't you let on to Brother John, though. I'll go for a bowl of water, Brother Thomas, and see you inside.'

Brother Cyprian, sitting in his chair in his favourite place beside the lavender hedge, sheltered from draughts by the infirmary wall, watched Brother Tom with inscrutable eyes.

'It's a funny thing, Cedric,' he remarked as Brother Tom passed him. 'I can never understand what they want with all these cattle. There's such a lot of cows in here today.'

Tom glanced round wildly, half-expecting to see a breakaway invasion from the farm.

'Oh, Mother of God!' he said. 'I never wiped Father Gerald's nose!'

He could have hugged Brother Michael when he walked in through the door half an hour later.

'Has everything been all right, Tom?' Michael enquired, his friendly smile and calm voice restoring a sense of sanity to Tom's ruffled spirit.

Brother Edward spoke before Tom had a chance to reply. 'He's been just grand,' he said. 'He's managed fine. Drinks are all out except Peregrine's. You'll maybe take his to him, Brother Thomas? Take some wine for yourself as well. I'll give you a call when Brother John's here, and you can get back to your ploughing.'

Peregrine was still sleeping when Brother Tom came into his room. Two of the little cats were stretched out asleep in the warmth on the floor, one with its paws up against the warm stones of the built-up hearth.

Tom sat down in the cushioned chair and sipped his wine. He reached forward for two more logs to place on the fire, and put his feet up on the hearth. The room was full of contentment and peace.

'Be m-y gues-t.'

Tom looked across to the bed. The dark grey eyes were open, smiling at him.

'G-etting un-der th-eir f-eet, were y-ou?'

Tom laughed. 'Yes. Badly. I've brought your wine. Can you drink it lying down?'

'I d-on't kn-ow. N-ot eas-ily, I th-ink. A ch-oice betw-een l-ying on m-y r-ight side and sp-illing it, or pr-opping m-ys-elf up on m-y l-eft elbow and n-ot being able to l-ift m-y hand to m-y m-outh.'

'Don't spill it. I've mopped up more mess this morning

than I hope to see for a very long time. On your left elbow,
and I'll feed it to you.'

'Y-es. If it f-alls tow-ards the l-eft side of m-y m-outh, it
doesn't f-all out again.'

Tom knelt beside the bed, holding the cup of wine to his
friend's mouth, saddened by the helplessness, moved by
the holy intimacy of that communion.

*'Calix benedictionis, cui benedicimus, nonne communicatio san-
guinis Christe est?'* he whispered softly.

Peregrine lifted his face from the cup, looked at him, his
eyes depths of awe, fear almost.

'I h-ave th-ought so. It s-eems too pr-esumptuous, but I
have th-ought it s-o. In our s-orrow, in our d-ying, in our
l-ove, is h-is real pr-esence. *"Ecce Agnus Dei."* Th-ank y-ou,
T-om.'

Tom sat down by the fire again, watching one of the
kittens as it yawned, white needles of teeth and a delicate
curl of pink tongue contrasting with the sleek black fur. He
drained the last of his wine.

'That's good: better than ale and water. Better than
Brother Walafrid's strange brews.'

'Y-es. Th-ere are s-ome cons-olations to l-iving in th-e
inf-irm-ary. Y-ou m-ust come and s-ee me again at this
time of d-ay.'

'Mmm. I think I will. I'll fetch some more logs for this
fire, shall I? Will I find some more apple logs, do you
think?'

'Ask Br-other M-ichael. H-e kindl-y panders to m-y
wh-ims. I f-ear you might get sh-ort shr-ift w-ith Brother
J-ohn today.'

'Brother John's not back yet. That's why I'm hanging
about here drinking your wine. I must get back up to the
farm as soon as he returns; he'll not be long, I imagine.
Anyway, I'll get those logs while I'm here; leave you with
your fire well supplied.'

When Tom returned with the apple logs for the fire, he

found Brother John sitting in Peregrine's chair, talking to him. 'I'll look at that sore patch later.'

'Th-ank you.'

There was a slight tension in the air. Tom dropped the logs into the basket. 'Should I go?' he said.

'No, it's all right, Brother Thomas. I mustn't stay long. I've only just come back from my bed. I must make myself useful about the place in a minute. I've come to make my apologies, really. You used to say to us in Chapter, Father, "Courtesy is the flower of Christian charity." I don't know how many times I've heard you say that. I did listen, and I did take it in, though you might not have thought so this morning. I'm sorry. The way I spoke to you was inexcusable. I can only say that I was very tired, and you were...' Brother John's face broke into a grin '...obnoxious! Awkward? I've never known anything like it! Anyway, I'm sorry. Please forgive me.'

Peregrine smiled. 'Y-ou're s-upposed to give m-e a chance to adm-it m-y own obn-oxious beh-aviour. I sh-ould listen to m-y own s-ermons. I ask y-our pardon also.'

'I've got some news for you too. I've been talking to Father Chad. He asked whether I thought you might be ready to give the homily at Chapter in early November.'

'Wh-wh-at d-d-id y-y-ou s-s-s-ay?'

'Yes. Of course.'

Peregrine said nothing, but looked at Brother John with his eyes shining. He turned his head away, and looked into the fire.

'Y-ou are n-ot b-eguiling m-e w-ith f-alse h-opes? Can I r-r-eally d-o it?'

'Yes. You really can. If you take your time, your speech is clear enough. You've had enough time to meditate and pray!'

'Wh-at ab-out th-e wr-etched inc-ontin-ence? I'd die if I wet m-yself in Ch-apter.'

Brother John shook his head. 'Not a problem. The Chapter meeting isn't that long—you could probably get through it all right anyway; but we'll wash you till you smell as sweet as a rose, and send you in a chair so well padded the Great Flood would go unnoticed, just in case of any unfortunate mishap. November 1st. Father Chad says that day's Chapter is full of dreary stuff about exclusion from table and the oratory. "Speak about what you like," he said. Yes?'

'Y-es. Oh, y-es pl-ease.'

'All right. I'll tell him. Now then, I must get some work done. Brother Thomas, are you away up to the farm? Thank you for staying so long. You've been a great help.'

'I'm not too sure about that, but yes, I must be going now. Goodbye, Father.'

'Goodb-ye T-om.' But Peregrine spoke absently, and did not look at him. Tom left him gazing into the fire, his eyes burning with excitement, absorbed in thought.

VII

The Course Run

Throughout October Tom was ploughing. Brother Germanus took over the milking, the pigs and the hens, and kept a watch on the sheep, feeding them in the evenings now the growth of the grass had stopped. They had been put to the tup and were in lamb now, precious sources of revenue and meat.

Brother Prudentius saw to the apple harvest, the abbey school turning out as willing labour again. The loft above the wood store in the kitchen yard had been filled with apples, row upon row of them, green and red and russet; carefully set on the racks so that none should touch its neighbour and any rot be contained. Brother Walafrid passed his days making cider and brewing ale, tending the wines he had started in fruitful September.

Every spare minute Brother Germanus had he spent chopping wood, sawing and splitting logs. Severe frosts had held off so far, and the brothers hastened with the tasks that grew so much harder in the bitter cold to come.

By the end of October, the fields showed neat strips, ploughed, harrowed and sown. Plenty remained to be done, but they could afford to relax a little, and Brother Tom and Brother Stephen were able to spend a day mending the roof of the byre.

In the evenings, Brother Tom snatched an hour with Father Peregrine, but spent those hours for the most part fast asleep with his feet up on the hearth. He had his own chair in that room now, his own Office-book and ale mug.

Peregrine would talk to him as he dozed. He knew Tom was not listening, but his mind buzzed with Scripture and theology, his whole being dancing like a moth round the dreadful, attractive flame of hope and fear, teaching the brethren in Chapter again.

He must have prepared thirty sermons in the long, empty days of waiting, his mind singing again with theology, philosophy, analogies and quotations.

Sometimes he found himself petrified before the dread of his speech scrambling in the stress of the moment, and sick at the thought of being wheeled in before their eyes. He would not wholly admit his terror of appearing too pitifully grotesque, too much a freak to be seen; but neither could he wholly suppress that fear. His sleep was tormented and destroyed by nightmares of incontinence. He dreamed of sitting in the abbot's chair on its dais, all Brother John's careful padding left behind in the infirmary chair they had brought him in, fighting the sudden, desperate urge to urinate, struggling to keep his mind on his talk as his stuttering speech fragmented into nonsense before the polite silence of the brethren.

Always in his dream there would be that watching, listening, sceptical silence sitting in judgement on him, his disintegrated speech finally stuttering into nothing as, appalled, he felt his bladder emptying, on and on, a great sea of it running down the floor of the Chapter House, and the brethren in silence raising their pitying eyes from the stinking yellow river, to watch with curiosity his tears of mortification at the torture of his public shame.

He would wake from this dream night after night, his bed soaked in sweat and urine, and have to force himself to ring his bell to summon the infirmary brother, glad the shadows of night hid his face burning with shame as he mumbled his confession of incontinence. At first, he had been unable to bring himself to call the night brother, but

Brother Michael had insisted gently, 'You *must* tell us. If you leave it till morning we're likely to lose the mattress as well, and heaven knows we've enough to do without spending the day making mattresses. We could come in and check you at intervals in the night, but I don't think you want that either, do you?'

And he had shaken his head, speechless in the humiliation.

'What is it?' Brother Michael had asked him. 'What's upset you?...It's this blessed Chapter talk, isn't it? You don't have to do it, you know. Would you rather not?'

And even more costly than the shame had been the admission: 'Broth-er, I w-ant to do it m-ore th-an anything.'

He tried out his ideas on Brother Tom as Tom dozed before the fire.

'D-oes F-ather Ch-ad keep th-eir v-ow of pov-erty bef-ore them? They sh-ould never forget poverty. To be p-oor in spirit...Obedience...he w-ill have spoken to th-em of obedience. It is eas-ier to talk about. Ch-astity...T-om, has h-e talked to th-em about ch-astity? Th-ey need to h-ave called to m-ind the f-ire of th-e first love f-or God, s-ingle, h-umble adorat-ion. Celibac-y w-ithout insp-ira-tion an-d tendern-ess is as soul destr-oying as C-ormac's porridge.

'H-as he sp-oken to them of th-e Tr-inity? Of pers-everance? Has he talked about h-onesty? T-om? T-om? Oh, g-o b-ack to sl-eep, y-ou usel-ess l-ump.'

'Mm? What? I'm not asleep. What did you say?' 'H-as h-e talked to th-em about l-ove, T-om; s-uffering love?'

'Pardon? Who?'

'F-ather Ch-ad.'

'Father Chad talk about suffering love? Well...he may have said something that I missed, but...I'd be inclined to doubt it.'

Tom threw another log on the fire and settled peace-fully back into his chair.

'Th-en I sh-ould talk to th-em about th-at. Th-e l-ove of J-esus. Love that gives and goes on g-iving. Th-e def-enceless, humble, r-oyal l-ove of Jes-us. Love h-as n-o def-ences, T-om. Y-ou know it's l-ove when it h-urts.'

'Mmm...good idea...you talk to them about that.'

'Y-ou th-ink so? Tr-uly?'

'What? Oh, yes...' Tom's eyes were closing in spite of his best efforts to pay attention. 'Sounds good to me...loving when it hurts...' and he was asleep, and nothing roused him again until the Compline bell rang.

The two of them spent every evening in October in this fashion: Tom working hard on the farm and bone-weary by the end of the day, Peregrine restless in the longing and dread of working again, growing more and more nervous as the first of November approached.

The night of October thirtieth Tom found him in a state of unbearable tension.

'Talk to him, for mercy's sake,' said Brother John. 'He's driving us all crazy with this talk of his. We should never have given him so much time to stew over it. He's thought of nothing else since I don't know when, and talked of nothing else either. Mind you, he changes it every five minutes. He's been so on edge today; tore Martin off a strip for some silly little thing—completely lost his temper. I'll be glad when Thursday's over and he's got it out of his system. That's if we survive tomorrow!'

Brother Tom went into the room and found Peregrine brooding, lost in thought, his chin resting in his hand, scowling in concentration.

'Byre roof's as good as new,' Tom commented cheerfully. 'And we should have a good crop of winter wheat if...'

'T-om, wh-at did Augus-tine s-ay in th-e book of h-is confessions, ab-out th-e inc-arnation? L-oving G-od in things th-at d-elight...um..."He m-ade th-is w-orld, and is not f-ar off"...oh...*M-ementote ist-ud, et conf-undam-ini: r-edite praevaricator-es ad cor*...um, it's Is-aiah, isn't it? B-ut what ch-apter? Oh, I c-an't r-emember it, and I us-ed to know it s-o w-ell.'

He shook his head impatiently, his mouth twitching in frustration. 'C-an't y-ou rem-ember?'

'What? Augustine or Isaiah? Either way, the answer's no. What do you want to know that for, anyway? You're not trying to impress the Pope. It's only a homily to a handful of monks who are weary after the harvest. All they need to know is how to find the grace to tolerate each other and stay awake through the reading of the martyrology. I guarantee you there'll not be a man in Chapter but his heart'll sink if you start quoting St Augustine in Latin.'

'Tr-uly? Do y-ou th-ink s-o?'

'No. I know it. Don't spin theological marvels for them, just talk to them about Jesus. They like it better.'

'M-aybe...I w-ish I c-ould r-em-ember it, th-ough. Do y-ou th-ink I'll g-et th-rough it all r-ight?'

'Yes. I'm sure you will. Stop worrying about it.'

'I'm afr-aid of...'

'Of what?'

Peregrine sat with his shoulders hunched, his head bent, hiding his face.

'Afraid of what?'

'Inc-ontin-ence.'

'That'll be all right. Brother John said so. You should trust him.'

'B-ut, if it's n-ot...'

'It will be.'

Peregrine sat hunched in brooding silence. He spoke only once more in the rest of that evening.

'T-om...I'm t-errified,' he said.

He scarcely looked up to say goodnight when Tom left him to go to Compline. His face was fixed in a frown, staring beyond his present reality, as he groped helplessly in his memory for forgotten teachings, sayings of the Fathers; strove in futility to remember the Athanasian Creed and the famous Corinthians passage on love. To his horror, he found he couldn't even remember whether it came in the first or second epistle. It all vanished into shadows that mocked him and eluded him. He hardly noticed Tom go.

The Chapter for the following day, October thirty-first, concerned the details of exclusion from the common table for minor faults. Brother Tom made himself as comfortable as he could in his stall, and prepared to hear Father Chad's careful dissertation on this subject. Tom could not restrain himself from the reflection that anyone who had sat opposite Brother Richard eating pottage might be tempted to commit a minor fault with the sole object of securing exclusion from the common table, but he chided himself for his cynicism, and bent his attention repentantly to Father Chad's homily, which proved to be, as he anticipated, exceedingly dull but mercifully brief.

After his homily, in the business part of the meeting, Father Chad explained to the brethren that Father Peregrine was to address them the following day in Chapter; said that this should be seen as an encouraging sign of recovery, and though they must not expect too much too soon, they might take hope from this beginning of seeing him returned to them from his long and distressing period of sickness. There was no other significant business that day.

Once released from Chapter, Brother Tom spent the morning with Brother Stephen building a rick to store some turnips and mangels for which there was no more space in the stone shed in the farmyard. They spread a layer of straw, thick enough to protect the roots from ground-frost, and then layered the roots and straw into a stack. There had been no hard frosts as yet, but winter was coming. The two men sweated as they worked, carting the roots and forking the straw, but their hands were red and rough with the cold.

That job done, they fetched the tumbrils out of storage in the barn. The air nipped with a promise of frost now, and the days were coming when the cattle would be housed in the foldyard, feeding on hay and roots, stolid, patient beasts, their breath hanging in steam on the winter cold. Their hay would be forked into the high, freestanding racks, and the roots chopped and fed to them in the wooden tumbrils, great feedtroughs that stood on tall legs near the wall of the foldyard.

After that, the morning was all but spent, and Brother Tom went into the dairy to help Brother Germanus, who had set himself the task of scrubbing it out in an effort to rebuff the sarcasm of the kitchen brothers.

'Brother Thomas!' A voice hailed him loudly from the farmyard. 'Brother Thomas!'

Tom looked puzzled. 'That's Martin Jonson,' he said. No monk would stand in the middle of the yard and shout. 'What's afoot, I wonder? They're perhaps needing me in the infirmary. Father's like a cat on hot bricks about this Chapter address tomorrow.'

Brother Germanus followed him out into the farmyard, where Martin was still calling.

'I'm here, Martin. Is something wrong?'

'Aye, I'll say there is. Father Columba's took bad: he's had another seizure. Carrying on something shocking he was this morning. We couldn't do a thing to suit him. But, "let it be", says Brother Michael, "let it be"—although I can tell you Brother John was looking pretty tight-lipped by the time we got to the morning drink.

'And there he was, would you believe, he threw his cup of wine across the room, and all because he couldn't remember how to say some ticklish business in Latin! "Well, here's a pretty kettle of fish," I says to him. "You can't have this sort of going on, not even if you've forgot your own *name*." And do you know, he swore at me something atrocious—words no man of his calling should even know, not by rights. Fair gobstruck I was.

'Still, Brother Michael, bless him, he's the patience of a saint. "Don't take it ill, Martin," he says to me, just like that, "don't take it ill," and he was on his knees by the old villain, talking to him as gentle as you please. And what we should have done if there'd been but Brother John and me there I don't like to think. Still, we shall never know, shall we?

'Any road, the long and the short of it is, he was took bad again. You should have seen him; eh, it was ghastly! Vomiting he was, and his face as purple as a pulpit cushion, his eyes turned up in his head and his mouth blowing in and out like a flapping sail.

'So I said I'd come for you. Brother Michael seemed to think you might like to know, being his friend like, so much as you brothers have friends, if you know what I mean.

'Are you all right, Brother Thomas? You don't look too good yourself.'

Tom stood with his fists clenched and his face drained of colour, staring at nothing. Everything that made up reality, the solid reassurance of his body, the breeze on his skin, the smells of beasts and hay and earth, the grey banking clouds and the mud under his feet; in that moment he lost it all. There was nothing left to him but the thunder of his heartbeat in the derelict shell of his life.

'He is...he is still alive?' he whispered.

'Oh yes, he's bad, but he's with us—just like before: helpless as a babe in arms, his face grey and his wits gone. But he's not dead. Not yet, any road.'

'I'll come,' said Tom. 'Go down ahead of me, and tell Brother Michael I'll come.' He could not bear to walk down the hill in Martin's company.

He went back into the dairy, Brother Germanus shadowing him anxiously, and like a man in a dream he picked up the yard-brush he had been using on the floor, and propped it with meticulous care and precision against the wall.

'I'm sorry I won't be able to help you finish this job,' he

said, his voice polite, remote; someone else's voice from far away.

'Don't you worry about that,' replied Brother Germanus. 'Father Columba needs you with him by the sound of it.'

'Yes,' said Tom. He was unsure whether he spoke very slowly, or if it was just that the whole universe had slowed down, stopped all its bustle and colour, condensed all its movement into one slow, agonised, wailing cry. 'Yes,' he said again. 'There may still be something I can do for him. I promised him I would do what I could.'

He stood still for a moment, Brother Germanus watching uneasily the haunted gazing of his face. Then he took a deep breath and smiled at Germanus. 'Well,' he said, 'I'd better go and see what I can do.'

He walked down the hill, cocooned in terror, aware of nothing but the nauseous fluttering of his stomach, the beating of his heart; purposing nothing but that his legs should not give way under him, should carry him into that room, where he might behold that grey, distorted face, and wait a chance to be left alone with the battle-weary, wrecked remains of his friend.

He came to the infirmary, where everything was business as usual: the old men out in their chairs encased in blankets, woolly grey bonnets framing the faces yellow and withered, or veinous purple, of their nodding, dozing heads, and Brother Edward moving among them, rousing them for their cup of wine.

Inside the building, Tom paused at the door of Peregrine's room, trying to get his body back under control, master the shaking, refuse the icy nausea. He closed his eyes for a moment. 'Help me then, help me,' he whispered; and he opened the door.

Brother John stood by the bed, bending over the form that lay there. He had his hand laid on Peregrine's brow, his face thoughtful.

'Hotter than ever,' he said, without looking up to see who had entered. 'This doesn't look good.'

He took his hand away and lifted the sick man's eyelids, one by one, moving aside slightly so that the daylight might shine in on the eyes.

They had laid him on his right side on the bed, his left arm and leg cushioned on pillows. Brother John laid his hand on the still, twisted hand on the pillow, rubbing it gently.

'Peregrine,' he said, 'Peregrine. Can you hear me?'

He waited, looking down at his patient. Tom was moved by a sudden impulse of gratitude for the look on John's face; the gravity, the respect, the sadness. Brother John looked up.

'Tom, I'm sorry. I didn't realise it was you. Martin told you?'

'Yes. Can I . . . can I stay with him for a while?'

'Of course. Brother Michael and I will sit with him through this morning, but I ought to get some sleep this afternoon in case he needs me through the night. Why don't you go and get a bite to eat, and come back and sit with him this afternoon?'

'Eat? Maybe . . . John, will he live?'

Brother John shook his head. 'Who can tell? He's very ill; burning up quite a fever now. Pulse is slow . . . bounding. Pulled through it last time though, didn't he?'

'And if he lives?' Tom's voice was husky. He could not iron out the tremor in it.

'Again, you can't say. How many times must a ship be dashed against the rocks before it finally tears apart? Each time is one step nearer the last time. Each battering brings further disintegration. All we can say for sure is that right up to the end, before anything else, this broken, helpless, suffering being is a living soul, a house of God's spirit, needy of tenderness, worthy of respect. I don't know, Tom. I just don't know.'

He looked down again at the man on the bed. The

sound of the slow, stertorous breathing was the only intrusion on the utter silence.

With an effort, Brother Tom forced himself to take the steps—one, two, three, four, five—that brought him round the bed where he could see Peregrine's face, clammy and colourless except for the slight, unnatural flush of fever in the cheeks. His lips vibrated with every breath, but the blowing in and out of the paralysed side of his face had been masked by lying him on his right side.

Tom gazed at him, saying nothing. Cold—it seemed so cold today. Brother John laid a hand on his shoulder. 'Get yourself something to eat, Tom. I dare say you don't feel like it, but he could be days like this.'

Tom shook his head. 'No,' he said, 'he won't.'

Brother John squeezed his shoulder. 'Have some food. You must. I can't trust you to be alert to sit with him if you haven't eaten. No one can say how long he'll be before we see a change. Go on with you. There's the bell for Sext now. Come back after the meal.'

Nobody disobeyed Brother John. He had the calm authority that went with responsibility. Tom went to chapel, then to the refectory with all the others, and forced down as much food as he could bear.

When he returned to the infirmary in the afternoon, he found Brother Michael sitting with Father Peregrine. He had a smile for Tom, as always.

'Hello, Brother. I'm glad you've come. He mustn't be left alone, and although it's quiet now, someone may need me later. We turned him only just now before Brother John went, so there's nothing to do but sit with him and keep a watch, keep the fire going and not let his lips get too dry.'

They sat, Brother Michael in Peregrine's chair and Tom in his own chair, mostly in silence. On the hour Martin came in, and the three of them turned the sick man and changed the padding and the sheet when necessary. Apart from that they just sat and kept watch.

Tom waited, the palms of his hands sweating, for the moment when Brother Michael would leave the room; leave him alone with his promise, his task. But the moment never came. For the first time Tom could remember in all his visits to the infirmary, no bell rang. The afternoon drifted by in tranquillity, the light in the room swelling to a glorious tawny gold as the day drew towards its close.

Once, Brother Edward came in to ask Brother Michael to help Martin change a wet bed. Tom's heart beat faster, but Edward said, 'I'll stay here and keep vigil with Brother Thomas till you're back. There's nothing to do for Peregrine, I know, but I'll share the watch over him a while.'

Brother Edward did not leave until Brother Michael returned, and Brother Michael stayed with Tom while Martin and Brother Edward set out the evening meal trays.

'It's a miracle how quiet it is today,' he remarked once to Brother Tom. 'Well, you know what it's like here. Some days we're rushed off our feet. I don't think I've ever known it this quiet.'

By the time the sun was sinking and the bell began to toll for Vespers, Brother John was back.

He came directly to Peregrine's room.

'No change? Ah well.' He bent over the unconscious man, making his own checks.

'We'll give him a wash, shall we, while the others are eating? Edward and Martin can do the feeders, then one of us can help settle them in to bed. No, he's not much different, is he? Still hot—I don't like the look of that. I don't think there's much point in trying to force fever herbs down him, though; not till he shows more signs of life than this. I'd hate to choke him.'

He looked at Brother Tom. 'Thank you, Brother, for staying. We'll look after him now till tomorrow. Go to Vespers and then get some supper and some rest. If you'd like to come the same time tomorrow, that would be a help.'

He saw Tom's hesitation and added, 'I will call you, don't worry. If there's any change at all, I'll let you know.'

They were waiting for him to go, Tom could see it. They didn't want the intrusion of his company while they washed and examined their patient. He dithered a moment longer, then helplessly he left. It would have to wait until tomorrow.

As he sat in the Chapter meeting the next day, Tom wondered if this was what hell was like; a grey suffering limbo of exclusion.

He listened to Father Chad's homily, but did not hear what he said, and did not take in the announcements. He registered Peregrine's name being mentioned once or twice in suitably grave tones, but nothing else.

Up on the farm he muddled through his chores, walking down the hill like a sleepwalker when the bell rang for Sext. The other men left him alone when they found their kindly questions met by his dazed, bewildered murmur, 'He's... I don't know... I don't know...'

After the midday meal, he returned doggedly to the infirmary, where he was met by Brother John.

'I'm glad you've come. I would have sent for you if you hadn't come anyway. You'll see a change in him. We must get some of the men bathed this afternoon, so I'll be glad to have you sit with him. Brother Michael will come and help me as soon as you relieve him.'

This was it then. Tom's mouth was dry and his knees turned to water as he approached the room. He felt his courage ebbing away from him, his resolve melting.

'All right, Tom?' Brother Michael smiled at him as he entered the room.

Tom's eyes were drawn to the bed, his attention riveted by the racket of breathing that filled the room.

Peregrine lay on his back in the bed, his head and arms supported on pillows. His head was propped slightly to one side, the mouth fallen ajar, his eyes half-open, dull, sightless. A vein pulsed under the scrawny skin of his neck. His face was yellow and seemed to have shrunk. Each breath he drew was a rattling labour, an unnatural, jerky heaving of his chest, separated from the next breath by an age of silence.

Tom looked in horror and sadness at the grievous, pitiful struggle; gazed without moving, without speaking. Yes, there was a change.

Brother Michael watched Tom, took in the tautness of his face, the look in his eyes that gazed across desert spaces of desolation.

Michael nodded. 'I know,' he said, 'I know.'

Tom was roused to panic for a moment, and looked at him, horrified, but Michael didn't know. 'It's the same for all of us,' he said.

And then Brother Michael left, promising to return later when the baths were done. 'I'm not sure how long I'll be,' he said, 'but you can ring his bell if you need me, or you're worried about anything. We're not turning him every hour now. No need for that any more.'

Tom watched him go, waited until the door clicked shut, gave him time to walk away. Then he moved slowly to the bedside. He put out his hand and touched the pillows that supported the unconscious man. Those under his arms were lumpy, solid, real monastic pillows, but the one under his head was filled with down, soft and light. Tom slid his hand under Peregrine's head. It felt unpleasant, sweaty. He lifted it slightly, leaning over him, and with his other hand he tugged the pillow free. He clasped it to him, holding his breath, his heart thudding as he lowered Peregrine's head back down onto the bed. Without the support of the pillow under his head, his mouth fell open even further. Tom could see inside it. There were brownish, dry patches on his tongue, and little drifts of sticky white saliva. The skin on the lips was tight and dry, cracking.

Holding the pillow in his arm, Tom reached over the bed to the bedside table, where a sponge lay in a bowl of water. He squeezed it lightly and carried it to Peregrine's mouth, dripping a trickle of water onto the parched tongue, gently moistening the cracked lips. Then he replaced the sponge in the bowl.

'It's because I promised you,' he whispered. 'It's only because I promised you.'

He stood there, very close to the bed, clutching the pillow in both hands, holding it ready as he looked down at the bleak, withdrawn, shrunken face.

He swallowed convulsively, his heart hammering and his head wobbling in uncontrollable agitation.

He couldn't do it.

After a while, he backed away from the bed, still gripping the pillow. He sat down on the low stool beside Peregrine's chair, his eyes fixed on Peregrine's face, watching the tough, insistent tic of the pulse in his neck, listening to the arduous labour of his breathing, watching the dead grey absence of his eyes, half-expecting even now to see them waken to a flicker of humour, anger, tenderness.

His grief and frozen helplessness grew until they overwhelmed him; till grief was no more part of him, but he was all grief, had become absorbed into grief, had no more being beyond this moment. Enfeebled of all power to act, he began, unawares, to rock, clinging to the pillow for comfort, past knowing or thinking, seeing nothing, hearing nothing but that face and that harsh, erratic breath.

'Oh God, give me the courage to do this thing,' he whispered in agony. 'Damn me if you like, but first give me the courage to do what I promised...oh God...for he always kept faith with me.'

He had no idea how long he sat there on the chair, clutching the pillow to him, his body rocking in grief. The golden light of afternoon filled the room and then in time subsided until the place grew dim with the violet shadows of evening, and cold. The slow, harsh breathing went on and on; a breath rasping in...the slow wheezing rattle of the outbreath...a long, long pause; impossibly long...another painful indrawing of breath. On and on.

It seemed that the diminution of human life to its last extremity was a grim wrestling with God. For did they not share the same breath, God and man? Neither, it seemed, was willing to let go, and Tom could not find the courage to come between them and break the hold that anchored this man to life.

He did not look round when the latch of the door clicked. He heard it, and yet he did not, everything in him absorbed in the slow, rattling travail of breathing that had become the heart of the cosmos.

'It's a hard, slow climb for him, isn't it?'

He glanced up then, at the sound of Brother John's voice.

'Mm?'

'Not an easy one.' Brother John looked down at Tom's haggard, distracted face. 'Shall we put that pillow under his head?' he said gently. 'It might help to make him a bit more comfortable.'

Tom sat without speaking. He looked at Brother John, then stared down at the pillow as if he'd never seen it before, dazed with grief. And he realised with slow, appalled remorse that he had missed the opportunity. His consciousness filled with the realisation that he'd left it too late. The chance had come and gone, and he had squandered it on his own distress; and now it was too late.

'I couldn't do it,' he said, gazing stupidly at the pillow. He raised his eyes, bewildered with grief, to Brother John's face. 'I promised him, but I can't...I...I've failed him...I can't do it.'

Brother John knelt down beside him and took his hands between his own. Tom's eyes searched his, yearning for refuge in John's kindness and sanity, but there was nothing, anywhere, to ease the heartache that was bursting inside him.

'Promised him what, Tom?'

Brother John's eyes looked steadily back into his, full of warmth and understanding. But warmth and understanding belonged to a dead past, to a man who had not broken his promises, failed his friend in the time of his most helpless extremity. In this cold landscape of grief and regret, warmth perished, and understanding starved; there was no comfort in all the world.

'Promised him what, Tom?'

'I promised him that...if he had another seizure...if he was helpless...dumb...incontinent...I would finish it for him. He said...he couldn't face it again. He said, hemlock, a pillow on his face, anything...and I said I would. I *promised*...but I can't...when it comes to it, I just can't...and *listen* to him...'

Brother John nodded. 'I know.'

He chafed Tom's cold hands gently between his own. 'You don't have to do it, Brother,' he said quietly. 'He's dying. This is the end now. This is it. He'll be gone before the dawn. Stay with him. You haven't failed him, Tom— far from it. Don't leave him now. I'll go and get a fresh bowl of water to wash his face and moisten his mouth. Stay with him and say whatever you still need to now, then I'll fetch Father Chad for the last rites, have them send word to his family. Help me then; let's put this pillow back under his head.'

Stiff and cold and weary, Tom rose to his feet and approached the bed. With gentle competence, Brother John slid one hand under Peregrine's head, one under his shoulder, and raised him sufficiently for Tom to replace the pillow on the bed. They both stood there looking down at the dying face, all the life in it shrunken back, conserved for the one arduous work of breath. His skin lay, a toneless shroud on the bones of his face, his eyes half-open, unfocused, dull as stone.

'Will he hear me? Does he know anything?'

Brother John looked thoughtfully, a long time, at the sick man. He put a hand to Peregrine's brow, smoothed it tenderly.

'Do you hear us, Father? Do you know we're here? Or is everything you have going into this fight for breath? We aren't sure, neither of us...but in case you can hear us, in case you know...we want you to know—we love you.

'Stay with him, Tom. Say goodbye. I won't be too long.'

He glanced at the dying fire, slipped out of the room, and went in search of Brother Michael.

'He's going, Brother. I'll go and fetch Father Chad, though I dare say he'd rather have had Theodore if I can work it tactfully. Make up the fire in case we're there through the night, and keep an eye on Brother Thomas. It's almost too much for him, I think. Oh, and you'd better take him a light. It's nigh on dark in there.'

'It won't be long now, Father,' Tom whispered as Brother John left the room. 'Brother John says it won't be long. Just a little while, and God can have his breath back, and the Earth can have her dust back, and all this hell will be over. I suppose...you won't miss me, where you're going. I don't know how I'm going to get along without you. I always did mess things up. Thank you for the help you gave me. Thank you for the man you were. Thank you for your courage, and your honesty, and your compassion...Father...goodbye. I can't tell you how much I love you.'

He reached over for the sponge and squeezed a little water between Peregrine's lips, wiped the sponge gently along his lips to moisten them. He dropped the sponge back in its bowl, and carefully with his fingers wiped away the trickle of water that dribbled from Peregrine's mouth. He lifted his hand and traced with his fingertips along the ridge of his friend's cheekbone, along his eyebrow; turned his hand over and stroked with the back of his fingers the hollow of his temple and down the sunken, toneless cheek to the bone of his jaw; a slow, rapt contemplation of tenderness.

'Father...I'll tell them what you said. "Love has no defences—you only know it's love when it hurts." I won't forget.

'Oh Jesu...Son of God, Son of Man...you have been his Lord for so long, master and man. Forgive him that his courage failed and he tried to take a way out of this long misery. Forgive me that I would have helped him but that my courage failed too. Jesus...Jesus, he loved you in Gethsemane, pleading that the cup be taken from you...he loved you for the faltering of your courage...in your utter humanity, he saw God...

'Look...Jesus, in mercy, look at him...look...oh Jesu...have mercy on your man.'

And then the night. The long, slow watch of the night: last rites, anointing, prayer of absolution from all earthly weight of sin. And the watching and waiting, the painful rattling breaths measuring out the hours of the night.

Until, as the first grey finger of day came stealing in, he drew breath, and they waited...waited...but he did not breathe again. In the dreary uncertain light of dawn, before the sunrise, he was gone.

Tom, who had thought before that those eyes looked lifeless, dull, gazed down on them now and saw beyond doubting, Peregrine was gone. Even his helplessness, his blind, broken suffering he had taken with him: those belonged with his breath, were part of the breath of God in him. They were God's helplessness, God's brokenness; and he had taken them back to himself. Peregrine had left nothing behind but this husk of flesh, a cast-off, finished corpse. And it was to that last trace of his presence among them that his brothers must now address their respect.

'Tom? Would you like to do the last offices for him, with me?'

Tom nodded in silence. He could not take his eyes from

that dead face; could not take in that this was the end...the end.

'Brother Michael, will you bring me the things I shall need? Send Martin to tell Brother Basil and Father Chad. Tell him to remind Father Chad he had family; Melissa Langton, and there is a brother still living.

'What do we do with his ring? Leave it on while he's lying in the chapel, isn't it, and take it off for burial? I think that's what we did with Abbot Gregory.

'All right then, Tom; have you ever done this before?'

'No.'

'We want everything off the bed, pillows, blankets and everything, so we can see what we're doing; that's right. Now it'll take both of us to get his clothes off—very unwieldy is a corpse. Cut the shirt. We'll burn it. No sense in heaving him about unnecessarily. Ah, Michael, thank you.

'What shall I put in his hands, Tom, to lay him in the chapel? Some men, I lay out with their rosary in their fingers, or fold their hands over their Office book, or a crucifix, depending on the special character of their devotion. I laid out Father Matthew with a copy of the Rule.'

Tom pondered the question.

'Nothing,' he said finally. 'He should have nothing in his hands. That's how he wanted to live.'

Brother John nodded. 'Yes. I think you're right. Now then, we have to plug anything that might leak—I'll do that—then you can help me wash him.'

Together they washed him, dressed him in his best habit, combed his hair. They laid him on a clean linen sheet, and folded his hands on his breast, closed his eyes and weighted them down, bound his jaw.

'Pass me that ball of thread, would you?' said Brother John as he fastened the dead man's sandals on his feet.

Tom watched as Brother John cut a length of the linen thread and tied it in a neat figure of eight round the big toes and the ankles, unobtrusively binding the feet into place.

'There. Done.' Brother John stood back and cast a critical eye over his work.

'Right then, we must set to and get this room clear. There'll be a string of people in even before we can have him lying out in the chapel, I should think. Martin can help me with that though. The fire's all but dead, but I'll souse the ashes. We certainly don't want it warm in here.' He shot a quick, appraising glance in Tom's direction. 'Will you like to sit a moment quietly with him, while I go and get that organised?'

Tom nodded, and Brother John left him, shutting the door behind him.

Left alone, he stood by the bed, his eyes travelling slowly over the motionless form of death. The ivory stillness of the toes; the misshapen fingers stark against the blackness of the habit, decorated with the opulent, bejewelled abbot's ring; the sharp, jutting outline of the hawkish nose. With his cold, trembling fingers Tom traced the line of the savage scar that ran the length of the right side of the face.

'Gone...' he murmured in amazement. 'Gone...for ever...'

Then, in the depths of his numbed, chill disbelief, he felt the first sharp stirrings of a pain too cruel to be borne, the jagged, rending legacy of love.

I don't know how I'm going to get through this, he thought as he turned away from the bed.

He stooped and untied the knotted tatter of string that had been the kittens' plaything, from the arm of Peregrine's chair. For a moment he paused. Brother Basil had begun tolling the church bell; the dolorous, repetitive tolling of the bell for the passing of the dead. He rolled up the scrap of string and put it in his pocket.

Then he left the room and, closing the door behind him, went in search of Brother John.

'Where have you put his crutch?' he asked him when he found him.

'His crutch? It's in the back room with the wheeled chairs and walking sticks and so on. Why?'

'Can I take it?'

Brother John looked at him. Brother Tom was not a man to be patted on the back and soothed like a child. If this would ease his suffering, why not?

'Yes, you can take it.'

At the funeral five days later, with its solemn requiem Mass, attended by villagers, Peregrine's family, the bishop, representatives from other religious houses and local dignitaries of all sorts, Tom stood sealed in remote, indifferent impassivity. He followed the bier with the other brethren up the winding path under the beech trees to the burial ground, and stood with the others in the raw, blowing drizzle, watching the last remains lowered into the earth, and the clay shovelled in. There had been some argument about that, because Father Chad had thought it more fitting to inter him in a vault in the church; but Brother Tom had insisted that he would have preferred to be buried with the ordinary brothers, out here on the hill, under the stars.

Tom was glad he had won that one, but apart from that, the burial had been of little consequence to him. He had said his farewell two days ago after Vespers, when he had lit a fire behind the vegetable garden, of dry, dead weeds, bean haulm and rose prunings. He had cut back the rosemary bushes and brought the trimmings green to the fire. Into the incense of their fragrant smoke he had place the little coil of knotted string and the wooden crutch. He had watched as the string charred and spurted into flame, and the crutch blackened and caught fire, the worn, shiny leather pad of the armrest and the leather pad on the foot being the last parts to ignite. He fed the fire until they were completely consumed, and stood for a long time looking up at the smoke of it rising to the stars.

Then at last, he took a stick and raked through the ashes until he found the little metal casing from the foot of the crutch, and this he wrapped carefully in his handkerchief, and he placed it in his pocket before he went to Compline.

VIII

Winter

Father Theodore sat by the fire in the abbot's house drinking Brother Walafrid's blackberry wine. Father Chad had asked him to come and report on the progress of the young men who formed the present novitiate.

When Father Matthew died, Theodore had been a surprising choice as his successor. The obedience of Novice Master was exacting, demanding a man of considerable spiritual stature and wisdom, a man of unsentimental kindness, of both scholarly ability and common sense. Theodore; shy, clumsy and forgetful, had not been the most obvious choice. Father Chad remembered Peregrine defending his decision to some of the more sceptical among the brethren: 'I know he's a young man, but there may be good in that. The lads who come here may find a sympathy in his youth. Further to that, there is scarcely a man in this community who suffered so much in his novitiate year as Father Theodore, and so much by the fault, or at least the weakness, of his Novice Master.

'I want a man who has struggled to persevere, a man who knows what it is to bear the cost of another's weakness. I think I have that in Father Theodore. He will serve the novitiate well.'

And it had been a good choice, Father Chad acknowledged with mild astonishment.

'All is well then? You have no anxieties?' he asked him now.

'No.' Theodore shook his head. 'For the moment they are working well, praying devoutly, living contentedly. No doubt trials and difficulties will assail them, but just now we have tranquillity.'

'Good. Good; I'm glad of that. That's good.'

Theodore, experienced by now in detecting unspoken unease, gazed steadfastly into the fire, not looking at Father Chad, waiting for him to speak out whatever was on his mind.

'Father Theodore...this...this has nothing to do with the novitiate, but...'

'Yes?' Theo smiled encouragingly.

'This is a matter of confidence, you understand. I rely on your absolute discretion.'

'Of course.'

'I am not happy about Brother Thomas. He used to be such a cheerful, easygoing soul. Now he looks shut in, withdrawn from us. He has lost all his joie de vivre, all his zest for living.'

Theodore frowned in puzzlement. 'Well, he...well, naturally he has, Father. He's grieving.'

'Yes, but...this is the third week of Advent. He should be recovered by now, surely?'

'Why? Has Advent got some special healing power I haven't heard about?' said Theodore. 'I'm sorry,' he added hastily, seeing Father Chad's startled displeasure at the discourtesy of his sarcasm. 'Father Peregrine is but six weeks buried. Brother Tom will take longer than that to pick up the dropped stitches of his life again, I think. He's bound to feel a little unravelled for a while. Give him time. Perhaps he needs a chance to talk it over.'

'With me?' Father Chad sounded doubtful. And not without reason, Theodore had to admit.

'You are his abbot, for now anyway. I doubt if he will make it easy for you, but I think you ought to try.'

Father Chad nodded gloomily. 'And if I get nowhere?'

'I could have a word with him. Or Brother John.'

Father Chad sipped his wine, staring at the yellow flames of the ash logs burning on the hearth. Administering the business of the abbey had its difficulties, but it was easy compared with the pastoral care of men in grief or crisis of faith.

'I don't know what to say to him,' he admitted.

'Ask him.' Theodore spoke as diplomatically as he could. Father Chad was not an arrogant man, but Theo must not be seen to have too much of an edge over his superior in this matter of the nurturing of the souls in his care. 'Allow him to talk to you freely about Father Peregrine, about the effect on him of that loss. He loved him very much. He will be full of memories, sadness, tenderness that need to be spoken out.'

And you think if I ask him, he will be able to talk to me?'

'Yes…' said Theodore, slowly. If you ask him the right way, he thought, but he didn't say it.

'He'll be up at the farm all day. I'll catch him at Vespers. I'll try.'

With very little confidence in the usefulness of the interview, Theodore watched at the end of Vespers as Father Chad laid a detaining hand on Brother Tom's arm, beseeching his co-operation with the peculiar ghastliness of a nervous smile. He watched Brother Tom's guarded acquiescence, and saw the two of them leave the chapel with negligible hope of frank self-exposure. Brother Tom, in Theo's judgement, was about as likely to show Father Chad his soft underbelly as he was to take up embroidery. In this assessment of the situation he was right.

'Sit yourself down, Brother Thomas,' said Father Chad. He had intended a warm and reassuring welcome, but his voice slid into a disconcerting falsetto under pressure of his apprehension.

Brother Tom sat down in silence in the chair that

Father Chad indicated by the fire. He looked at the ash logs burning in the grate, then looked down at his hands with lowered head. He had a fair idea of the purpose of this summons, and he did not want his heartache forced into the open by Father Chad or anybody.

Aware that his unco-operative silence might seem more than a little rude, he glanced up with a forced and sickly smile.

'Thank you,' he said. He could think of nothing else to say. Encouraged by this crumb of compliance, Father Chad cleared his throat and began his pastoral consultation.

'I've been worried about you, Brother,' he said sympathetically. 'You haven't been your usual cheerful self at all these last six weeks.'

Tom raised his head and stared at him incredulously.

'I'm not surprised, of course; of course I'm not surprised,' Father Chad added hurriedly. 'It is quite understandable: you were very fond of Father... um...Columba.' As he came to say the man's name, Father Chad stumbled over his anxiety to do the correct thing. As acting abbot of the community it seemed more proper to refer to the deceased man by his name in religion than by the affectionate informality of 'Father Peregrine'. Tom, hearing the hesitation, wondered in amazement if Father Chad had actually forgotten Peregrine's name.

'Yes,' he said, in the pause left for his reply, which was lengthening into embarrassment. 'Yes. I was very fond of him.'

'Good. Good. Well, that's natural and right, of course.' Father Chad's voice carried the insincere effusiveness of anxiety. It matched his smile.

'However...all of us have to, um, count our blessings in circumstances like this; to...er...you know—look on the bright side and put a brave face on things and...um...so forth.'

Father Chad was a timid man, not at his best in such

circumstances as these: but he was not a fool. He struggled to repress the twinges of irritation and resentment that were awakened by the expression on Brother Tom's face. Brother Tom looked as though he thought Father Chad had all the intelligent sensitivity and discernment of an earwig.

'I *have* been putting a brave face on it,' said Brother Tom. 'At least, I thought I had. What would you like me to do differently?'

'No, no, no!' Father Chad wished he had had the humility to ask Father Theodore to join in this conversation. 'Don't misunderstand me, Brother. This is not a rebuke. It is only that, although you have not complained or given any cause for complaint in your work or prayer, nevertheless your unhappiness is very evident. I am your abbot, for now anyway. Brother Thomas, I know you don't like it, but you ought to confide in me and tell me what's on your heart. It says so in the Rule.'

Brother Tom was sufficiently self-indulgent to allow himself the tiniest twitch of the eybrows. This small twitch was so expressive that it plunged Father Chad into a sense of total inadequacy.

'So it does,' said Brother Tom. He lifted his eyes calmly to look Father Chad in the face. 'What would you like me to tell you?'

Why is this going so wrong? Father Chad floundered in desperation. I knew it wouldn't be easy for him, but why do I want to shake him and shout at him? I mustn't let him see how I feel. I must try to understand.

'Well…' he replied with forced benevolence, 'well…um…perhaps you would like to talk to me freely about Father…um—Columba, about the effect on you of that loss. You loved him very much. You must be full of memories, sadness, tenderness that need to be spoken out.'

Tom looked away quickly into the fire, biting his lip.

The hurt of bereavement was intolerably raw still. He could not bear it touched.

'He always burned apple logs,' he said at last. Father Chad smiled.

'Really? Apple logs, mm? Good, good.' There followed a silence in which Father Chad cleared his throat uneasily.

'That, um, that wasn't quite the kind of thing I was thinking of,' he said. 'I was wondering more about how you felt about him. Um, I thought you should tell me how you feel now; um, what hurts most, you know, and the memories you had of times together. That sort of thing.'

Tom swallowed. 'Oh,' he murmured, 'that sort of thing.'

'I beg your pardon?' Father Chad's face creased into the nervous smile. 'I'm sorry, I didn't quite catch what you said...'

But Tom shook his head. 'Nothing.'

He picked up the iron poker from the hearth and prodded moodily at the fire. 'What hurts most,' he said, 'is that he's dead.'

Father Chad laughed, then stopped himself abruptly, unsure if the remark had been intentionally humorous. He cleared his throat again. 'Ah yes; yes, I can understand that. Um... tell me about it.' His face twitched in alarm at Tom's sharp intake of breath. 'Are you all right, Brother? You sound as though something hurt you.'

Tom passed his hand across his face and sighed. He decided that he might as well give Father Chad what he wanted simply in order to secure his escape.

'How I felt about him? I loved him. Sometimes I was angry with him, at my wits' end with him. Sometimes he made me feel very small, very ashamed. Sometimes he tore my heart open with pity. He taught me to love in darkness, showed me that it is possible to find a little spring of hope in the most arid place of despair, just by loving; by consenting to be defenceless... permitting the pain and the wonder of loving and being loved. All

that...but mostly I just loved him without knowing why.
I loved his crazy smile and the way his eyes could dance
with laughter. I loved the way he looked like a bad-
tempered bird when things were going wrong. I loved his
faith.

'And what hurts most is facing up to the fact that I will
never hear that slow, careful voice struggling its way back
to speech—"T-om. Th-ank y-ou, T-om." Never. As long
as I live, never again. Never see those eyes smiling, "T-ell
m-e about it."

'What else did you want to know? Memories? I remember the night we went out to look at the stars...the hunger
and ecstasy in his eyes, the sigh in his voice, "Oh, mon
Dieu; oh le bien." And the scent of rosemary. I remember
lying with him in the grass below the burial ground,
talking about his death, about God...I remember him
lying on his bed naked in the firelight, the oil shining on
his body, the sound of him weeping, and Brother Michael
talking to him, quietly. I remember another time he wept,
holding him in my arms, and I felt as though his pain
would divide my soul in two. Those wretched blackberries. I remember holding his hand, before he learned to
speak again, and the extraordinary cost of caressing it
with real tenderness, such a simple thing, but it took
courage to do...

'I remember how Martin used to drive him to distrac-
tion...I remember how jealous I was that it was Theodore, not me, who taught him to speak again...silly...'

Tom looked up at Father Chad, all the extravagant
torment of unbearable grief in his eyes. He felt the pain of
it swell relentlessly inside him; the by now familiar agony
of hurting so intense he felt it would split him apart,
dislocate his reason.

Father Chad was looking at him with considerable
concern, clearly disturbed, shocked even, by what he had
just heard. He cleared his throat and, anchoring his voice

with an effort to a normal masculine pitch, began his
cautious reply.

'Thank you for being so, um, open with me, er, Brother
Thomas. What you have said is very moving of course, but
I must, er, confess, it disturbs me just a *little*
bit...um...concerning, er, as it were the, er, um, *nature* of
your closeness to Father Columba.' He cleared his throat,
crossed his legs, avoiding Tom's eyes.

'As you know, our Rule is very insistent on a most
prudent modesty...guarding against particular friendships...against too, er, *demonstrative* forms of affection, and
certainly against, er, um, nakedness. I feel I ought really
to ask you whether this extreme affection was in all ways,
er, in your view, quite proper?'

Father Chad would never have believed it possible for
one man to pack so much contempt into his gaze. He had
an extraordinary sense of having shrivelled to a state of
being so cheap and so dirty that he had no rightful existence in the order of creation at all.

'What are you suggesting?' Tom asked him coldly. The
simple question demanded an answer of a bald honesty
that Father Chad squirmed to think of.

'Presumably you are asking me if the relationship I had
with Father Peregrine was of a homosexual nature?'

Father Chad felt as though his tongue had dried up,
cemented to the roof of his mouth. All he had to say was,
'Yes.' He could not bring himself to say it. It seemed to
him as if some mischievous force had picked up his
attempt at pastoral counselling and worried it to bits,
leaving his room all strewn about with pain and indignation, disgust and distrust and distress.

He made himself look at Brother Tom. 'That, um, was
what I was asking, but I see by your reaction that I may
have been wrong, er...'

'Father Peregrine,' said Tom, with a sudden, unexpected smile, 'was not that way inclined. Neither am I.
We both took our vow of chastity seriously. Particular

friendship... I don't know. Towards the end of his life, without friendship, what would he have had? But certainly, it was perfectly proper. He was naked because he had bedsores, and limbs deformed by paralysis, and he ached all over. Brother Michael was tending to him. There was nothing erotic about it, you may take my word.'

'Quite. Quite, I see. Good. Er, good. Well, um—oh dear, is that the Compline bell? No? Oh dear... I thought it was...'

Father Chad's hands fluttered in a small gesture of helplessness. He felt totally at sea. Perhaps, he thought, it would be possible to redeem the situation by moving on to a less critical topic of conversation.

'Has Brother Stephen told you of our new plans for the farm?' he asked brightly.

Tom frowned. 'No,' he said, with a note of surprise in his voice. It was not like Stephen to forget to mention farming matters to Brother Tom.

'Hasn't he?' Father Chad looked at Tom in alarm, wondering if he had made a blunder, racking his brains to think of some reason why Brother Stephen might have thought it more prudent to say nothing about the plans to Brother Tom. He could think of none.

'Yes, we met last week. We have decided on looking at it again that the dovecote really does need rebuilding to a larger size. Also I have been up to the buildings by the boundary, and I can quite understand from the way Brother Stephen explained it that they all need to come down. We need a good-sized barn, with three threshing floors and a granary up there, as well as new cow housing.'

Tom said nothing to this. His face was fixed in a smile of bitterness. He looked older than his thirty-three years.

'I am surprised Brother Stephen said nothing to you. Perhaps it slipped his mind.'

'Yes. Maybe so. And then again, maybe he remembered Father saying, "Over my dead body will you build a

barn with three threshing floors." Perhaps he has the
grace to blush. So—with what is this work to be paid for?'

Father Chad pulled a glum face. 'Well, this is the
problem of course. We shall rely on selling corrodies,
which I know Father—er—Columba was reluctant to
do.'

'Reluctant? He wouldn't hear of it!'

'No…still, these are troubled times. Heavy taxes and
so forth, you know. He was not a well man, and of course,
his disability kept him rather confined here. It may be that
he did not realise how common a thing it is to sell corrodies these days.'

'What ever do you mean? Of course he knew! It was
seeing all the houses round about going into debt and
cluttering the place up with worldly people that made him
so desperate to stay free of it. I…Father
Chad…please…please may I go?'

Tom got to his feet. He was shaking, his hands clenched
into fists. He hardly knew how to contain his anger and
grief. He knew only that he had to get out before he hit
Father Chad; before he did something really stupid.

Father Chad looked up at him. He had an unwelcome
suspicion that Father Peregrine, under the same circumstances, would not have permitted Tom to go anywhere.
Even so, it was a relief to hear his own voice saying, 'Of
course, Brother Thomas; this is not an easy time for you—
you must be very tired,' in spite of the embarrassing
quaver in it.

'Thank you for your time,' said Brother Tom, with a
valiant attempt at humble courtesy, and left.

He did not see Theodore sitting in the cloister in the
wintry darkness. He did not even register that the Compline bell was ringing. He walked swiftly along the cloister, out through the passage beside the Chapter House,
and then ran up the hill to the farm; ran till the frosty
night air hurt like a knife in his throat, ran till he had a
stitch in his side and he gasped for breath. He stopped

then, up on the hill, looking down on the farmyard in the moonlight, the silence of winter all around him. An owl floated overhead on noiseless wings. A fox's bark carried on the tingling air. He stood, his body heaving, regaining his breath.

Then, slowly, he walked down the hill again. It was too cold to stand still. The cold ached in his ears, numbed his toes.

He walked down to the farmyard. He could hear the shifting and blowing of the cows in the byre as he came alongside it. He opened the barn door and went in. The fragrance of the hay hung on the air, distilled memory of dusty summer days. Weary, numb, defeated, Tom trailed into the barn and sat in the warmth of the hay, his knees drawn up to his chest, his forehead resting on his knees and his arms wrapped tightly round his shins, contracted to a ball of aching misery.

He sat there motionless, containing the sorrow, the impossible, breaking weight of sorrow that he could not dodge or escape or put down. The spaces of the night widened away from him, until he became the beating heart of a universe of bereavement, the core of a vast, immortal, pitiless night.

Bird of death, the owl, as it came curving down on silent wings, with cool, unerring precision seizing the little grey mouse that scuttered among the hay. A small noise, a disturbance of the hay, piteous squeak of terror, and it was over. Tom raised his head and saw the owl fly through the moonbeams that shone in at the doorway, a limp scrap of frailty in its talons.

He also saw someone standing in the doorway, silhouetted in the moonlight, looking in.

'Tom?'

It was Theodore's voice. Tom watched him silently from the dark place where he crouched.

'Tom?'

It seemed churlish to hide from him. Tom felt half-inclined to call out to him; and half-possessed by the silences of an empty, finished world.

'Tom?'

Tom compromised. He shifted his position in the hay. Let him hear that if he wanted to. He heard it. 'Tom.' Theodore came into the barn. He walked forward uncertainly into the darkness.

'Theo, I'm here.'

Theodore came towards his voice, peering in the dim light afforded by the open door until he made out the blot of black dark amid the darkness that was Brother Tom.

'Tom?'

He sat down in the hay beside him. An immense, dragging weariness filled Brother Tom at the prospect of explanations, questions, futile commiseration. But Theodore said nothing. He unclasped his cloak, turned it upside down so that the wide hem of it might spread over the shoulders of both of them. Only then did Tom become aware that he had been shivering. His shivering increased, became uncontrollable, and Theodore took him in his arms, with the cloak wrapped about them, saying nothing still.

It was only there, hidden in Theodore's arms, in the sheltering cloak, hidden in the silent dark of the barn, that Tom uncovered the wound of grief that savaged the very bowels of him, and allowed his face hidden in Theodore's shoulder to wear the agonised mask of mourning, allowed the tears that ached in his throat to scald his eyes, until he clung to Theo in the sobbing anguish of his torn, abandoned soul. And Theodore did not speak, did not move, did not intrude upon that molten place of pain in which a man's soul is recast.

Eventually, it was finished. Tom sat back in the hay, drained of everything, exhausted.

'I didn't know anything could hurt this much,' he said. He lay down on the fragrant hay, his face, his throat, his belly aching from the labour of weeping.

The last six weeks had been full of the kind words and sympathetic counsel of the brethren; well-intentioned words ranging from, 'It's a blessed release for him, Brother. He's better off where he is,' to, 'I expect it's a relief to you to be free of all that extra work in the infirmary.' Theodore's company had an intriguing novelty about it in that he said nothing at all beyond the simple statement of his presence.

'D'you remember what he said about having your heart ripped open?' said Tom after a while.

'Yes, I do.' Theodore sat rubbing his ankle, easing the pins and needles that had resulted from sitting awkwardly immobile for a considerable length of time. 'He said it was part of the necessary pain of following Jesus.'

'Ripped open. That's what it feels like. Other times it doesn't feel like anything. I walk around like a man lost in the fog; things that were familiar looking alien and bizarre. My life doesn't feel like home any more. I feel as though I've been cast out of my own heart, wandering. And then the grief comes again, swelling and rising inside me till I'm maddened with it. Last night...last night I lay on my bed tearing at my belly with my hands, retching, trying to void myself of the pain of it...

'Five minutes. If I could talk to him just for five minutes. "Th-ank y-ou, T-om...T-ell m-e about it...L-ove h-as n-o def-enc-es, T-om. Y-ou kn-ow it's l-ove wh-en it h-h-urts." He...he...oh, I'm sorry...' The wash of it overwhelmed him again. He lay on his back feeling the tears welling hot in his eyes, and trickling cold down into his ears, weeping helplessly, torn open with grief.

'Psalm a hundred and twenty-nine,' said Theo. ' *"Supra dorsum meum..."* um...how does it go? *"Supra dorsum..."* '

'What ever are you talking about?' Tom's voice quavered peevishly between his tears.

'Psalm a hundred and twenty-nine. "The ploughers have ploughed upon my back, and made long furrows." '

Tom sniffed, and considered this, sniffed again. 'Yes...' he said. 'That just about says it.'

'I'll expect to see you looking like a horse with a green mane in the spring, then. And a blond hedgehog by next harvest.'

Tom felt offended by this inappropriate levity, and faintly guilty at his own, equally inappropriate, faint stirring of amusement. He was not sure how to respond. He hunted for his handkerchief and blew his nose.

'You know,' said Theo into the darkness, 'how Martin likes to have one of the brothers say grace over the food; in Latin. It has to be in Latin. He can't speak a word of Latin you know, but he thinks it's needful for blessing. I was there one day; in September, it must have been, because Father was just struggling with speech—he had it, but it was very unclear still. And Martin brought him his meal; fish, rather overcooked, and some very tough beans, the end of the season, and a hunk of Cormac's bread, chopped...and soaked to a mush. He beamed down at Father, and he said, "Now then, you be a good lad, and let's hear *you* say grace today."

'Father looked up at him, and I was a bit worried for a minute: it was so insultingly patronising; I thought he would be angry. But he smiled at Martin—the sweetest smile, and it was a bit of a relief, you know.

'He composed his face into the most dignified, sepulchral solemnity, and he said, *"L-L-amentat-iones J-er-emiae, c-cap-ut pr-im-um; V-ide D-Dom-ine quon-iam tr-ibul-or, c-conturb-atus est v-enter m-m-m-eus...in n-om-ine P-Patr-is, et F-il-io, et Sp-ir-itui S-ancto, am-m-en."* And he made the sign of the cross over his food with all the pomp and ceremony of a bishop. Martin was delighted. I couldn't figure out what he'd said at first, his speech was so stuttering and laboured still, but gradually it dawned on me. It was that verse from the first chapter of Lamentations, "Behold, oh Lord, my tribulation, and how my bowels shudder...in the name of the Father, and of the Son, and of the Holy

Spirit, Amen." I don't know how I kept a straight face. I thought I'd choke before Martin was out of the room, but he, he didn't bat an eyelid. He didn't eat it either.'

Tom smiled. It felt strange. His face wasn't used to smiling. His eyes were sore and swollen. He began to laugh, but his breath caught in a sob. 'He was awful to Martin,' he said.

'No,' said Theo. 'He took more than he gave.'

Tom wiped the cold tears out of his ears with his handkerchief. 'He couldn't always see the funny side of it,' he said, 'but we brought him up here to the farm one day, me and Stephen. It was only about the second time I'd brought him out. He was so touchy about meeting people. But he consented to come up here. The harvest was in, it was halfway through September, and Stephen and I were just pottering about doing odd jobs, so I thought it would be good for him, nice to be out of doors and have a bit of company. We wheeled the chair up as far as it would go, and then carried him to the grass beside the track up above the orchard, in the shelter of the wall.

'We left him there and came back down here to swill out the milking shed and scrub the milk barrels clean. We'd left enough chores to keep us busy round the yard for a while, knowing he would be there.

'Then Stephen and I went down to the pasture to have a look at one of the cows, she'd a bad foot. While we were there, Brother Germanus came tearing down to the field: "Brother Thomas! Brother Thomas!" he was shouting, and he as white as a sheet. We ran to meet him. He was puffing and blowing, "Oh God, come quick," he said. "Father Columba's in some kind of fit. I don't know what to do, he looks terrible."

'Stephen and I looked at each other, and we went up there at a run. I think he felt as cold and sick as I did. As we came up by the orchard, I could hear this thrashing about and garbled shouting, and when we got round the corner, sure enough there he was, rolling about on the grass, making a terrible row, calling and shouting, all nonsense. I knelt down beside him and started to soothe him as best I could, but he was pushing me away with his hand and going on and on at me, writhing about on the ground. It was odd you know, because his eyes didn't look glazed or anything, but there was obviously something badly wrong with him. He looked at my face and at Brother Stephen's and he stopped shouting, and he started to laugh. For one hideous moment I thought he'd gone insane; wondered if there was some kind of fit you could have with his illness to make you lose your mind.

' "T-om," he managed to say at last, and I was so relieved. He closed his eyes, and made a real effort to get his speech working, calm himself enough to make some sense. "F-or th-e l-ove of G-G-od, m-an," he said, "w-ill y-ou g-g-et m-e off th-is a-ants' n-est?" '

'We had to take all his clothes off and everything. They were all over him.'

Tom chuckled at the memory. 'Brother John was disgusted with us. We'd made him promise not to tell, but he was covered in bites.'

Resonant and clear on the tingling wintry air, the Matins bell began to sound in the abbey below them.

'Midnight?' said Tom, startled. 'It's not midnight already?'

'I searched for you a long time before I found you,' said Theodore. 'And you were a long time weeping.'

Tom scrambled to his feet. 'We'd better go down, Theo. They'll miss us from our beds and our places in chapel.'

Theo sat up in the hay. 'If you feel ready. There's no harder work than grieving. We can stay here if you like.'

'No.' Tom was brushing the hay from his clothes, bending over to shake it from his hair. 'No. Come on, Theo, get all the hay off you, straighten yourself up. It...it's just something Father Chad said this evening. I think I'd have a lot of explaining to do if he had reason to think I'd been out of my bed, spending half the night with you in the barn—especially you, with the novitiate and everything.

'Come on—please. I don't want another long session with him. Not just now.'

Tom fastened the barn door to keep out the animals, and they hastened down the track to the abbey.

As they approached the cloister, Tom made Theodore stop, and he inspected him anxiously in the moonlight. 'You've got hay in your hair still, look.'

'Have I? I'm surprised you can tell the difference.'

'No, I'm serious, Theo. Turn round, let me look at the back of you. Truly, I think I shall be in trouble if you appear with me in chapel looking as though you've just been having a tumble in the hay. Have a look at me. Am I all tidy?'

'Brother, you look charming. I suspect your nose and your eyes, which are rather swollen, may also be rather red, but it's hard to say by the light of the moon. Apart from that detail you look positively elegant.'

'Oh, for mercy's sake, the bell's stopped. Come on.'

Father Chad, Tom was relieved to see as he took his place in chapel, looked almost as crumpled and bleary-eyed as he did himself.

They were in silence, so Tom could not speak to Theodore again, but he sought him out the next day, climbing the stairs to the novitiate to find him in the few minutes before Vespers began, after the Novitiate Chapter. He was grateful to find him alone. The novices had already gone down to chapel.

'Theo—thank you…last night…. Thank you.'

Theodore smiled, the kindness in his eyes enfolding Tom with a gentleness and understanding that was almost unbearable. Tom bit his lip. 'Don't be too kind to me. I can't…I'm a bit shaky still.'

'Give yourself time,' said Theo. 'You can always come up and find me here if you need me. You know how it is for the novices—they spend half their lives in bits. They won't think anything of it.' He hesitated. 'Father Per-egrine...'

'Yes?'

'He...he was worried about you. He spoke to me about it one day. He said that he never knew when he might be taken ill again, and he was worried once Brother Francis went away to the seminary, that if he died while Francis was away you might have no one you could turn to. He told me to look after you. He said I was to remind you, if you needed some comfort, that you'd helped him to start living again. He couldn't have faced it without you. He said that the breath of God in you is a gift of life, a holy kiss to be passed on. He said you'd know what he meant. And he said to tell you that the sorrow of grief is a bitter crucifixion, but that the loving had been joyous, and one day would be again.

'He told me to behold your grief without embarrass-ment, to help you not to run away from your pain. He told me...he said that it would be the comfort of my love that led your anguish out into compassion, instead of it fester-ing to destruction. He said to tell you that a man in grief is like a man with bedsores. It costs him to reveal it, but he needs help with it. He said you'd know what he meant. And he said to remind you of the thing you said last night. That love has no defences, and you only know it's love when it hurts.'

Author's Note

In the life of the church, some people easily find an identity, a place to belong, while others find themselves marginalised, forgotten, relegated to the outside place of loneliness and aching rejection, which was how Jesus characterised hell.

This happens in part because the church community organises itself around meetings. Who cannot participate in such meetings? Children, who get bored easily. The deaf, who cannot hear, and cannot lipread or sign when seated in rows. The mentally handicapped, who may make unusual or inappropriate noises or interruptions. The incontinent, who may not be able to make it through the meeting, yet may not be able to leave quickly and quietly to reach distant toilets. It is such as these, the citizens of the kingdom of heaven, whose path into the church family we misguidedly obstruct.

The story of *The Long Fall* is about the isolating and humiliating nature of such disablement. In the story I have tried to write sensitively and respectfully of some of the most difficult, and common, aspects of human suffering. One of the problems of such writing lies in deciding just how explicit to be.

For example, it very often happens that someone who suffers from post-stroke aphasia may swear, very graphically, before the control of the rest of his speech returns. As speech returns, it sometimes happens that he may say things that would have been unacceptable to him before, of a sexual nature perhaps, or other improprieties. Along with incontinence as well as impairment of mobility, such things can make it impossibly hard to find the comfortable place in the fellowship of the church community that he once enjoyed.

Not to write about these things would compound the conspiracy of silence by which so many are excluded from the loving circle of fellowship. Yet to write too explicitly would cause offence, by the inclusion of swearwords and indecent language.

In *The Long Fall* I have tried to present an authentic picture. That is to say, a realism which includes the reality of the tender compassion of God, as well as the grittiness and tears of the reality of human suffering. It is my sincere wish that you may not be offended in any way by this portrayal of reality.

Penelope Wilcock

The Hawk And The Dove

by Penelope Wilcock

'Lifts and transports us into another world...I was hungry to read more.'

- JANE GRAYSHON

THE HAWK. An aristocrat of the thirteenth century and a renegade from his own passions, Peregrine entered monastic life still fierce and proud. When thugs from his past beat and crippled him, they left him helpless as a child. Bereft of his independence, he could finally teach true strength to his brothers.

THE DOVE. Melissa is a modern teenager, direct descendent of the hawkish abbot, who encounters the same struggles he did. As she listens to her mother's stories of her distant ancestor, Mellissa discovers that times do not change: that people, pride, resentment and love stay much the same, and that it is the grace of God on the inside that changes things.

'I enjoyed reading this book and saw once again more of Jesus - for me always the final test of a good book.'

- ROGER FORSTER

'Not only a joy to read, but also the kind of experience from which you come away feeling cleansed, whole and determined to live life more generously.'

- JOYCE HUGGETT

Minstrel
Published by Kingsway

The Wounds Of God

by Penelope Wilcock

'Clarity, simplicity and depth...Penelope Wilcock is a genuine storyteller. I loved this book and so will many, many others.' **ADRIAN PLASS**

Abbot Peregrine was an aristocrat, scholar, priest and authoritative leader of men. He could be fierce and intimidating, but there was also a tenderness about him that he had learned in the bitter school of suffering. A man with a broken body, he was familiar with fear and pain.

The monks of his community, sharing Peregrine's path of poverty, chastity and obedience, wrestled with pride, faced disillusionment, tasted grief and struggled with despair.

Yet they, and Peregrine, persevere. Each glimpses the love that stands firm in disappointment and grief: the steady love of the wounded God.

Minstrel
Published by Kingsway